RED DAHLIA

by

T.A. Bound

RED DAHLIA

Copyright © 2022 T.A. Bound

This is a work of historical fiction. I base the main character upon a historical person, as interpreted by the author. All other places, characters and events are entirely fictional.

To request permissions, contact the publisher at Tbound@protectingyourrights.org.

Paperback: 979-8-9853936-2-0
Ebook: 979-8-9853936-3-7

First paperback edition June 2022.

Cover art by Photographia
Cover Model Erika Jarrell
Photographs by Photographia

Excerpt from" Deceased" by T.A. Bound.
Reprinted by permission.

*I dedicate this book to my Tanya. Without her support,
this story would not have been possible.*

CONTENTS

THE BODY

Kansas City, Missouri

1949

A lone scream pierced the foggy morning calm.

The scream broke the still air five minutes after Benji Tucker burst back through the kitchen door he left moments before on his normal route to the school bus. Spoiling those few precious minutes of tranquility that dwelled between his bus departure time and when she needed to head to hers. Clad in his yellow rain slicker, dripping from his brief foray outdoors, his return annoyed Sophie as she hurried to get herself ready for work; her bus left fifteen minutes after Benji's, so any interruption on a weekday posed an existential threat to her tight schedule.

"What did you forget?"

Instead of answering, his little feet thudded down the wooden hall floor toward her room. At the doorway he stopped, hood back and hair wet, his face ghastly pale and twisted into an unfamiliar grimace. If not for his expression, she might have yelled at him for trailing water everywhere, but his wide, terror-filled eyes stopped her.

"Mama, there's a dead lady!"

"What are you talking about?"

"Down by the new houses, in an empty lot. I saw her!"

Benji cut through the corner of this new housing development every morning to reach his school bus stop.

Still mostly vacant lots, the developer planned hundreds more houses, although construction had begun on fewer than a third.

"Where is this lady?"

"In a vacant yard. Nobody is around. I discovered her!" His excited voice welled with a touch of pride. "Should we call the police?"

In other circumstances, she might have dismissed his fanciful story, a rainy-day version of a scary campfire tale, but his voice, his face, his entire manner were so atypical, so odd for Benji. And something convinced him to slog back home through this miserable weather rather than catching his bus. Yet, she had no intention of embarrassing herself by calling the police because her eight-year-old mistook some old clothes for a dead body.

"Let me grab my coat. You can show me on my way to my bus. But be quick about it—your bus will be here any minute!"

In fact, by then his school bus almost certainly had come and gone without him, but nothing they could do about it now. If so, he'd ride along on hers to a connecting intersection.

Through the heavy mist, she took Benji by the hand and had him lead her to this supposed dead lady. Sophie expected little more than to identify what an imaginative third-grader confused for a corpse, then hurry on to a busy day at work. A broken mannequin or, at worst, someone's Labrador Retriever killed after tangling with a car. At least the steady drizzle had let up, leaving only eerie remnants of fog hanging heavy over the city. The development stretched for blocks beyond Crest Avenue. Where a forest once grew had been cleared and, beyond that, new roads scarred the flat terrain in a rigid grid pattern. Benji led her to the second of those fresh asphalt wounds and turned left.

Several already completed houses stood on one side of the road with others under construction, and she wondered whether anyone had moved into any of them yet. Benji pulled her across to the far side, where only one completed house had a For Sale sign jabbed into its fresh, sprouting lawn, the rest of the block still under construction. Past one house with a sign in its yard lay a stretch of bare, vacant lots. Two or three, she guessed, where tall grass planted when the ground had been cleared and —spared the mower's blade since—struggled against ambitious weeds.

"There," Benji pointed and dug in his heels. Near the center of those vacant lots, something partial and white lay hidden among the weeds and fog.

Odd—the peculiar shape did resemble a body from a distance, but they were too distant for an exact identification. A trail of bent grass topped with long V-shaped seeds marked where Benji had ventured earlier. Together, they retraced his footsteps.

"Is that a mannequin?"

Shaking his head with gusto, Benji refused to venture one step further, although his path through the grass indicated he earlier risked approaching ten feet closer. The sight intrigued Sophie, because she could see how he mistook this for a body, but from thirty feet she still struggled to comprehend what the tall weeds concealed. Whatever it might be appeared disassembled, although why someone might go through the trouble to discard an old, broken department store mannequin in such an unlikely spot made no sense.

Wary now, she crept toward the pale figure, each step giving it clearer form. The form of a woman, although the object was two separate pieces. Not quite white, more the color of lard. Something lay across it, red and green.

Drenched red hair streamed out from the head like rays from a cold, wet sun, and pale blue eyes stared glassy and unseeing into the mist.

That is when her scream pierced the fog.

THE BUS STATION

Along a dark wall which a smashed light on a phone pole was supposed to reach, several shadows watched a bus lurch to a squeaking halt at 9:48 p.m.

Right on time.

Air sighed from somewhere underneath, and the narrow door swiveled inward. The first passengers off rushed into the waiting arms of parents, spouses or to their children, everyone all eager smiles as they departed the platform, sharing stories of the trip with loved ones. Behind them shuffled the solitary travelers—most businessmen and salesmen. Moving without eagerness, weary and relieved to be back home, or at least an overnight stop where a bed awaited. Or a friendly bar nearby.

In the shadows along the edge of the platform, those figures maintained their vigil, unobserved by the departing throng. At every bus station in the country, such men sought the final group to file off buses at their terminal stops. People are so predictable and perform the same unknowing routine regardless whether the bus route terminated in a small town or the largest: New York, Chicago, L.A.

Occasional exceptions aside, those last few stepping off the buses are invariably the desirable ones.

A teenage boy descended the four stairs from the Greyhound Bus to the otherwise empty platform, eyes darting about, toting an old cardboard suitcase old enough to have belonged to his parents when they were his age. Perhaps his mother or father once carried their possessions in this same bag from the Dust Bowl to wherever they set down new roots. The nervous kid had the uncertain air of a high school sophomore.

A heavyset older man exchanged glances with the other two shadowy figures alongside. "This looks like mine."

The shorter man, dark and stout, the hint of a pencil-thin mustache visible in the gloom, chuckled. "How can you tell he ain't our type?" He elbowed the taller man beside him in an effort to coax a laugh confirming how hilarious his joke was.

It failed. Beside him, the taller man continued his watch, supporting an elbow in one hand, the other balled into a fist under his chin as the fat man waddled off after the teenager.

Two teenage girls stepped off together. Both dressed in pretty pastel dresses, one yellow, the other powder blue, elbows locked together. One step in the lead, the taller of the two appeared a year or two older, as well, and like the boy before her, hesitated long enough to check both ways before taking the irrevocable step onto the concrete platform and into her new life. The younger one, in the jaunty yellow dress, jumped to the ground, far more eager to get underway.

The short, thickset man asked, "They yours?"

"Maybe." His eyes remained focused on the last passenger, lingering halfway back among the seats, who stood facing the far side of the bus; impossible to guess from the shadows what problem delayed her. The driver swiveled in his seat, craning his head back at her as well. From the look of it, using valuable extra seconds packing something back into her suitcase as her last chance to build up her nerve.

The wary pair of girls made their way toward the station and ventured inside. The shorter man watched their every step, then turned his attention back to the bus. "Hurry up, will ya?" His elbow jabbed the taller figure again. "What's the matter, Kid —wind blowing the wrong way?"

"Something like that. You going to let those two get away?"

"I figured the one in blue was the one you were looking for. Besides, I can't always leave the prime cuts for you."

Turning to gaze down at him, the taller shadow did chuckle this time. "If I can't save 'em all from you, just allow me to salvage the most precious gems."

The stocky man snorted unpleasantly at such an unnecessary dig. "One of these days I'm gonna find out what the hell you do with 'em. Never seen 'em on the streets with the others. Donnie says you send 'em to New York or Hollywood."

"Well, Donnie's a knucklehead. You never know, though—sometimes empty heads come up sevens."

"Wake up, ace, here she comes." The shorter man may not have modeled his style of speech after Edward G. Robinson with intent, but nevertheless achieved the result. "Now we're cooking with gas—take a look at that cookie!"

Descending the steps gingerly as walking the plank, this girl looked to be about the same age as that boy the chubby man ran off after, although she had one of those faces that could be a year or two either way, still rounded by baby fat, although with a figure near fully ripe. Very blonde with light eyes, although the distance and poor lighting made it impossible to determine the color. Those eyes scanned around before she took that last step from the safety of the bus, stopping upon the two faint outlines watching her.

The Kid tilted his head back an inch, and he made that weird sniffing sound he always made. That is why the stockier of the two ribbed The Kid about the wind. No one knew why he did it, some of the regulars assuming it was his *tell*, like that twitch some gamblers get after drawing the wild card while sitting on an inside straight flush. Others believed he actually smelled something, but most dismissed it as a mere manifestation of his overall eccentricity. The Kid was a strange one. Almost creepy.

"Jeeze Louise, don't tell me you can smell her from here."

"Can't you?"

"Yeah, sure, Kid. Smells like vanilla and lettuce. Lettuce with President McKinley's ugly mug printed on it." Only four years before, soon after the Japanese surrendered, the Treasury Department ceased printing the $500 bills featuring a scowling McKinley, but every two-bit gangster still had a stash socked away for a rainy day.

"That's your problem, buddy—you've been sniffing for money so long the inside of your nose is coated with a layer of printer's ink." He waved his hand in front of his nose, the way grandmas check a soup's aroma before serving it. "Wine connoisseurs call it bouquet. Now, you'd better get moving before those two babydolls go poof into the night!"

"You better watch it, Kid! Somebody might begin thinking you are getting too big for your britches."

"They might still be inside! Consider it as your ship came in: two for one."

The shorter guy hurried off, disappearing into the station hot on the trail of two gullible teenagers in search of a fresh start. The blonde started in that direction, too, but lurched to a halt when the goon entered the station, which she hoped offered her refuge. Then the pretty teenager made Lot's wife's mistake, looking back as the taller man stepped from the shadows.

"You look lost."

"No, it's swell. I'm meeting someone."

"You sure are. What's your name?"

"Jeanette."

"What are you so afraid of, Jeanette?"

"Nothing… I just don't talk to strangers."

"Oh, I see. A wise precaution. And the folks you expected are running a little late." She nodded while swiveling her head to scan the empty platform in search of a cop or station agent. "Then how about I wait here with you until they show up? So many unsavory characters frequent this place after dark."

"No, I'll be fine."

"You're scared of me, aren't you?"

"Not at all."

"Then why won't you even look at me?" Her eyes fluttered up, briefly meeting his. Brilliant green as a 7Up bottle. "Listen, we'll stay right here. Bright lights, station manager around here somewhere. Until your friends show up. Keep each other company while you let me chase off the goons."

His eyes rolled toward where the stocky man had hurried

away, no doubt still lying in wait, and the corners of her mouth curled up slightly. "Inside?"

"Sure. They have chairs in there, better than these uncomfortable concrete benches."

More comfortable than the worn seat on the bus, too, and so brightly lit. The goon had vanished, as had the other two girls from the bus. The tall guy looked strong but with a pleasant smile and handsome face. Not at all scary. Like a college student, with gorgeous eyes of blue that were bright and safe. Except no college kid would have such an expensive, double-breasted Navy suit, the kind George Raft might wear on the silver screen. He took the seat beside hers. "What is your name?"

"They call me The Kid."

"Why?"

"I guess because I'm older than I look. How old do you think I am?"

"Maybe twenty-one?"

"Blackjack," he said, and that made her giggle. "You always that good at guessing?"

"Tonight must be my lucky night."

"You can say that again. Hey, let me guess who is meeting you here… your aunt. No, aunt and uncle on your mother's side."

"Can I be honest?"

"I don't know, can you?"

That brought the hint of a smile, but it lasted only a second before reality set back in. "There isn't anyone meeting me here."

"I see." Quiet descended. Inside, the bus station might as well have been a crypt. "I had to leave home, too."

"Really? Why?"

"Oh, it's a long story, one so strange you won't believe, so what's the point?"

"Where is the YWCA? Is it nearby?"

"Not far. Can I tell you something?" Her head bobbed in tiny, rapid movements, and he leaned close, eyes boring directly into hers. A chilly breeze blew through the door and swept a newspaper off a wooden bench onto the floor.

Eyes reveal so much about someone. His were so deep.

THE COPS

Dead bodies have a bad habit of luring morbid vultures.

A phalanx of uniformed officers held the crowd of reporters, photographers, and curious neighbors at bay and in the street when Scott Branford arrived. As one of the lead detectives of the busy Kansas City Homicide-Robbery Squad, he lost count of the number of these calls he responded to over the years. This one sounded different, though. The captain sent Detective Ralph Stringer along with him, which was odd enough.

Branford worked alone.

"Sounds like we may have a maniac on the loose," the captain warned them. "Don't let the press turn this into a circus."

Along the way, he lost Stringer in the morning rush-hour traffic. Their unmarked Hudsons equipped with neither lights nor sirens, so drivers did not get out of their way like they did for black & whites. A year or two before, the very concept of morning rush hour in this city would have sounded ridiculous.

"Hope you didn't eat breakfast," Sergeant Gallagher greeted him at the scene and pointed. "Thank Greene and Smitty for the puke over there."

"Just coffee for me, Gallagher," the detective answered. He pronounced it *Gallaher*, the Irish pronunciation the Sergeant preferred. "That bad, huh?"

"Never seen anything like it. The work of a lunatic, if you ask me."

Not one for hyperbole, Gallagher had seen it all in his lengthy career as a cop, first in New York then, after serving in the Pacific during the war, when he settled out here for what he hoped to be the promise of a quieter life. "Coming from you, Sarge, that's saying something."

"Worst I've ever seen this side of Okinawa. We've got a regular Black Dahlia here." The veteran patted him on the shoulder before turning his attention to a couple of pesky beat reporters trying to work their way around through adjoining back yards.

Two years before, the infamous murder and savage butchery of Elizabeth Short out in L.A. gripped the entire population from coast to coast. In fact, most people could recite from memory every gory detail of the discovery of her mutilated body in eerily similar circumstances along a residential street in the City of Angels. Much like this street. For two years the killer evaded justice, and no suspects meant the homicidal maniac who butchered that poor woman was still on the loose… somewhere. The last thing Kansas City needed was for that madman to show up here.

Even Gallagher's warning failed to adequately prepare the homicide detective the awful sight when he lifted the large tarpaulin covering the body.

In life, she must have been lovely. Young—twenty, twenty-five tops—slender yet shapely with movie-star looks. Her skin so devoid of color in death, she might have been sculpted from paraffin wax. The unnervingly precise way her body had been laid out. Posed. Arms out at her sides, one straight, the other bent up at a 90-degree angle with her palm up, exposing a gash running alongside the tendon on the inside of her wrist. Hair arranged in a meticulous halo around her head. Legs crossed at the ankles completed the impression of a debauched crucifix.

But her most obvious feature was her body had been severed in the middle. Cut clean in two, through the stomach, her hips lay almost three feet distant from her lower ribs. Across her chest, placed between blood-drained breasts, a fresh red rose with its vibrant colors formed a stark comparison.

No, posed was not the right word. Displayed.

"Jesus Christ," Stringer exclaimed. "One of the patrolmen said Black Dahlia to me, and I thought he was jerking my chain."

"Yeah, she looks exactly like what we have here. You don't suppose he came to KC, do you?"

"That's all we need. What have we got?"

"Outside the obvious, not sure. I only beat you by a couple of minutes. Didn't the killer carve up the Black Dahlia's face?"

"Like a clown, they say. Ear to ear grin, and mutilated in other ways, too. This one's only cut in half."

"Not quite." Branford pointed to her wrist. "One wound visible there. Looks like someone worked her over good, but with fists, not a weapon. Notice anything missing?"

"Blood," Stringer said, his eyes scouring the grass and dirt around the corpse.

"Bingo. Not a drop. The rain doesn't explain that because it never rained hard enough to wash this much blood away."

"So he killed her somewhere else."

"We have a winner. Someone killed her, did this to her, then dumped her for some unlucky slob to stumble over. In this case, a kid on his way to elementary school. Got the kind of lesson the don't teach in class today. Let's get a grid search going: tire tracks, muddy footprints, cigarette butts—that sort of thing."

Stringer looked up as a white panel truck pulled to a stop. "I'll get Gallagher on it. Coroner's here."

"About time. Clear everyone not part of the grid search off the property and make sure no one gets by them until we finish. And make sure photographers can't snap a picture of her. The mayor will kill us if this," his open hand waved in a circle over her, "winds up on the front page." Just then, a head popped above the wooden fence along the rear of the property line from the adjoining lot. "Hey! Down from there! Someone get that man off the fence!"

Two uniformed officers jogged toward the back. "Go around, stay off this area," Stringer waved a wide circular motion to the two cops, who veered to the edge of the lot, staying close to the house under construction a hundred feet distant.

"Burns warned us not to make this a circus," Branford said. "Looks like the Chief will be disappointed."

†

Sophie Tucker shivered in the rear seat of a squad car alongside Benji. They'd been there so long. Had the police forgotten about them? Not that anyone could blame them, dealing with what Benji had found and she burned into her memory with her own eyes. At least the reporters were distracted from two civilians sitting in one of a dozen or more police cars lining the block. A half hour ago, the cops moved most of those patrol cars along the curb near the coroner's wagon to serve as a barrier blocking all the scavengers filling the street, shouting questions at the officers as they came and went.

A front door opened and a man in a tan trench coat stuck his head in and tipped a sodden gray hat. "Sophie Tucker?"

"Yes?"

"Detective Branford, homicide. We have a few questions for you, if you don't mind. Can we go somewhere we can talk?"

"Our house?"

"We were thinking of the station."

"We live only two blocks from here."

"Alright, I'll have the officer drive you home—I understand you walked here."

"Thank you; we don't have a car."

"We'll be right behind."

The two cars slipped away amidst little notice, thanks to the distraction of the coroner having yet to load the disassembled pieces lying in the field into the meat wagon. Inside the duplex, Sophie asked, "Is it okay if he goes to his room? I don't want him hearing all this."

"Sure. If we need anything from him, we can interview him afterward."

"Go change into some dry clothes, honey." When he

disappeared down the hall, she motioned them to the couch while she sat in an armchair; the detectives sat far apart on the ends, an empty cushion separating them. "How am I supposed to explain why he missed school today?"

"Your son found her? Benji is it?"

"Benjamin. Named after his father."

"Husband?"

As shaky hands lit a Lucky Strike between pursed lips, she shook her head. "Widow. He died in France two weeks after D-Day. Benji was two. A week before his birthday."

"How did he find her?"

"That's on the route to his bus. Came running home saying he found a dead lady. I didn't believe him, but he's not the sort of boy who makes up stories. So, I went to see what brought on his panic."

"Did you see anyone? Anything out of the ordinary?"

"Other than a woman sawed in half, you mean?"

Stringer clarified, "Any cars? Footprints? That sort of thing?"

"Nothing. I followed the trail Benji left through the wet grass earlier. Only closer than where he stopped. Who would do that to another human being?"

"That's what we intend to find out," Branford said. "Benji's path in the grass was still visible? No other marks where anyone else had walked through the field?"

"Not that I saw. Just the one trail that stopped short of the... of her."

"Must have beaten the rain," Stringer said when they left. "That explains the missing footprints in the mud."

"What time did it start raining?"

Stringer shrugged his shoulders. "Went to bed around midnight; it was still dry then." They rode together in Branford's car to the Tucker residence, so they both got in together for the ride back.

"Let's give the coroner a couple of hours to get ready. Back to the murder scene to check for witnesses? I asked the uniformed cops to canvas the area to dig up any neighbors who saw anything."

"Sounds like a plan, Stan."

†

Light rain fell since before daybreak, offering most construction workers the day off, save for one house two blocks away which already had a roof, where work on the interior continued as normal. Few residents had moved into this brand-new development, intended to provide housing for a huge, modern factory being built nearby. All that would change in a few months, as the lots were selling like hotcakes, thanks in no small part to the low down-payment rates offered to war veterans. But families had yet to move onto this block, making witnesses hard to come by.

The beat cops had flagged a couple of promising leads, albeit no eyewitnesses. Most promising: a man living several blocks away.

"My dog was whining to go out," he told the detectives. "He runs, and since these houses don't come with fenced yards, until we can fence it, I need to walk him."

Branford asked, "Tell us what you saw."

"A car drove by. An Auburn boattail. Nice condition, late 30s; that's what caught my eye. That and the fact that no one is on the road at 2:30 in the morning. Dark red, but looked black as night until he passed under that streetlight down the block."

"2:30? Are you usually up at that hour?"

"Yeah. Don't sleep well."

Branford asked, "Where did you serve?"

"101st. D-Day to Bastogne. Sent home from there. Shrapnel."

"I get it; same happens to me. Italy myself. First Infantry. Big Red One," Bradford motioned with his eyes and a tilt of the head. "This guy had it easy over in the Pacific. Iwo Jima. Did you see who was driving this old Auburn?"

"Not well. The streetlight is down past here, so all I could see is one guy driving alone. Light hair. Young. Younger than us."

"How young? A kid?"

"No. Maybe twenty, something like that. Hard to tell for sure."

"Where did this Auburn boattail go?"

"Who knows? My dog shits, I take him back in. Far as I know, he kept driving straight."

Stringer asked, "Towards where we found Jane Doe?"

"That's why I mentioned something to the officer there at the scene. It was out of place. Who drives this block that late at night, toward exactly where cops find a dead body the next morning? Not many old Auburns in this neighborhood. Don't get me wrong, the houses are great…"

"Just not built for someone driving a car that costs $2500."

"Bingo."

"Tell you what: if you see that red Auburn again, jot down the license plate and give us a ring. One of us will probably be awake, so we'll swing on by and have a chat with the driver."

THE VICTIM

The city shelled out the cost for a modern coroner's office after the war, less than two years before. A couple of gleaming factories and all the new residents flooding in with the post-war boom brought with them massive new tax revenues. The city spared no expense, equipping the lab with the latest refrigerated storage filling one wall with individual stainless-steel doors that opened into sliding slabs. Two examining tables, still-sparkling blue tile floors, and the latest scientific equipment arrayed on black countertops opposite the freezer bank. A stark contrast to the grim tasks performed behind its doors.

Stan Rhodes had Jane Doe laid out on the table.

"You boys outdid yourself this time," the coroner greeted them.

Stringer moved an ashtray to the edge of the counter nearest the examining table and flicked ashes into it. "What can we say? We're overachievers, Stan. What can you tell us?"

"I'll have more after the autopsy. Can I convince you to stick around?"

Bradford grinned. "We'll take a pass. Give us something to work with. Somebody already told the press she's been cut into pieces, so there's a lot of heat simmering with this one."

"Well, I need not explain the obvious. Clean bisection at the waist. External examination revealed a couple of other wounds—one to her wrist, another back here." Rhodes lifted hair several shades lighter, now dried out of the rain, and turned her head to the left, revealing a half-inch gash behind the ear. "Both incisions are to veins, which may help explain perhaps the most unusual finding—other than being cut completely in half."

Stringer asked, "What's that?"

"This body has been completely exsanguinated. Look here." Rhodes rolled the torso half to reveal the back. "Notice anything missing?"

"No lividity?" Branford wrinkled his brow.

"Bingo. Give this man a kewpie doll."

Stringer bent down to inspect the back. "What does that mean?"

"Either massive blood loss caused her death or someone immediately drained all her blood post-mortem."

One eyebrow raised, Stringer asked, "Like by cutting her in half?"

"No. This was post-mortem, not the cause of death. And since blood stops flowing the instant the heart stops pumping it, severing a corpse will not drain all the blood from inside. No, she was intentionally drained of blood."

"Through the wounds to her neck and wrist?"

"Another kewpie doll for Detective Branford. Like she was butchered. Funny thing about butchering a deer or a hog—you slit the artery, not the vein. Heck, most people just slice the entire neck; these wounds hardly seem enough to explain such a dramatic loss of blood. Several contusions to her face and chest, too, abrasions without blood, the bruises are not pronounced."

"Let's hope the full autopsy will give you some idea how that happened," Stringer said.

"What else can you tell us?"

"Nothing to help ID her, if that's where you're heading. No marks or scars. I'll send over fingerprints, but my gut tells me she has no arrest record. Oh, someone washed her body post mortem."

"Washed?" Branford's puzzled expression only grew more intense. "Like scrubbed?"

"Bathed, scrubbed. She smells of soap, and not a trace of blood is anywhere on her externally—nothing else, for that matter, other than dirt and grass from the crime scene. Which is not where he killed and butchered her."

"Yeah, we knew that," Branford explained. "No blood on the ground there. So the killer has plenty of time to carve her up, then transports her body where he displays it for his audience to see. Like another very famous crime victim."

"Someone needed to say it. Glad it wasn't me," the coroner deadpanned.

"Here's what's eating me, Doc: what level of, um, skill does someone need to slice a woman in half like this?"

"Ah, the very question that the Black Dahlia herself raised. Is this a hemicorporectomy requiring medical knowledge, or is this simple butchery? Not as easy a question to answer as you might hope," the coroner pointed to the exposed, severed ends of the spine. "See how clean the spinal transection between the second and third lumbar vertebrae is? What this suggests clinically: either the person who did this has extensive medical knowledge or it is the result of dumb luck."

Branford pressed the issue. "Give your odds of each."

"Dumb luck? 70%. Both these other lacerations accurately piercing veins gives me pause. Let's bump it up to 40% medical training, considering those. Could a doctor have done this? Absolutely. Did these mutilations require a surgeon's hand? Probably not. Perhaps a closer examination during the full autopsy will draw a clearer picture."

With a tap of the gurney next to Jane Doe's feet, Stringer said, "Well, don't let us hold you up from that, we've got an Auburn to track down."

The coroner raised one eyebrow. "An Auburn?"

"A witness saw a boattail in the vicinity," Branford explained. "Probably nothing, so keep it under your hat. A lead's a lead, but he left us so little to work with, we'll take any luck we can get."

"Good luck. Whoever did this—get him off our streets."

Pointing a loaded finger at Rhodes with a kick as it fired, Stringer said, "That's the plan, Stan."

†

The grand scheme involved starting with doctors owning Auburns and expanding out from there. Like the Spruce Goose, this plan barely got off the ground. Turns out Auburn produced a grand total of only 143 Speedsters before the company fell victim to the Depression. The hard part was locating one in Missouri. Of those 143, only two boattails were registered in the state. Neither of those was red.

"Red was not a factory option on the boattail." His partner leaned on Branford's desk to break the bad news. "Their color choices were more conservative in the thirties, likely because driving a snazzy convertible while half the country was out of work is ostentatious enough without painting it bright red."

"Could be from out of state."

"Or someone could have repainted it with Jane Doe's blood. In either case, I asked the captain to wire every police department in Missouri and the surrounding states to be on the lookout for our red Auburn. Gave me a look like he thought I'd been drinking, but he put Saldano on it. If it's on the road, we'll find it."

†

Afternoon editions of the Kansas City Star and papers around the state all ran their own versions of the same eight-column banner headline. By five p.m., Jane Doe had a name.

Red Dahlia.

Wire services broadcast the grisly story far and wide. Similar headlines across the country carved her name in stone before the sun set. By the next morning, her name was on everyone's lips in every corner of the country. Everyone knew in their guts the Black Dahlia's murderer now roamed the streets of Missouri in search of his next victim.

Kansas City did not lack for murders. Over the last few months, the homicide squad experienced an alarming spike in the number of murdered and missing young women. Many cleared already, with boyfriends and husbands the most commonly arrested, but a few defied easy solution. Two of those involved wounds to the wrist or neck, although neither were cut in half or otherwise mutilated, and across the Mississippi River in Kansas, a young woman had been killed by a puncture wound to the neck reminiscent of Jane Doe's.

"What do you make of this, Stringer?"

The detective took the file Branford handed him and began flipping through the pages. "Emily Sonntag. That puncture wound looks like Jane Doe's. Garcia's handling this?"

"Sure is. He's on lunch break, but the injury is not the only similarity. Another pretty girl, this one twenty-four. Cause of death is blood loss—not as complete as Jane, but then again, Miss Sonntag was not sliced in two. Check out that witness statement."

Stringer flipped to it. "Last seen in the company of an unidentified male, age around twenty-one, height six-foot to six-one. Expensive dark suit, fair hair. Think he is our boattail driver?"

"Makes you wonder, doesn't it? One last seen with a mystery blond, the other found near where a mystery blond was seen driving a car that had no business being there. Know what I am thinking?"

"We need to start shaking down tall blond men?"

"Too many—that will take forever. What we really need is Garcia's witness to sit down with a sketch artist."

None of those other murders captured the community's imagination the way a Red Dahlia found in a rain-soaked vacant lot did. Rumors embellished every aspect of Jane's murder at the speed of sound, from her wounds to fantastical stories of messages written on her body in lipstick or blood. Hysteria spreads more rapidly than a forest fire on a windy day.

Perhaps the most surprising thing was the number of missing redheads. Calls began pouring in soon as the news hit the wires. First routed to Branford and Stringer, after about twenty such calls, the captain began distributing them throughout the department to free up the two lead detectives. The chance call still slipped through.

"Homicide, Branford."

A tentative voice on the line said, "Hi, I may know who the Red Dahlia is. Are you the one investigating her murder?"

"I am. Let me get your name?"

"Lida Santelli. My sister went missing. Carmen Santelli. She lives in Kansas City, on Elm Street."

"How long has your sister been missing?"

"Two weeks. She's thirty. She has black hair, but she always liked red hair; I think she may have dyed it…"

"Okay, I have some good news for you. Carmen is not our Jane Doe."

"How can you be sure?"

"Because Jane Doe did not dye her hair. If you want to put in a missing person report for your sister, you can call Jackson four, three three…"

"No, that will be okay. I'm sure she will turn up—she always does." Click.

Still shaking his head as Stringer walked up, Branford said, "Does it sound to you like people actually want their missing loved one to be Jane Doe?" So far, the department had refrained from referring to the victim as Red Dahlia.

"Well, you might want to come with me—Jane Doe's husband is downstairs.

†

"Leslie has been acting strange for a few weeks. Staying out late, acting drunk when she gets home, although she swears she hasn't been drinking and her breath is clean."

Richard Haas fidgeted with a white gold wedding ring. He looked to be about forty, dressed in an expensive suit and spotless silk tie, seeming to Branford an unlikely match for the young woman on the slab downstairs. "What makes you suspect your wife may be our Jane Doe?"

"She never came home three days ago, and Leslie has long red hair, like the papers say Red Dahlia has."

Still skeptical, he asked, "Why didn't you report her as a missing person?"

"See, here's the thing." His voice lowered, and he leaned forward on his elbows as if conveying a secret. "I suspect she's got a guy, been two-timing me. When we married, she was still in high school. Sweet sixteen. After graduation, gals like her don't last long on the market, not with a million soldiers returning home from war in their uniforms covered with medals. Her parents found themselves in some financial difficulty, and as a result, I was in a position to offer them some help. One thing led to another, and…"

With a nod, Stringer said, "Show him the picture, Mr. Haas."

A wedding photo from the photo flip in his wallet showed a beaming Haas holding a stony-faced bride in all white with his arms around her stomach, pulled tight to his chest. After studying the small photograph with a jaundiced eye, Branford asked, "Your wife is blonde?"

"I like platinum blondes. Been a Jean Harlow fan for years. Back then, she dyed her hair for me, but a couple of years ago, she started refusing. Naturally, it is light auburn, the one thing I never liked about her."

"Aside from sneaking around town, maybe with another guy?"

"Well, yeah."

"Any clue who this other man is?"

"No idea. See, she never had a chance to sow her wild oats. I didn't like it, but what's a guy to do? I come home from working late and there's a note. *Going out with the girls. Don't wait up.* What can I do, lock her in the basement?"

"What do you think, Branford? Mrs. Haas does resemble Jane Doe."

Rather than answering, he asked another question. "Mr.

Haas, has your wife ever tried to harm herself?"

The husband responded with an adamant tone, offended by such an insulting question. "Of course not!"

"Are you sure?" Every instinct in Branford's body told him the man was lying to cover up something.

"Okay, right after the first time she pulled that crap with her friends, we had this big blow-up. I didn't really hurt her or anything, just made sure she understood I was serious. You know. Well, she overreacts to everything. The next night I come home to find her in the bath, blood everywhere. She only did it for attention; she wasn't trying to cause herself harm."

"Did what?"

"She slashed her wrist, okay? There, I said it." Haas slumped back in the chair with his arms clenched across his chest. "Damn thing never did heal right. I wrapped it up, and the bleeding stopped, but it never scabbed over. Still looks raw, even now."

"Mr. Haas," Branford said, "will you come with us? We need to see if you can identify her remains."

A few minutes later, down in the basement, Branford handed Hass his handkerchief to wrap around his bleeding fist. From the sound of it, several bones in his hand broke when the Red Dahlia's husband punched the concrete block wall of the coroner's viewing room.

"What kind of monster does this to a woman?"

"That's what we aim to find out," Stringer assured the grieving widower. "We are going to need a list of your wife's friends—starting with those girls she spent time with over the last few weeks."

THE BUTTERFLY

A small trickle of viscous, bluish-red liquid crept toward Jeanette's chin from one corner of her pallid pink lips. Most of her blood red lipstick had worn off, revealing the more alluring, natural tint beneath. Her tongue flicked out, alluringly catching the drop before it got too far. She giggled.

"I can hear my parents now, angry and telling me how unladylike my behavior is."

The Kid leaned on the table; he hadn't taken his eyes off her since they sat down. "They are wrong; it is very ladylike."

"These blueberry pancakes are delicious. How did you convince them to whip up some this late?"

Funny how blueberries resemble blood. Intact, the berry is the darkest blue, but when cooked and pierced by a fork, the juice runs down the golden-brown surface and the white interior a dark red as if the berry itself is bleeding from its wounds.

"I'll let you in on a little secret." He leaned closer, wagging his finger until she, too, leaned, mirroring him, her emerald eyes a foot from his. He whispered. "This place serves breakfast 24 hours a day."

Her eyes lit up, her mouth forming an O that threatened to turn into a smile. "That's it? What's so secret about that?"

"They do it for me, because I frequent the place at all hours. Sometimes I will order an omelet at three in the morning. Other nights," he dipped his finger into the blood-tinged maple syrup on her plate and sucked it off, "I prefer something sweet."

"If I come here tomorrow night—without you—and order more pancakes, will they refuse to serve me?"

"Probably not. Jane, our waitress—she has the memory of an elephant. She will never forget you came here with me."

"Why do they do this for you?"

"The owner and I are... close. A few years ago, she was much like you: alone, frightened, didn't know anyone in town. I helped her. Now, she owns this cafe."

"We don't have these in Diamond, Missouri. I've seen diners like this in the movies, but never have eaten in one." During the war, this shiny aluminum restaurant rolled the rails across the Midwest as the dining and kitchen cars of a train. Hundreds of its passengers soldiers and sailors heading off to war, and more than a few who never returned from Italy or France or some island in the Pacific. Now it was Main Street Diner, open 24/7 and serving breakfast all day and all night to a few select customers.

"What do they have in Diamond?"

"Nothing. Nothing at all. You've heard of a one-stoplight town? Well, Diamond still hasn't gotten its traffic light yet." When he scoffed, she said, "No kidding! We have a stop sign and a train stop—freight only—where they load cattle and wheat and vegetables. And a general store. That's about it. Our claim to fame is Bonnie & Clyde robbed our bank once, during the Depression. It's abandoned now; I guess they bankrupted it. Supposedly made off with something like five thousand dollars."

"No kidding?"

"So help me!" She held one hand, palm facing him, and for a minute she stared back at him, but then her sheepish eyes fell to the remainder of her pancakes. "Why are you treating me so nicely?"

"Why wouldn't I be nice to you? Aren't other people nice to you?"

"If they were, do you think I'd be here now? People accuse me of putting on airs, spending too much time reading and earning good grades in school rather than goofing off with my classmates; acting like I'm someone special..."

"You are special."

A flicker of a grin crossed her lips. "Thank you for noticing. My step-father is a real creep. He didn't think I was special. I wanted to stay to help protect my little sister, but it was too late. She is special, apparently. Daddy died in the war and my Mama needed someone to run the farm, so it's not her fault; not really." She paused. "Anywho, now I'm here, the need to worry about those things behind me."

"How true. Your past is behind you. All that's left is your future."

"You never answered me."

"Why I'm so nice?"

"Yes. Why me?"

"Simple, really. When you stepped off the bus, do you remember another man waiting on the platform?"

"That guy who looked like a boxer with his nose punched in? I was wondering who he was and what he was doing there."

"Joey. He's a pimp."

"What's a pimp?"

"Joey takes in girls like you—runaways, orphans, juvenile delinquents. Pretty girls, mostly. Puts them in debt and forces them to work off their debts to him."

"What kind of work?"

"Prostitution, stag films, that sort of thing."

Her head dropped to give him top-eye as if questioning whether he was lying. "He was planning to do that… to me?" Her fork clattered on her plate. "Oh, no—I am not that kind of girl!"

"Of course not. I knew right away."

"How do you know this Joey? The way you were standing there together when the bus pulled in, I assumed you were friends."

"Joey and I go way back. He's not so bad, far as pimps go. Fancies himself a comedian, a regular Abbott and Costello, although he's better at pimping. When he saw you and wanted to have you, I told him to scram."

"Is that what this is about?"

"What what is about?"

Her arm waved in a sweeping circle around the room, then over her half-eaten stack of pancakes. "This—all of it. Am I in your debt now?"

"I am not like Joey. I am not a pimp, nor will I ask you to let other men use your body like a common whore. When I said you are special, that was no lie."

"So you just run around saving girls from being tricked into becoming prostitutes? Are you some kind of Batman, a caped crusader fighting evildoers?"

"Not exactly."

"Then what exactly are you, and why are you so interested in helping me?"

"Maybe it's easier if I show you than trying to explain it to you."

"No, I don't think so. Don't misunderstand, I appreciate all you've done for me. Maybe I should be heading to the YWCA now."

His eyes looked so sad, the way puppy dogs do, only a brilliant, wonderful blue. Beautiful and the way he gazed without blinking, as though nothing else existed. Nothing in the entire world. Although it was a cool evening and she put her cotton sweater on when the bus arrived here, beads of sweat formed on her forehead and temples.

"Are you finished with your pancakes?"

"I think so."

"Then let me show you something else. Someplace you'll enjoy much more than the Y. A place like home—a home the way it should be, where you are valued and treasured. Where you will always be special."

Her mother warned Jeanette about smooth-talking men like him who lived in the city and preyed upon pretty girls. Deadly black spiders laying in wait for a beautiful butterfly to flutter into its web, ensnaring it and preying upon it. Naive girls like her. She didn't believe it—not really. And while she now experienced it, felt the power of his gaze upon her, rather than fear, she felt relaxed, comfortable, tingly in a strange, pleasant way.

None of the boys back home could compete with The Kid, and when one side of his mouth smiled, sweet and innocent as a boy half his age, she wondered if she might in fact melt. A total gentleman, too, the way he held open the car door, lifting her skirt in to make sure not to close it in the door. Like his finely tailored suit that fit him just so, his car also spoke of money and class and safety.

Truth was, when she left home, she dreamed of meeting someone just like him here in the city. A man who would sweep her off her feet, the way it happens in a Frank Capra movie. An older man, but not too old. Like him. After all, she had not given up her life at home to become a secretary or continue in school like nothing happened. And she certainly did not come all this way, spending every spare penny she saved up from babysitting, only to prostitute herself to line some pimp's pockets.

Stupid as The Kid sounded, even his name had the panache of a movie character. A young hero climbing his way to the top, maybe even doing something slightly shady along the way. A crook with a heart of gold. As long as it wasn't too shady, a possibility adding to the excitement of her adventure. As he strode around to the driver's side, she pinched herself to make sure she was not dreaming, snoozing in the back of the Greyhound still miles away from arriving here in town.

Do butterflies realize their fate when their wings first touch the sticky outer strands of a web?

THE GHOST

"You see, there she was: twenty-one, married to a man twice her age who is having a fling with his secretary." She leaned forward and lowered her voice to let them in on a secret. "They have a baby together, Dick and the secretary, but I'm not supposed to know about that, so it didn't come from me."

Lucy and Barb seemed unlikely best friends of a respectable married woman like Leslie Haas. Perhaps a simple case of looks being deceiving as ladies of the night.

Both wore their dark hair permed; Barb's into a Lauren Bacall wave and Lucy still with a roll that framed her face, likely unchanged since the war. If able to overlook their penchant for too much lipstick and rouge, two lovely dishes. Barb's dress buttoned down the front for easy access, which she left unbuttoned from the cleavage up. From the pristine condition of the upper three buttonholes, those buttons had never penetrated those holes.

The initial impression they gave was that Leslie's angelic face, her hair arranged as a halo and her body laid out in a position resembling a perversion of the crucified Christ may have been intended to convey an obscene, false image of the deceased.

But why?

Both Branford and Stringer were eager to take part in this interview, if for no other reason than beautiful women's habit of hunting in packs. No doubt these two had plenty of experience handling men, best when outnumbering their prey. Branford, as lead detective, took control. Women love a man in control. "So she decided to sow her wild oats, as her husband calls it?”

"Leslie never had her chance to have any fun, if you know what I mean." Barb gave a slow wink, the kind that is open to interpretation. "When the secretary's baby came, she never complained. Instead, she took advantage of the free time. Her husband practically moved in over there. Don't get me wrong, she is a nice girl, not too wild."

"But she knew men," Stringer finished for her, changing the tense to past. Whether once good girl or bad, she now was no longer either.

"Oh, sure. The boys love her! When we go out? Well, the rest of us are invisible around her." The detectives suspected Barb had never been invisible, and were she to begin to suspect she went unnoticed, might free the next button.

"Were there a lot of guys?" Branford directed his question at Lucy to confirm what her friend said. Lucy had green eyes, ringed with a narrow band of golden hazel.

"Everyone wanted to meet her, to dance with her. I'm sure detectives with your experience know how that is."

"Sure do. It's more common than you might imagine. Were there any guys in particular? Maybe a tall blond?"

The two turned to each other, nodded, and answered together. "Raul."

"Who's Raul?"

"Oh, he's super sweet." Lucy's painted lids batted like she had something in her eye. "Quite mysterious-like. Leslie monopolizes him—likes to keep him all to herself."

"For good reason," her friend added. "He's a proper gentleman. Handsome, too, and younger. Cultured. Says he grew up on a farm, but talks real educated."

"He wouldn't hurt a fly, if that's what you are thinking. He's more a lover than a fighter." The expression Lucy wore divulged that Leslie had not been the only one infatuated by the mysterious Raul.

Nose and forehead wrinkled like she smelled something bad, Barb asked, "What about Albert? He's pretty questionable."

Branford tilted his head. "Albert?"

"I don't think it's his real name. He's one of the married ones, I'm sure." And Lucy seemed the type to have plenty of married gentlemen friends.

A sour expression spoiling her face, Barb added, "A lot of men go by fake names. They're usually easy to spot."

Her friend concurred. "I saw one guy named 'Steve' at the market, and when I said 'Hi, Steve,' it was like he had been struck stone deaf."

Before she chased this Steve down a rabbit hole he had no interest in, Branford steered her back. "Tell us about this Raul. Has he got a last name?"

"Something Spanish or Italian, I think," Barb said. "I'm so bad with names, exspecially foreign ones."

Lucy's eyes searched the ceiling for the answer. "Silver, maybe? That's not it, but something close. I only heard it once."

"What about this Albert?" Stringer asked. "Know anything more about him?"

"He's not my type; let's leave it at that." Barb nodded in agreement, but Lucy lost her struggle to leave it at that, for she continued, "He only had eyes for Leslie. Never had a minute for me. A lot of guys are like that."

"Too many," Barb agreed.

"What else can you tell us about this Raul? I don't suppose you have an address?" When they denied knowing where he lived, Branford asked, "What does he look like?"

"Not like a Raul, that's for sure."

"What do you mean?"

"When you hear Raul, you think Latin lover. Rudolph Valentino or José Ferrer. Tall, dark and handsome. Well, Raul is two out of three."

"Which two?"

"Tall and handsome. To tell the truth, he looks straight out of one of those Nazi SS recruiting posters from during the war."

"So he's fair-haired?"

"And dreamy blue eyes. Looks so strange on a Raul."

The other detective dug deeper. "What about a car? Have you seen if he owns one?"

"Sorry, I don't know much about cars. All I know is it's an old car, but very nice."

"Like an Auburn Speedster?"

"I don't know."

"Maybe."

Barb's eyes searched the ceiling for answers, which seemed to work for her. "Red. But not fire-engine red. Dark, like a rose."

†

From their window on the second-floor, a portion of which was home to the homicide department, they watched the two sashay toward the bus stop down the block. "What did you make of those floozies?"

"Other than they're not telling us the entire story?"

Stringer picked something from his teeth, examined it, and flicked it away. "Barb was a working girl. Ran into her a few times when I was working vice a couple years ago. Didn't seem to recognize me; then again, she has the memory of an absentminded goldfish."

"Let's dig around into Lucy's background, too."

"You think she's hooking, too?"

Branford craned his neck as they made their way down the block. "Wouldn't surprise me. And if she's working…"

"Maybe Leslie Haas was their co-worker."

A sip from his coffee, then Branford replied, "Wouldn't be the first time a young woman in her shoes steps out on a lousy husband, then enjoys her additional source of spending money. Maybe build up a nest egg so she can leave that worthless two-timer to his family with the secretary. Start a new life for herself down in New Orleans; maybe head west."

Stringer took a box of matches from his pocket to light the cigarette dancing in one corner of his mouth. "Surprised you didn't see it."

"See what?"

"That they're working girls." An exhaled blue cloud extinguished the match. "What's the matter—worried your Mama might suspect something if you can spot a hooker?"

His temporary partner leaned forward, eyes bulging, then without a word turned and stormed down the hall at double-time.

The younger detective called after him, "Was it something I said?"

Lt. Nash, at his nearby desk, narrowed his eyes. "Don't mention his mother."

"What did I say?"

"That his mother might suspect something," he spat out.

"What of it? He's old enough to have outgrown his knickerbockers."

Nash's pencil drummed the desk like Gene Krupa. "Have you worked with him before?"

"Nope. This is our first case."

"Well, consider yourself warned." Then Nash, too, stood and disappeared down the hall in another direction.

†

Several hours later, back at the station, Stringer made a breakthrough. He brought it to his partner's desk. "A Raul di Silva registered a 1936 Auburn Speedster down in New Orleans. Bought it new and registered it again every year until 1942."

"Then what?"

"Then nothing. He stopped registering it, and if he's registered it since, it isn't in Louisiana."

"A lot happened in 1942."

"You can say that again. That's the year I joined the Marines. Think Raul signed up?"

"I guess that depends on whether he was twenty-five or sixty-five."

"Or 4-F."

"Sounds like we need to talk to someone down in New Orleans."

†

Branford had a few contacts down in the Big Easy, so he worked the phone. Afterward, he tracked down Stringer in the records room down in the basement.

"How did I know Raul di Silva would turn out to be a ghost?"

"I expected no less from Raul. What did your sources tell you?"

"Seem odd to you, no one in New Orleans knows Raul di Silva? Usually someone well-off enough to afford an Auburn leaves a mark."

"What do you mean, no one knows him?"

"No real estate, no arrest record, didn't register for the draft. It's like his entire existence consisted of owning a car, registering it once a year until he went up in a puff of smoke."

"And then reappears in the dead of night within spitting distance of where two halves of a pretty redhead are discovered a few hours later." Stringer's dark eyes rolled. "What about the car's registered address?"

With a slow shake of his head and a sigh, Branford said, "That's where it starts getting weird. The police tell me the place has been abandoned since the mid-30s. It's well-known—the local kids say it's haunted, the same reputation every spooky old abandoned house ends up with if unoccupied long enough. Someone owns it, but no one has lived there in nearly twenty years. Nobody picked up on the fact that a car was registered to an empty house; following up on those things takes valuable energy."

"So Raul is a ghost who registers his car at a haunted house, then falls off the map for seven years, until he shows up here, has a left-handed honeymoon with a working girl who ends up cut in half?"

"That about sums it up."

With a chuckle, Stringer said, "I've never arrested a ghost before."

"This one just keeps getting better all the time," Bradford said, then pounded the table with the fleshy part of his fist, hard enough to make the elderly sergeant in charge of records jump.

THE INFORMANTS

Branford tracked down Stringer at the stained coffee pot, scorching on the lone electric eye down in the vice squad. Why they deserved their own coffee pot but homicide-robbery didn't was the subject of heated discussion, most of it around said coffee pot and glowing-hot burner.

"Remember what those two dames told us about Leslie Haas? Turns out it may have been pure horseshit."

"What have ya got?"

"Come down to the interrogation room. There's somebody you will find very interesting. Did you leave me any coffee in the pot?"

"Might have left you half a cup."

"Good, because you aren't going to want to waste valuable time waiting for another pot to percolate."

A disheveled man sat at the lone table in the interrogation room, his reflection off the mirror on the opposite wall forming a double as they walked in. "Henry Donohue, meet Detective Stringer."

"Hiya. Say, do you have any more java?"

"Sorry, this is the last of it." Branford took a seat across from him and explained to his partner, "Henry here worked for that fleabag hotel down on Rosemont..."

"The King's Inn," Henry added, still hoping for a cup of java.

"Right, The King's Inn. Where royalty stays when they visit the Paris of the Plains. How much do they charge per hour, Henry?"

"Buck fifty. Two fifty for a half day."

"Affordable, too. So, aside from kings and queens and the Prince of Wales, tell Detective Stringer who else frequented this establishment."

"The Red Dahlia. She was one of them working girls. Worked for Joey Four Fingers, we called him. Joey Pants I think is his real name."

"Well, well, well. Joey Pentangeli. She was one of his hookers?"

"Oh, yeah. A real beauty, too. Word on the street, she is a natural redhead—that's why Joey charges top dollar for her. Well, that and she was his gal."

One of Stringer's eyebrows raised. "Oh, really—his gal?"

"That was the scuttlebutt. He always stuck around when she was working, never let her out of his sight. Once some clown got a little rough with her, and Joey escorted him out to the alley behind the building. Worked him over real good. Never have seen that guy since."

"Did you turn in a missing persons report on that guy?"

Palms up in the air, Henry answered, "Hey, none of my business, you know? Happened outside. I assume he crawled home afterwards. If he took a swim in the river, I don't know nothing about that."

"We don't give a damn about a John who roughhouses the ladies of the night; we are interested in Leslie Haas, a/k/a Red Dahlia."

"Yeah, that's what I figured. When they canned me..."

Branford chuckled. "Tell Stringer what earned you a pink slip."

"You see, we got this buzzer left over from Prohibition. Still works and all. One day vice comes in, and when they show up, whoever's working the front desk is responsible for hitting the buzzer. Rings down to the boss. Well, I was dealing with these two drunk fucks out in front of the desk when vice bursts in. So they have me against the wall, patting me down like I'm packing. Hell, the shotgun's under the counter, so I don't carry a piece when I'm working…"

"Get around to the point, Henry."

"Right, so vice goes in while I'm up against the wall, and they go downstairs and find the boss' son running his weekly poker game down there. So they take him in on gambling charges. Turns out he had a warrant on him from Georgia. I mean, who the fuck's got a warrant in Georgia? Shot some clown in Savannah, they say, so now he's on some prison farm chain gang down south. Needless to say, the boss found fault with my job performance."

"And that's why you are here?"

"Well, there is a thousand-dollar reward, and money's tight these days."

"The reward is for information about the killer, not about the victim," Stringer deadpanned.

"Oh."

Branford smiled with genuine empathy. "There's always a catch, Henry."

"Well, you guys won't tell where you got this, will ya? Like, if you give a reward?"

"Now Henry, would we still be in business if we let slip where we get our information?"

Branford added, "Everything is in strict confidence. Hence, the word *confidential* in confidential informant. And if your information helps us catch the butcher who killed Leslie Haas, we'll hand you an envelope stuffed with cash and no one will ever know."

"Good. In that case, you might want to take a look at Joey Four Fingers. Something was wrong with the guy for a couple of days before Red Dahlia showed up dead in someone's yard. Had a real chip on his shoulder, and most times he's a funny guy; you know, wisecracking and joking with everyone like he's Bob Hope. Last time he had his gal in there, you'd think he was at a funeral. Next thing I know, his dame is on the front pages 'cause someone filleted her like a fish. Haven't seen him since, although I got fired, so who knows after that." He emphasized with a shrug of his shoulders.

"What's the word on Joey since then?"

"That's the thing: nobody's seen him. I asked, 'cause of his gal being killed and all. If he's in town, he's holed up somewhere out of sight."

"So you think he whacked his gal?"

"Joey's got a temper—I don't need to tell you guys that. Everyone knows. Wouldn't be the first time a pimp snaps his cap if his gal likes a John, comments on how good he is in the sack, how big he is, that kinda thing."

"No, it sure would not," Branford agreed. "Tell you what, Henry: if this leads anywhere, I will personally slip a grand into your pocket and no one but the three of us will know about it. How's that sound?"

From the hopeful expression on the unemployed desk clerk's face, it was the best news he heard all day.

†

Hard as it was to contain their excitement about the first solid lead they had, but to Branford, it did not ring true.

"Can you imagine Joey Pentangeli with his steak knife, sawing a woman in half? That ain't his style. Let alone his own gal. Bash her face in for saying a John was hung like a horse— sure, I'd buy it. Cut off her head? Okay, I'm with you. Carefully carve her up like that injury we saw?"

His reluctance did not sit well with Stringer. "So, after two weeks of nothing, you're willing to ignore all that?"

"Did I say anything about forgetting it? Henry's information, if it holds up, might lead to the break we needed, but he's got it all wrong. Joey may be a butcher, but he's not the kind of butcher we're looking for."

After mulling that possibility over in his mind, Stringer asked, "So, what's your point?"

"Point is, Joey knows who the butcher is. Why do you think he's gone underground? Something went down. Something very bad. Maybe Joey hired someone to take care of his lady friend, or maybe it was something else. If you decide to send someone like Joey a message, how do you do it?"

"Hacking his gal in two is quite a loud message."

"Reminds me of the message the Mob sent a couple of years ago when they blew Bugsy Siegel's head off in Virginia Hill's living room. They used an M-1 Carbine, for crying out loud! They say one of his eyes was rolling around all the way on the other side of the room."

With a dubious expression, Stringer asked, "You sayin' this was a mob hit?"

"Are you working a better angle?"

"We need to get our hands on Joey Four Fingers, don't we?"

"Yup. I wonder if he still has all four fingers? Heck, from the sound of it, we should hurry before Joey starts turning up in pieces around town."

†

Henry was right about one thing: Joey Pentangeli had vanished. According to the various stories on the street, smart money had him either in Havana or New York, buried somewhere north of town, or else floating downriver toward the Gulf of Mexico. Given those choices, they started dragging the river first.

On a hunch, Branford asked one informant whether he knew of any connection between Joey Four Fingers and Raul di Silva.

"Oh sure, they know each other."

"And how are they acquainted?"

"They both work the bus terminal. Joey gets lots of his girls there. Runaways are his specialty. He has a thing for the younger ones; people pay top dollar for the kids and they don't give as much lip as the older broads."

"So Raul's a pimp?"

"Who knows? Real strange agent, that guy. None of his

girls ever show up working the streets or in any of the whorehouses around town. What he does with 'em, no one knows. Plenty of people ask questions, but nobody has real answers about the guy. Keeps mostly to himself, doesn't seem to be involved in any rackets, stays outta trouble. Just collects girls. Real particular, too. Always takes the pick of the litter."

"Pimps like Joey let Raul skim the cream of the crop?" Stringer's mixed metaphor made Branford cringe a little, but nonetheless drove the point across.

"Yeah. Everyone's a little scared of the guy. He's been in his share of tussles over the years and no one ever lands a glove on him. Tore a guy's arm half off about two years back. He's a strange cat, that one. Hates being called Raul, so everyone calls him The Kid, 'cause he looks like he's eighteen, twenty tops. Been around since the war, though, so he's gotta be older than that. Good looking kid, too. Pretty gals always go for a pretty guy, know what I mean?"

"Yeah," Stringer answered, even if no answer was required. "Ain't that the truth?"

†

Along the riverbanks, while uniformed officers searched among logs, rocks and underbrush, boats dragged hooks through the mud on the bottom of the Missouri River searching for Joey Four Fingers, the detectives focused on the enigmatic name that kept popping up in their investigation while observing police boats zigzagging across the water.

Their confidential informant knew more about him than anyone in the precinct house. Not a single arrest or any other contact with the police they could unearth, and Lord knows they tried. Part of the reason the captain assigned Stringer to this case was his uncanny research ability. Due more to knowing an astounding network of people with access to information than his ability to dig it up himself, the detective went to work on his contacts.

Took him less than a day to uncover information that only enhanced their bewilderment.

"Take a gander at this." It didn't matter to Stringer that Branford was eating a sandwich with his phone propped to his ear with one shoulder.

His free arm reached for the official-looking document. "What is this?"

"Raul di Silva is dead."

"Let me call you back," he said and dropped the phone in its cradle to focus on the document.

"What?"

"Yeah, you heard me right. Doing pretty good for a dead guy, too. According to the State of Louisiana, he died of polio in 1932. He was seven."

"How can we be sure this is our Raul di Silva?"

"Because he's the only one anywhere near the right age. They say a guy by that name lives down in Miami, where he retired at the end of the war. He's in his seventies."

"Hey, maybe he just looks great for his age."

Branford stared at the papers scattered over his desk, shaking his head. "Our perp uses an alias because he hates his bogus name? Doesn't make a lick of sense."

"Your Crescent City ghost theory is sounding better all the time."

THE ROSES

It was a strange place. The house itself was picturesque, a stately Victorian built from brick with a porch painted white wrapping all the way around the front and one side. Fit for a Hollywood movie. Shutters of black at each window, several closed up on the second floor, which struck her as odd. From the outside, it resembled any other house in this tony neighborhood.

Two residents shared this house with The Kid. Two girls, both older than her, the elder, Kat, perhaps a few years older than him. The younger was a colored girl named Grace, with skin the color of coffee with extra cream. Maybe a mulatto, from her exotic look, although she had only heard about them herself, making certainty impossible. At first, she figured Grace must be The Kid's maid, although she did not wear the uniform of a domestic. In fact, like Kat, she wore a fancy dress fit to attend a fancy party.

It's not that she had never seen colored people before, just never one as pretty as Grace. Both girls were so gorgeous she paled alongside them, awkward and plain, and in her mind had trouble deciding which was the prettier of the two.

"Why don't you girls show Jeanette to the guest room? The one on the left."

Before she could pick it up from where The Kid placed it, Kat snatched up her suitcase and started toward the stairs. "Come on, let's get you settled!"

Kat placed her bag on the bed and flopped down next to it while Grace opened the shutters. "This room gets morning sun. You will love the view."

"Thank you." The furnishings were antique and in pristine condition, the bed a canopy held up by four hand-tooled posts and a double wedding-ring quilt, white with pastel color rings. "It's lovely."

"He appreciates beautiful things." Grace giggled as if Kat referred to an inside joke.

"I am confused. Are you... who are you to The Kid?" Turning to the older one, she asked, "Is one of you his wife?"

"Oh, no," answered Kat.

"We're just friends."

In a cryptic manner, Grace added, "Like you."

"But you live here?"

"Yes." Both nodded.

"And The Kid does, too?"

"Of course; it is his house," Grace said.

"Where I come from, if a man lived with a single lady, the sheriff would drag them to jail—let alone two ladies."

"Three," Kat corrected her.

"I'm just here until..." she stopped, unable to explain what she was doing there, despite being a massive, undeniable upgrade from her sketchy plan to spend her first night in a strange city at the Y.

In fact, thinking back, she could not recall why she chose to accept his invitation, generous as opening his house to her might be. A fog lifted from her, leaving instead in its place a weight, crushing in its heft. None of this made sense, unless this stranger intended to make her part of some suburban harem right here in Kansas City. Stories of horrific things taking place in big cities provided endless fascination in small towns— including her own—but could it be possible such tall tales were real?

A pimp targeted her before even setting foot in the city, so what form of debauchery was *not* possible here?

"How long have you been here?"

"A year for me," Grace answered, "but she's been here longer."

"Almost two."

"Until now, just the two of you? Plus The Kid, of course."

"Oh no," Grace laughed.

"Heavens no," Kat concurred. "He's always bringing strays home with him."

"There are others?"

Grace smiled. "Not now. They move on. Some go home to where they came from; city life isn't for everyone. A couple are married now…"

"Did he take you to Main Street Diner?" When Jeanette nodded, Kat continued. "The lady who owns it was here when I arrived. Now she has her own house over on Oak Street."

"Does he expect you—us—does he take liberties with you?" Both girls laughed, loud and free. "What's so funny?"

Grace asked, her manner friendly, lighthearted, "Have you been with a man?"

"Of course not! I'm only fifteen!"

Turning to Kat, Grace said, "He has an eye, doesn't he?"

"Honey, lots of girls your age have experience in those things, whether they want it or not. Not us," Kat waved her hand between herself and Grace. "We're still virgins. The Kid has a knack for picking us out. That's why he chooses us. I have no clue how he spots us."

"All his strays are virgins. At least they claim to be."

Weird as it might seem, to someone from a big city in particular, a person picking random girls of her age in her small town stood a good chance of selecting an inexperienced girl. The same in most small towns. Plenty of exceptions, of course: fast girls and drunken fathers and the occasional slick-talking boyfriend whose clever manipulation convinces girlfriends to give in to their base instincts. But small towns clung to valued traditions from the simpler times big cities were rapidly abandoning.

Perhaps The Kid had cultivated a knack for spotting those girls.

But why?

"Oh! I see," Jeanette said, embarrassed by her naivety. "I've never met one before. We don't have them in Diamond. You can't tell them from regular people, can you?"

After a confused, wordless exchange between them, Grace and Kat together asked, "What?"

"We don't have queers in Diamond. Well, we did once, but the men in town…"

Both girls laughed so hard that Kat fell back across the bed and Grace collapsed nearby. They spoke, but spasms of mirth made their words incomprehensible for several minutes. Grace got hold of herself enough to say, "She thinks he's queer," which ignited another eruption, Kat slapping the colored girl on the shoulder with such playful familiarity it made Jeanette uneasy. They acted like friends—the closest of friends.

When they regained control at last, she asked, "If he hasn't made a pass at either of you or anyone else staying here, how do you know he isn't… you know?" She chose not to repeat the word to avoid setting them off one more time.

Once again, they exchanged a knowing glance and, almost coordinated with perfect timing, said together, "Oh, we know."

"But you said…"

"Obviously, we said too much. Don't worry, he is a gentleman," Kat assured her. "He didn't bring you here for the purpose you assume. In fact, most girls coming through here find his problem to be quite the opposite."

More confused than ever, nothing making a lick of sense and her hosts laughing at her as a country rube, Jeanette frowned. "If he doesn't make passes at you, what is the problem?"

"Most of the girls end up wishing he desires them in that way. He has that effect on people."

"If he lives in a house with dolls like you and doesn't try anything fresh, then how can you be so sure he isn't queer?"

Once again, they laughed, although more sarcastically than with humor, until Grace said, "Give it a few days. We can talk about it then."

†

In the morning, a knock on her door awakened her, followed by someone calling out, "Breakfast."

Before the stove, Eddie stood wearing a white apron. "Sure hope French toast is okay. Coffee?"

"Please." Kat and Grace were already at the table. "What time is it?"

"Seven," he answered, pouring from the unusual pot on the rear burner.

"I've never seen a coffee pot like that." Tall and narrow, flat unpainted metal sides formed in an octagonal shape, rather than the typical rounded form.

"This is the kind they use in Europe." The way he said it sounded like he was ready to launch into a story, but flipped the toast sizzling on the griddle instead.

"You must be an early bird."

He smiled. "Hardly. Go sit down; it's almost ready."

"Oh my gosh, this is the best French toast I have ever had," she said through a mouthful once he served them. Too late, she remembered to cover her mouth, and when she did, upturned corners of her lips peeked past the red and white checkerboard of the napkin.

"He makes it from special bread with his own secret spices," Grace explained.

"He's a chef," Kat added.

"Oh, I wondered what sort of work you did."

"It's not my work; it's a hobby of sorts, the way I occupy my free time."

"And he has plenty of free time," Grace said with a smirk.

"Then what sort of work do you do?"

"Well, I've tried a few things. Was even a sailor once. One of these days I'll grow up and find a job I enjoy. I have some money saved up, so there's no rush."

Must have inherited it, she assumed. Owning a house like

this at his age? This place was almost a mansion. In a small town like Diamond, such a fine house would cost at least $25,000. Higher-priced in a fine district in a big city, where everything is so much more expensive. She wanted to delve deeper into her mysterious host but, evasive as he had been with every other question she asked him, didn't bother.

When finished, Kat and Grace washed the dishes in what seemed a normal routine, but when Jeanette offered to help, Kat shooed her away. "You're our guest; guests don't clean up."

Still at the table, Eddie leaned back, fists stretched taut above his head, and yawned loud enough to be heard across the street. "If it's okay with you, I think I'll go upstairs and lie down."

"Goodnight, sweetie," Grace extended her cheek as he went by, and his kiss was innocent, but he laid a provocative hand low on her back, repeating the same with Kat before retiring upstairs.

"7:30 in the morning and he's just going to bed?"

"His schedule takes some getting used to," Grace said.

From her experience thus far, his odd schedule might be the only thing requiring any period of adjustment.

†

On her knees by the row of rose bushes she planted along the property line to divide their yards, Mrs. Peabody pruned a few unsightly stray branches to even them out. Often on pleasant evenings, she busied herself working in her garden.

"Did I see you with a new girl?"

"Oh, you mean my sister? She just arrived from back home on last night's late Greyhound."

"Sister?" She scoffed. "Where is back home?"

"Oh, you've likely never heard of it."

"Try me."

"Now, Miss P," The Kid said with a grin, "why do I get the feeling you doubt me?"

The old widow watched him with the intensity reserved

for a snake found coiled under a rosebush. "Because it isn't proper, a man sharing a house with pretty young ladies. Not to mention that colored girl you've got stashed away in there."

"Gee, have I done something to offend you? Am I not a good neighbor?"

"Good neighbor?" She pushed herself up with one hand, brushing dirt off her knees once on her feet, and wagged the pruning shears in his direction. "Does a good neighbor run a house of ill-repute?"

"Ill-repute?? Wow!" For the past year, Mrs. Peabody derived immense pleasure from scolding him for various things she considered odd, but this evening she was in rare form, indeed. Once upon a time, her puritanical spying annoyed him. But like a ten-pound, fur-ball lapdog, Miss P was all bark and no bite. Over time, he learned to indulge the meddlesome neighborhood busybody with a sense of amusement.

Even if she lost her head and called the police, what could come of her meddling? Only two girls, each with their own rooms, living by choice in this lovely house rent-free. And a new girl who loves blueberry pancakes and French Toast who is thankful to have escaped becoming one of Joey Four Fingers' whores because he made sure to steer her away from that greasy pimp's clutches.

"Miss P, you need to get used to some changes now that the war is over and the fifties are approaching fast as a jet fighter. Things are different now."

"Not as different as you may think, young man! Other neighbors have noticed the strange goings-on and are none too happy about it."

"Have you even met the young ladies you have such a terrible opinion of? They are quite fine, upstanding, virtuous ladies with the strongest moral values, I can assure you. By the way, your roses are absolutely lovely this year." He stooped to take a whiff of a yellow flower in full bloom.

"Hmph!" Her pride in her garden overwhelmed her distaste for his lifestyle enough to allow the glimmer of a smile to brighten her face, so she turned and hurried away before he took notice.

THE BEEF

It began normally enough, much the way a car crash starts with an ordinary drive to work or the store.

Four men stood in the shadows watching passengers rush into the arms of loved ones or wander off into the night alone. Right away, they realized pickings were slim. One of those disappointments, when the talent disembarking that night's busses left a lot to be desired. On nights such as this one, they came up empty, with no prospects worth their while.

The guy everyone called Slick had been around for years and managed to eek out a decent living off dregs others passed up. No one asked how or begrudged him his little slice of success. A hopelessly lost homely girl lost stepped off, and Slick's radar spotted unlimited potential. Where The Kid smelled a girl who had been ridden hard and put away wet enough times to be a pro, Slick smelled profit in his niche market. The others did not share his reluctance to go home empty-handed.

"Rough night," Joey uncorked a flask and tipped it up. "Nothing compared to that dish you picked up last time, eh, Kid?"

"Can't win 'em all."

Joey kept up with him as they walked around the far side of the bus depot, toward the alley. "How's that blondie working out for you?"

"Wow," he stopped and turned to face Four Fingers, "that one really got under your craw, didn't she?"

"Not her," he answered, stepping too close. He jabbed The Kid in the center of the chest with a rigid, stabbing finger. "You do.”

Arms held out to the sides and with a tilt of his head, The Kid answered, “Alright, what’s your beef with me this time?”

“Some of us are getting sick of you always snatching up the pick of the litter.”

“Some of you? Who else?”

“All the guys say the same thing.”

“So they elected you to be their mouthpiece?”

“Some of ’em don’t have the guts to stand up to you.”

Arms crossed over his chest with a grin, The Kid asked, “Well, Joey, no one’s ever accused you of being a pansy, have they? Tell me, what’s really eating you?”

“Don’t think I don’t know about you and Red.”

“Oh, I get it. This is about Leslie.”

“I’m onto you, you creep. And don’t think you can get away with it, either.”

The Kid managed to stifle a growing grin. “What does your imagination tell you is going on between us?”

“It ain’t my imagination. You’ve got your sights set on her.”

This brought a wry chuckle. “Joey, you’ve got it all wrong. Sure, she’s easy on the eye, but I have no interest in stealing her away from you.”

“Damn right you ain’t stealing her. If you think I am going to let the one girl in my stable get away who’s prettier than any of the jailbait you collect, then you’re a lot dumber than you look.”

“Listen, Joey, everyone knows Leslie is your gal.” And yes, the smart move would have been to leave it at that, but seeing Joey’s dander worked up was amusing. “If it will make you feel any better, Leslie is not my type.”

“What’s that supposed to mean, wise guy? *Not my type*,” he mocked The Kid’s annoying Yankee accent, one no one could quite place. Strong but indistinct. Not Brooklyn or Boston, almost like a mixture of the two.

“Just what I said. She’s a dish, but not the kind of gal I am interested in.”

“Well, I’ll be sure to tell her you said that. What’s the

matter with her, pretty boy? Ain't she good enough for you?"

Recognizing this conversation had jumped the tracks but without quite understanding how or why, The Kid decided the time had come to tone it down a notch. When some guys start talking about women, the whole thing tends to go sideways in a big hurry. "What's gotten into you tonight, Joey?"

"You—always acting like you're better than everyone else. Looking down your pretty nose at us while you are no better than the rest. And another thing—what do you do with those girls? How come nobody ever sees them working out on the streets like the rest of the girls?"

"Oh, the truth finally comes out. You aren't worried about me stealing your gal; you believe I have some secret you want in on."

"Come on, Kid, you can tell me." His hand waved between them. "It'll be just between us."

"Now Joey, a man about town like you ought to know a gentleman never kisses and tells."

"Wanna know what some of the boys think?"

"I can't wait to hear this."

"Some think the reason they are never seen anywhere is because you've got 'em locked down in your basement for your own use, and when you are through with 'em, they end up floating down the Mississippi to New Orleans. Personally, I bet you bury 'em someplace out in the woods, because somebody'd have fished one out by now."

"You know what is most impressive?" The Kid's indifferent smile conveyed no trace of concern. "Here I was convinced your imagination was limited to concocting harebrained stories about luring your top earner away with a bigger, better deal. Isn't that what you're really worried about? Or are you afraid your gal might just fall for another guy?"

"Listen up, ace—the other guys may be scared of you after what happened to Rocco, but he don't have my connections."

The Kid snorted, a bit too loud. "Oh, so you're a syndicate man now? What, Binaggio's got you on his payroll? Next you'll tell me you're rubbing elbows with Gov. Smith?"

The mere mention of Charles Binaggio's name, the mob kingpin of Kansas City since before the war, was a bit of a street *faux pas*.

It was no secret he financed last year's gubernatorial campaign of Forrest Smith and used dirty tricks to ensure his candidate emerged the winner. Rumor had it he used Chicago money to the tune of a million dollars—maybe more. Even so, despite this successful campaign on the same ticket, when Binaggio hired a private train to take him all the way to Washington for Harry Truman's inauguration this past January, expecting a warm greeting for his diligent efforts, Truman made it clear he wanted nothing to do with the mobster by barring him from the celebration. Binaggio's fury over being slighted at the first inauguration shown on national television, robbed of the limelight of such a grand stage, had yet to show signs of abating.

As a result of this public humiliation, people were careful to avoid invoking his name. You never knew when word might filter back to him or the severity of his reaction if it did.

"Why don't you try me? Anyone who tries to rip me to shreds like you did to Rocco will end up wearing concrete shoes for a swim in the river. Same goes if you start poaching my girls."

"Take it easy, Joey. Nobody's trying to steal your girl, and I'm sure not aiming to kill you. Heck, for a whoremonger, you're not half bad. You're funny, and you've never gotten in my way. Not the way Rocco did."

During the summer the year before, while Binaggio was fixing the election, Rocco also trolled the bus terminal each evening. A hothead who never backed down from anyone, Rocco made it clear he did not welcome The Kid intruding on his territory. When The Kid refused to stop returning and taking with him the prettiest girls when he did, one night Rocco and two of his associates cornered him in this same alley. No one saw the details of what went down, but Rocco and one of his buddies ended up on the coroner's slab. His other associate still languished in a sanitarium. A nasty head injury left him unable to feed himself or even wipe his own ass. In fact, about the only function he was capable of performing these days was drooling on his bib at mealtime.

Under the law of the street, cops never learned how those stiffs wound up in the alley. That's why Joey made sure The Kid got a good gander at his snub-nose .38 packed in a shoulder holster.

"The same's not going to happen to me, you hear?"

Confident laughter was not among the responses Joey expected. "Is that why you brought along that pea-shooter? Funny, I gave you credit for being smarter than that."

"Listen, Whitey," his ire directed to The Kid's movie-star blond locks, "stay away from Red and you won't give me cause to use it. On second thought, don't show your pretty face 'round here no more, either. Not 'til you tell me what you're doing with them girls."

"I've got a better idea. How about we continue with same the agreement we've had for the past year, and I'll forget about your silly threats?"

"Don't play dumb, Kid. You're getting way too big for your britches, and somebody's gonna take you down a peg. You think I'm fooling?"

"No, but you're doing a darn good job convincing me you are a fool."

A pissing contest like this can only end one way. Two bighorn rams stood facing off in the narrow passageway, waiting for the first one to move. Without warning, the alleyway lit up bright as by a midday sun. From the direction of Troost Avenue at the far end of the alley, a 75,000-candlepower spotlight bright as a car high-beam aimed straight at them, as effective blinding them as it diverted their attention. Only one type of vehicle had such a light swivel-mounted like a ship's deck gun.

"Hey! Break it up down there!"

Joey spun, knees bent in preparation to make a run for

it. Eddie recognized how lousy an idea that was, so he said, "Everything's copacetic, officer. We're old friends just discussing a girl."

"Take it out of the alley. Come on, move it!"

Joey turned to him, and Eddie motioned toward the squad car with a tilt of his head. "You heard the man."

"This ain't over," the pimp said through lips pinched motionless as a ventriloquist. "You haven't heard the end of this."

The narrow alley, lined with grimy brick, emptied out at Troost, where the police cruiser idled at the curb, its blinding light still trained on the two men as they reached the sidewalk. Eager to slip away, Joey made a bee-line around the corner; The Kid, by contrast, with a polite tip of his fedora to the officer and turned in the opposite direction on the sidewalk.

THE KISS

In her young life, Jeanette never spent a day quite like this. Utter freedom!

A stroll through downtown where Kat and Grace took her sightseeing, skyscrapers blotting out the sun like towering mountains until midday. Although it was a calm, sunny day, wind whipped through the canyons between those massive office buildings, taller than anything she ever saw—no doubt taller than anything erected anywhere in her state. They took a ride on an electric streetcar—not because they needed to get around but because Jeanette had never seen one, let alone ridden on one.

Next, they took her for a shopping spree at The Grand-Leader and Famous-Barr department stores, for snacks at a quaint little tea shop in a small converted house just blocks from downtown, then to one of several boutiques where the salesgirls called them by name. No one minded a colored girl shopping with them, and, indeed, the shopgirls treated her the same as they did Kat, but she could not help notice the dearth of other colored shoppers in any of those boutiques, only at the gigantic department stores. In fact, from the transom of one of the shops hung a sign with WHITES ONLY printed in huge block letters, which they ignored and went inside, anyway.

"The Kid knows the owner," is all they offered by way of explanation.

Over lunch, at a restaurant on the third floor overlooking a busy street jammed with shiny new cars and delivery trucks, Jeanette had to ask, "Do you work?"

"Not right now," Kat answered, "but I may find a job soon. This last vacation has lasted longer than I planned."

"I don't have the same opportunities," Grace said. "The Kid refuses to let me do domestic work or teach, and not much else is open for me."

Kat interrupted, "What happened to nursing school? Didn't you decide that's what you were going to do?"

"That was last week, Honey. Maybe next week, too, but today I don't want to think about late nights' studying, or all those tests."

"If you don't work, how do you afford to go shopping?"

Grace asked Kat, "Should we tell her?" When the brunette nodded, she placed her small purse on her lap and produced from the inside pocket several metal rectangles, smaller than a playing card, which she fanned like a full deck. "Charga-Plates. The Kid has them for every decent store in town. As long as we don't go crazy, he lets us use them."

"What do you do with these doohickeys?"

"Buy things," Kat answered, enjoying having fun at a country bumpkin's expense, knowing only big city stores accept Charga-Plates.

Grace explained, "See, when you buy something, the store prints out a receipt. All you do is sign for it, and at the end of the month, the store sends The Kid a bill."

Wide-eyed at such a marvelous concept, Jeanette asked, "Can I see one?" Grace handed her the stack. At the bottom corner, embossed into the metal of each card, read the name Franklin Garland. "Is this him? The Kid?"

"Now you understand why he prefers being called Kid. If you want to annoy him, call him Frankie. Although I advise against it," the dark girl said as she scooped them up and put them back in her purse.

"What does he mean by *go crazy* with them?"

"Well, Kat here ran up a $200 dollar bill one month at Grand-Leader." Grace had a sly grin, while Kat's face clouded. "He made sure she never repeated that mistake.

At the sight of her friend's cheeks paling and her stony expression, Jeanette gasped. "What did he do? He didn't hit you..."

"The Kid does not hit you. Ever. He's gentle as a kitten. But sometimes when you are playing with a cute, fuzzy kitten, and you do something that aggravates it, those tiny, needle claws come out and dig into you. It doesn't really hurt, but you learn not to do whatever it was to that kitty again."

"What does that mean?"

This time, Grace answered for her. "It means The Kid won't raise a hand to us—or to you. But don't let his cute little face and soft fur fool you. Cuddly as kittens may be, remember they are wild animals who will drag a dead rat to the front door to show off their capabilities."

After shooting a scowl at Grace, one of those if-looks-could-kill expressions on her face, Kat said, "Anyone want to spend the afternoon at the art museum? Jeanette, you like art, don't you?"

"Only what is in picture books; I've never been to a museum."

†

That night, the ladies ate alone, which, they explained, happened several times a week. The Kid was not home, and Jeanette imagined him standing in the shadows of the bus platform, waiting for that night's bus to arrive. Did he prowl there every night? Certainly not, for if he did, the house would surely be stuffed to the rafters with runaways. But since neither of her housemates offered any explanation, after that awkward incident at lunch when she asked one question too many, decided against asking another.

After watching a brand-new television show called *The Lone Ranger*—a real treat for, until then, Jeanette had only watched TV a handful of times, most of those through glass storefront windows. The very idea of living in a house with a television she could watch from the comfort of a sofa? What a strange and wonderful new world. The future! Less awed, soon as the show ended, Grace announced she was heading to read in bed.

Kat yawned, stretched, and said, "Time for me to turn in, too. Turn out the lights when you go to bed. If you like to read, take whatever you want from his study. He must have a thousand books in there."

As she followed Grace out, she turned back. "Oh, don't go in The Kid's bedroom."

"Of course not," Jeanette answered. "I wouldn't dream of going in there."

"What I mean is, when he's gone. He's very private and considers it his personal sanctuary. Word to the wise," she warned, before heading up the staircase.

Still buzzing with energy and excitement from a day of adventure, Jeanette spent half an hour browsing through books lining two walls of the richly paneled study. A thousand may have been a gross underestimation of their number. Classics, books on science and nature, on every subject under the sun filled the shelves, along with novels for every taste. Filed with no rhyme or reason, in random order, although series were grouped together. When she came upon a copy of *Lady Chatterley's Lover*, she tilted it on the shelf, recognizing that this famous book is banned in the U.S.

Curious, she plucked it from the shelf and flipped it open, only to find it written in French—at least, she assumed it was French, although she had never seen anything printed in French other than the occasional quote in a book. After returning it to its spot, she chose *The Ides of March*, a recent release about the Roman Empire she heard so much about and retired with it upstairs.

As she unzipped her dress, it occurred to her she had not locked her door, a fact which gave a slight unease. A locked door at home came as second nature, what with her step-father and all. An instant chill ran through her, skin turning to gooseflesh all over her body. She discovered the door had one of those old-fashioned locks requiring a key to secure it from either side. Bent down, she peered out and, although dark, made out a shadow on the hall wall cast by the moonlight.

Without even a latch, she realized anyone could enter her room. Nice as everyone was here, they were still virtual strangers. And she could not lock them out.

In the front corner, a spot out of the line of sight from the other side of her keyhole, she slipped into her nightgown and climbed into bed to read by the glow of her bedside lamp.

When she drifted off, she could not guess, but something woke her. On her chest, the open book lay flat, preserving her place. The house was silent, although outside crickets chirped and, in the distance, an owl hooted its mournful call. Yet, she knew something stirred in the house, and held her breath, listening.

One of the wooden floorboards let out a slight creak. Not close, somewhere down the hall. Then again, closer this time. Then came a light rapping sound, answered by a hinge opening and closed so quietly, had she exhaled it may well have drowned out the sound. Muffled voices—whispers—too faint to make out whose or even if male or female, although she had the distinct impression of a masculine voice.

Try as she might to stay awake, waiting to hear some other sound—a giggle, the moaning of bedsprings, a scream—none came. Not until a knock on her door woke her. The book still lay on her chest and the light was on, although it was no longer necessary because pale, red morning light splashed on the wall next to the door. She remembered her mother predicted the weather by saying, "Red sun at night, sailor's delight. Red sun at morning, sailors take warning," as she stared at two glowing, window-shaped rectangles on the wall staring at her like crimson eyes.

"Wake up, sleepyhead," Grace called out in a cheerful voice, "time for breakfast!"

✝

That night, a storm rolled in, one of those summer storms that blow in to chase away the day's clear skies, thunder rumbling and lightning filling the sky with continuous flashes. The sort of evening Jeanette found perfect for reading a good book, just as long as the power held out. Close came the thunder, as flashes of lightning followed a split second later by the roar of a thunderclap, threatening to knock out their electricity at any moment.

A light tapping on her door made her jump, a bigger start than even the loudest booms from the storm. "Who's there?"

"It's me. May I come in?"

What was The Kid doing at her door after bedtime? "I'm already in bed"

"It will only take a moment." The door opened a crack. "Are you decent?"

Even with the covers pulled up over her chest, she shielded herself behind the book, which she pressed to her bosoms. "Is everything alright?"

"That's what I came to ask you. Quite a storm we're in for."

"I'm fine. In fact, it may be weird, but I love stormy nights."

"A kindred soul. Mind if I sit?" Rather than a chair, he sat on the foot of the bed, down next to her legs.

"Where have you been the last couple of days?"

"Oh, I've been about. Have Kat and Grace been showing you around?"

"The sure have."

"Getting along with everyone?"

"They are so nice. Back home, I never met a Negro socially, and…"

"Grace is quite special, isn't she?"

"Yes."

"Does that surprise you?"

"What do you mean?"

"This is your first time out of your hometown, isn't it?"

"First time."

"I've had a chance to travel. Quite a bit, in fact. All over the country, the world. What I've come to realize is people are people, no matter what color their skin."

"I guess it does surprise me how much we are alike."

"Exposure to new things—interesting people, new experiences—that's what makes life interesting, don't you agree? Isn't a desire to experience the unknown what drove you to leave Diamond? Take this book, for instance. Of the hundreds in my library, you chose one about a different time, an ancient and faraway place. A civilization now existing only in pages of books. Even the last living memory of this civilization has gone extinct."

A flash lit up the room, followed by an immediate, terrific boom. "Oh, that scared me!"

"Are you afraid of many things?"

"No, I don't believe so. Why do you ask?"

"Well, you are hiding behind that book, shielding yourself like you are afraid of me. Am I so scary, Jeannette?"

"No." Feeling burning cheeks, she realized her pink skin gave her away. "Well, maybe a little."

"There is no reason to fear me." He reached for the book, stopping before his fingers reached it. "May I?"

Jeanette only nodded, his eyes locked onto hers, and he lifted the book away.

"One of my talents is the ability to identify a pure heart. Yours is pure, is it not?"

"I suppose so…"

"Have you ever been in love?"

"No, have you?"

"Oh yes, a few times."

"What happened?"

"The same thing that always happens. Love always ends in heartbreak. Your heart, though, it is unbroken. Untouched. Yet you wish for a man to touch you, don't you?"

"Yes." Her voice cracked, despite her efforts to control it. "Now you are starting to scare me."

"Yet, you yearn for my touch, don't you?"

One second before, her answer would have been no. "Yes."

His hand rose again, as it was when he lifted the book from her breasts. "Don't be afraid, Jeanette."

His palm covered most of her upper chest, fingers splayed and reaching her throat. Slow, almost painfully so, his hand moved down between her breasts, pushing aside with a ginger touch, where his palm came to a stop. Outside, another flash bathed the room with brilliant blue light. Accompanied by a loud clicking sound, followed by the loudest clap of thunder imaginable. Beside her, the lightbulb flicked out, and when the flash faded, plunged the room into utter darkness.

His hand remained on her chest, touching her more intimately than any man had. "No one has ever touched me there. No man."

"Does my hand bother you?"

"No."

"You are telling the truth. Your heart is beating fast, but steady. Can you feel it? I can."

It thumped against the pressure of his hand. "I can; I feel it pounding."

"It is pure and untouched as your body, isn't it?"

"Yes." Emboldened and curious, his touch filled her with an unknown sensation. One forbidden to her. One she desired. "May I touch your heart?"

"You may," he answered, and her hand rose to his chest, mirroring his.

"I don't feel anything."

"Probably my clothes. Reach inside, see if you can feel it."

Strange as his request may be, she unbuttoned two buttons on his shirt, enough to reach his skin inside. Cool to the touch, a chill from his hand on her chest ran through her body, as well. But she felt its faint, slow beat. So indistinct, unlike any heartbeat she felt before.

"Do you wish for your heart to remain pure, Jeanette?"

"Yes, but I suspect you may have different plans."

"Suppose mine are—will you allow me to destroy what is beating inside your chest?"

"I bet you have broken a few hearts, haven't you?"

"Yours I wish to remain pure, beating, unharmed—if you will allow me."

"And if I want something else?"

"I can give you that, if that is what you desire."

"I want what you want, I think."

"Good," he said. It was dreamlike, and indeed, she must be dreaming, for he appeared behind her, but she did not see him move, although the room was so pitch black he had become little more than a shadow. His hand had not moved from her chest, not much anyway, and his other hand pulled her hair back behind her shoulder.

His lips were soft when he kissed her nape, following the gentle curve of her neck, sending a tingle through her body. He kissed again, higher this time. Higher still, kissing every inch of the side of her neck until his lips enveloped the skin behind her ear.

"No one's ever kissed me like that."

"Nor shall anyone else kiss you this way," he said.

That is the last thing she remembered.

THE INFERNO

Sometime during the night, as summer storms are wont to do, this one blew through, leaving scant traces by morning light. Scattered broken branches and torn leaves littered the still-wet ground, but otherwise there were few suggestions an intense thunderstorm pounded the area overnight. Hands of electric clocks ran two hours behind hand-wound ones, testament to how long the storm deprived the house of its electric life blood.

Smiling sugary as a child, Kat asked The Kid, "Are you using your car this morning?"

"No plans, other than some sleep," he answered. "Where are you off to?"

"We're in desperate need of perms. Jeanette, you're welcome to join us if you want your hair done."

"Not today," she answered. "That storm kept me up half the night, and I haven't the patience to sit still for a perm."

"Sure you won't join us?" Grace smiled as The Kid handed her roommate the keys, then seemed to realize the implied insult, adding to avoid misunderstanding, "Not that you need it, not with your gorgeous hair. We like to try all the latest styles is all."

"Thanks, maybe next time?" For reasons she could not put into words, she wished to stay here with her host. Eager for their trip, the ladies smiled and bundled themselves out the kitchen door to the spot where The Kid parked his brand-new Cadillac Series 62 Coupe, closer than in the separate garage in back. She refilled her cup and asked him, "Want some more coffee?"

From outside, a muffled thumping sound startled the morning birds, sending them to wing, angry and squawking. A second later, screams rent the morning calm.

On his feet in a flash, he flung open the back door. Acrid, vile smoke filled the kitchen. How The Kid reached the car before she made it even to the door she could not explain, but the gruesome sight in the driveway seared itself into her memory along with the flames engulfing the car.

Only the flailing hands of her housemates were visible through a curtain of fire filling the automobile's entire interior. Heat already blistered the paint on the door and, judging by The Kid's futile jerking on the door handle, either Kat had locked the driver's door or the metal had already begun buckling from the intense furnace, sealing the girls inside the inferno.

Those hands soon ceased thrashing about in the blinding flames, their screams dying out after a few unendurable seconds. After that, only her own screams reached Jeanette's ears. The Kid collapsed in the grass beside the driveway.

"The fire department," she yelled and sprinted to the phone on the kitchen wall. With no idea of the number, she dialed the operator. Before a voice answered her frantic call, The Kid's blackened, singed hand pushed down the metal hook to disconnect the call.

"Don't."

"But we must help them!"

"It's too late. No one can help them now."

"But the fire..."

"We cannot summon the fire department. Or the police. You are a runaway; they will send you home, probably arrest me for kidnapping you. They are runaways, too, same as you."

"We can't just let them..."

"What? They are gone, Jeanette."

"No! It's not true!" She knew, though, her words expressed only foolish hopefulness. No one could survive such a blaze. When her legs gave way, his powerful arms held her up. Never in her life had she witnessed so horrific a sight. In search of some meagre form of reassurance, her eyes looked up to him, The Kid's face twisted with fury and loss until almost unrecognizable. Only his eyes, although half-hidden beneath a set, low brow, remained the same, burning an incandescent blue.

"We must tell… someone."

"You do not understand," he answered, clinging her tight as if to prevent one or both of them from falling into an abyss.

"How did this happen? Cars don't just catch fire."

"It was meant for me. I know who did this," he said. In reply to the unspoken question on her face, he continued, "It seemed an idle threat—I never expected any of you to be in danger."

The fire burned itself out until nothing remained but a blackened, smoldering shell. At some point, every pane of glass had blown out. Few signs remained anyone had been in the car, only a few singed and scattered large bones, femurs and scattered fragments of pelvis on and among the dark springs which minutes before had been a fine leather bench seat. Even the chemical stench had burned itself out, although the harsh odor of burning rubber clung in the air, one tire still flickering with small flame.

"You must go; it is not safe for you here."

His words shocked her. "Go where?"

"Go home, Jeanette; you'll be safe there. If not, I will buy you a train ticket wherever you want to go. An airplane to the coast. It doesn't matter. For your own sake, you must be as far from me as possible."

It was the hardness of his face that shocked her as much as his words. "When?"

"Today—right now."

Mascara tears stained her cheeks down to her chin, eroding trails through the light makeup she applied only an hour before. "Who did this?"

"People who soon will be dead." His expression softened for the first time as he searched her eyes. "But you must be gone by then. I cannot allow you to be at risk when I take care of this or to be implicated in what I am planning to do. Nor can you be a part of this. Believe me, the man responsible for this will pay dearly."

Words failed her, so she held onto his body, if only to feel something other than numb. His eyes focused on the smoldering ruins. He spoke as if the skeletal remains could hear. "I tried. How I tried to leave this behind. To start fresh. To turn this curse into something good. Please forgive me."

He stroked her hair. "I am so sorry to have exposed one so innocent to such corruption." In answer, she held on tight as her arms allowed.

A circle of destruction spread in every direction from the car. Shrubs ten feet away already withered from the heat.

Inside, they held each other in timeless silence.

"Last night," she asked, trying to remember, "did you come to me?"

"Yes, I did."

"You kissed me and… touched me, didn't you?" He nodded. "Did you…?"

"No, you are still pure, my dear." He looked around the room. "After this, there is nothing keeping me here. If you wish for me to find you, then I will try. No promises, though, not with what I must do."

"I don't want to be alone."

"Nor do I, but we have lost the freedom to choose our own fate. That has been taken from us."

Out back, inside the charred hulk where lay the last traces of her friends, the truth of his statement made clear in the starkest, most tragic way possible.

†

The bartender at The Grand Hotel downtown made the best Brandy Daisy in town. Leslie still preferred this old favorite to the new Cosmopolitan, the current fad, and Jimmy, the

Grand's bartender, made the best Daisy in town. Its cherry red color seemed a natural fit as her signature drink.

Better still, The Grand catered to traveling businessmen —executives with plenty of cash burning holes in their pockets and an uncontrollable desire to spend it on companionship while so far from home. Perched on her seat at the bar on display for all to see, she had already gathered more than her fair share of attention. It was always the same, her flame locks and marble skin and a face capable of inspiring men to claim a willingness to die for.

Funny, Joey was nowhere to be seen. A heavyset man with salt and pepper hair and a tie loosened at the neck smiled and lifted his glass toward her. She winked. Time to get down to business.

"Hermitage Rye. Neat." The voice beside her made her jump; she had not heard anyone approaching. Raul leaned on the bar on her other side. "Hi, gorgeous."

"Oh, you startled me. What are you doing here?"

"Came looking for you." He had an unusual, serious look on his face. "Where's Joey tonight?"

"Still celebrating, I guess."

"Celebrating what?"

"Said he got rid of an annoyance. Something about a little fire took care of one of his problems. Don't know, don't care. His problems going up in flames mean one less thing for me to worry about, know what I mean?"

"I know exactly what you mean," he said, and she noticed he had not touched his glass. "You sure he didn't tell you what he did about this problem?"

A flick of her head cleared long, coppery locks off sensuous shoulders, exposed by a daring, off-the-shoulder blouse that suggested the absence of anything underneath. As further enticement, she crossed her legs, so the slit in her tight black skirt revealed one shapely thigh. "Honey, if you think he tells me more dirty details about he does than I spill the dirty details of how I spend my time when he's not around, you aren't half as bright as you look."

She spoke not to insult him, but emphasized her words as a compliment on his looks and intelligence. After all, her clientele was sophisticated and cultured enough to appreciate her exotic, ephemeral beauty over the more fashionable hourglass figures of the other girls. And if Raul possessed anything, it was class.

"Are you sure you haven't heard more?" The lapis of his pupils was particularly mesmerizing tonight.

Slender fingers reached out for his tie, playing with the charcoal silk with the familiarity of a wife. She laughed. "Oh, something about my competition. Not that I have competition, mind you." Her gaze rose back up to meet his. "Look, Joey treats me good, okay? If he thinks some bimbo stands in my way, then he can do what he needs to do. Better them than me is my motto."

When she realized how her answer darkened his expression, she sought to cheer him up. "Pull up a stool and join me for a drink?"

A hundred-dollar bill slid along the bar, which Raul tucked under her glass. "I have something different in mind."

†

As expected, the instant the story hit the papers, Joey Four Fingers knew whose body had been left in that field—one of ten lots Joey bought as investments and stood to make a killing on as the prices spiraled through the roof. Legitimate business for a hood with aspirations of legitimacy. He lay low in a remote cabin in the woods outside of town until a sketch appeared on the front pages of the still-unidentified corpse found in his yard. The moment he saw a drawing of Leslie's lifeless face, he knew in his bones.

The Kid was coming for him.

He'd make it down to Savannah, and from there, set sail for Havana, where he could drink rum by the barrel until this

fiasco blew over.
He had connections.

THE KILLER

Rare is the time when informants are unanimous on anything, but everyone they spoke to all echoed the same thing: no one had seen Joey Four Fingers or the mysterious Raul since Leslie Hass' severed corpse turned up in the middle of a vacant lot. If they didn't know better, the scuttlebutt might give the impression everyone recited the same script. Every rock the detectives kicked over came up empty.

The pimp and the ghost had both vanished into thin air.

Now facing the unpalatable prospect of the two most likely suspects in the murder of the Red Dahlia both missing, quite possibly dead, left the detectives in a quandary.

The only clue they had to go on was that the suspects both frequented the bus terminal, casting nets for runaways and small-town girls with heads full of big-city dreams. They arrived at the Greyhound station after nine, before the last of the night's buses arrived and while the full evening crew still manned their shifts.

"Yeah, I know who you're talking about," Darren North, the night station manager, answered. Salt and pepper hair suggesting middle-age, medium height and thin with taut features, he wore a blue tie with a short-sleeved dress shirt like people wore on Sundays during the summer when packed inside churches, few of which were outfitted with air-conditioning. "Didn't get his name; didn't ask. People called him Kid. Long as they don't cause trouble, those aren't the kind of guys you want to mess with. Some of them are connected."

Branford suspected more than apathy motivated his

ignorance. Pimps likely slipped him a few bucks to look the other way. "How frequently was he here?"

"Twice a week?" He shrugged his shoulders. "The Kid kept to himself, never caused any problems. Hardly noticed he was here."

"It isn't a problem for pimps to snatch little girls off the bus?"

"Look, we are responsible for getting passengers here safely. What they do after they arrive in town is more you guys' responsibility. We don't monitor who is there to meet the passengers."

Unable to restrain himself, Stringer rolled his eyes. "Mr. North, are you a churchgoing man?"

"Sure am."

"You know what these pimps do with them girls, right? Fifteen, sixteen…"

"Some younger," Branford added. "I've seen girls no older than nine or ten put out on the streets by these thugs."

The night manager huffed out a sigh, then spoke with the weary voice of a man who long ago surrendered his last trace of concern. "Look, I run a bus station. You're the cops; if you think someone is breaking the law here, you have my blessing to come arrest them. Police are always welcome here."

"So, it seems, are procurers for prostitution."

"I haven't the time for this; we still have several arrivals and departures this evening that need my attention." North turned to walk away. Then, perhaps pressured by a pang of conscience or he dug something from deep in his memory, added, "He drives a Cadillac. A new one. What do they call it? Series 62 I think? Two-door."

"What color?"

"He only came here at night." He motioned toward the parking lot, which had a few lights atop poles, casting most of the lot in poor light. "How many cars that fancy can be driving around town?"

✝

A stiff wind blew, a harbinger of an approaching storm this time of year. A gust whipped up a fleeting whirlwind of stray leaves and newspapers down the block. From the vantage point of their car two doors down, Branford and Stringer witnessed no activity for hours. The sun rose an hour ago, although a heavy cloud cover let in precious little light.

Inside the house, lights blinked out at 4:30, more than two hours ago. Far as they could determine, not a soul came or went, although the lights only switched on until an hour before that, suggesting either someone arrived home late or woke up hungry for a snack in the dead of night before crawling back into bed. Either way, they should still be asleep. Even if still awake, the wind made enough noise to drown out all else, and the way it whipped branches of trees and shrubs alike offered to provide sufficient cover if anyone inside was watching. "Whaddya say we sneak a peek in the garage and around back?"

"Good a time as any," Stringer agreed. His partner held onto his hat so the wind could not rip it from his head, but he left his in the safety of the unmarked Hudson Super 6 sedan. A car drove by, its driver eyeballing the strange men on the block at such an early hour with suspicion, so Branford waved.

Since access to the detached garage lay on the far side of the house, they decided to follow the driveway to find out what jumped out on their way. Of course, this risked passing by the kitchen while someone inside may be up early, frying their eggs and grits, as most houses in this neighborhood were designed with kitchens facing the rear. Ducking below windows, they made it around back. Using a windblown boxwood for cover, Branford poked his head around the corner. A half second later, he jerked it back.

"Found the Cadillac."

Aware of the prospect the suspect may be home, Stringer hugged the building a little tighter.

"It's in back. At least, it may be a Caddy. Hard to tell—it's been torched."

"Are you serious?"

"Burned to a shell. Check it out for yourself."

Criminals of the most devious sort are well acquainted with fire's effectiveness at destroying evidence. Torching an expensive, brand-spanking-new car such as this Caddy is an act of sheer desperation—something the state's most wanted murderer might write off. A necessary cost. They moved in for a closer look.

"Someone swept out," Branford whispered.

Knelt behind the fender, Stringer's full attention focused on the building, scanning the windows for any movement, making sure no one inside spotted them. "What do you mean, swept out?"

The beam of Branford's L-shaped flashlight, the one he carried with him through Europe during the war, lit up the car's interior. "All the ashes are gone from the front seat—well, the springs and seat frame. You can see brush marks in the soot. Back's full of ashes, though.

"Wonder what was in that front seat he wanted to hide?"

"Should we go ask, or should we check the garage first?"

In no mood for sarcasm, Stringer made his way to the garage window on the corner without acknowledging. Set high in the wall, he stood on tip-toes to peer inside. When he did, he frantically waved Branford over. Crouched down low, his partner hurried over.

"Auburn Boattail. Blood red. We've got our man!"

A locked back door posed no hindrance, for each detective carried their own set of tools and were experts at picking locks. Technically, they should get a warrant, but inside other girls might be held hostage, and every wasted minute only increased their danger.

Inside, all was dark and quiet, the silence broken only by wind whipping around corners, through branches and let in by the open door. Guns drawn, communicating by hand signals alone, they made their way through the first floor. Finding nothing, they kept their revolvers aimed toward the second floor as they crept upstairs.

The first bedroom bore all the signs of a woman's touch, flashlight beams lighting up pink everywhere, with makeup and hair brushes set out on the dresser. Same in the next room. Both looked like someone lived there, but empty of anyone inside. A nightgown draped over the back of a chair hung expecting someone to slip into it for bed.

"Is anyone home?" Despite whispering, Branford held one finger over his mouth to shush him. Two more doors in the hall ahead, one on either side. Fifty-fifty.

They chose right.

Although the face was unfamiliar, they recognized the perp. Blond, skin pale as an albino, with a young, handsome face. There was no mistaking this is the suspect every cop in the Midwest was searching for—whoever he may be. Make that The Kid they were looking for.

Branford's Smith & Wesson .38 trained on the figure shook, not from fear, but rather from the adrenaline of finding their killer. He should be trembling in fear, but he knew nothing about that. Their suspect lay on his bed, unmoved by two beams of light dancing over his face or the detectives shouted instructions to put his hands up. Then Branford noticed something on his face, smears on his chin and cheek. It looked like blood.

"Dammit! Is he dead?" His pistol held inches from the placid face, he shoved a shoulder, and still the man did not stir. "Shit!"

"What, did he kill himself?"

"Goddamn it!" Branford felt a wrist and his neck, but found no pulse. Hard as his heart pounded, perhaps his own masked the killer's. "Cuff him! I'll keep him covered."

Because he lay prone on his stomach, Stringer pulled both arms behind his body and cuffed his wrists tight. As he did so, he felt some resistance, an early sign of rigor mortis. "He's cold as inside an icebox."

"Maybe he's just blotto."

Stringer shook his head. "I've touched enough stiffs to know what a dead body feels like."

"Do you think he made us? Saw us out the window and knew the jig was up?"

"Hell if I know."

"It will cut the paperwork, so we should be glad he decided to commit hari-kari."

Angry fingers mussed Branford's hair. "I'm pissed! Screw the paperwork. I wanted to take this jagoff alive."

"What's your guess? Poison?"

"Sure. Looks like he hacked up some blood. Don't smell cyanide, though."

"Probably swallowed a handful of bennies."

"Who gets to call this in?"

"You're lead detective," Stringer answered. "Why don't you take the hon…"

His partner's sudden halt in the middle of a sentence distracted him from continuing searching around the room for evidence, and he shone his flashlight on him. Seeing his partner frozen, staring at the dead man on the bed, Branford swung his flashlight back toward the bed.

Two blue eyes stared back at him—eyes that moments ago were shut. "What the hell?"

The killer leapt from the bed with astonishing speed. Good thing they cuffed him, because neither had kept their guns trained on him, being dead and all. In two steps, he reached Branford and with lowered a shoulder, drove the detective against the far wall. Two gunshots rang out, then a third, but by then he was nothing but a blur disappearing down the dark hallway.

"Stop the bastard!"

Both cops sprinted after him. Fast as he was, arms cuffed behind his back slowed him from a pace that must be Olympic class when free to pump more speed out with them. Imagine how fast he might be, had he not been dead, a corpse sprawled across a bed moments before. Whatever he passed out from—drugs or alcohol—in the blink of an eye, it lost any effect on him.

The faster of the two was Stringer; avoiding being slammed into a wall by a freight train may have helped. Somehow, the quicker cop managed to lay a hand on a shoulder halfway down the stairs, enough to send the killer tumbling into the dark. He landed hard, on two feet, but one leg collapsed under him and he went down.

When they caught up with him, they understood why he was still down. One foot lay turned out at an unnatural angle. "Nice work, buddy," Branford said, panting hard from the burst of effort and sweating from the excitement. "You broke the killer's leg. I suppose you aren't willing to help us out by telling us where your phone is so we can call for an ambulance?"

An azure glare and, more unexpected, a smile on the murderer's face answered his question.

THE PRISONER

Captain Burns joined the growing police contingent at the hospital. "Nice work! This is the guy?"

"It's him—no doubt," Branford answered, sensing it in his gut.

"What's wrong with him?" His rank required the captain to feign interest in the homicidal maniac's welfare.

"Beats the hell out of us. He won't let the doc do anything but set his ankle. If he so much as tries to take his temperature, the guy goes berserk. The doctor wants to sedate him, but I told him to screw off. Slap a cast on his leg so we can drag his ass down to the station. Stringer and I have a bunch of questions for him—the last thing we need is for the sawbones to knock him out for hours."

"Good call. A nurse won't stand a chance if he's strong enough to toss you through a wall."

"It only smashed the plaster," Stringer said with a wink that set everyone laughing.

"I hear you missed him what, three times? While in the same room with him?"

"Give me a break; it was dark, and the guy is fast."

"Soon as you get him to sing," the captain said, "we're sending you back out to the shooting range. At least until you can hit something besides a wall inside the room you are standing in."

A doctor emerged and walked up to the assembled officers. "Your prisoner is ready to go, if you insist. We set the leg. Broke both bones above the ankle, but a simple break. Should heal up.

But I'd prefer you leave him here for now."

This brought a frown to the captain's face. "Will he survive a broken ankle if we take him to the station now?"

"That's the question. There are a number of strange things with your prisoner."

Branford asked, "What sort of strange things, Doc?"

"Well, his temperature, for one. And his pulse is curiously weak. He didn't realize it, but I took his pulse while setting his ankle. Most people don't know about the Dorsalis pedis pulse. You can measure it between the toes over the arch of the foot. He must have assumed I was making sure the bones were set properly. After what he's been through, painful at his injury must be, a pulse rate of 120 would not have surprised me. His pulse rate of 33 is hard to explain."

The captain crossed his arms. "Will he die if we take him with us?"

"Not from what I can see."

"Then, once you've finished gift-wrapping his ankle, we'll take him off your hands."

"No guarantees," the doctor said.

A firm hand on the doctor's shoulder, the captain said, "Doctor, if he only lives long enough for us to take his mug shot and book him downtown, that will be fine with me."

†

Stringer flipped the edges of the phone book pages, making a ripping sound. Must have been four inches thick. When he stopped in San Francisco for a few days when he shipped back from the Pacific, the size of the phone books there surprised him. They say New York's Yellow Pages are even thicker. This may be half the size of New York City's, but worked just fine.

The Kid's eyes, narrow as slits, bore into him with utter hatred.

"Look, Kid, we've been at this for what, eleven hours? If

you'd just be a good boy and answer our questions, we could wrap this up right now."

From his perch atop the table on The Kid's other side, Branford faced him with arms clenched over his chest. "Start with your name. We're sick of calling you Kid."

He said nothing, same as he ignored their thousands of repeated questions over the course of the day. While he was turned toward the other detective, Stringer raised the phone book with both hands and blind-sided him with all his strength. A direct hit on The Kid's ear. Hard enough to knock any other prisoner he'd interrogated out of the chair and onto the floor. The violent blow jerked his head, but he absorbed it as well as he'd taken dozens of other shots. More powerful ones. The detective's endurance was fading. He felt like the lead-off batter in a 200-inning baseball game.

To his partner, Stringer said, "It's official—The Kid's a moot."

"Mute. He's a mute."

"That's what I said."

"No, you said he's a moot. That's something different. This clown is definitely not moot."

A shin-high walking cast unbalanced his legs. It had to be a walking cast; crutches are so useful in the hands of dangerous felons. "Maybe we should smack him in the leg. He'll confess to kidnapping the Lindberg baby after a couple of whacks to that cast."

"Okay, knock it off, Stringer. From what we've seen, that really would be moot. This Kid is tougher than he looks."

Branford stood over him. Handcuffs still held The Kid's hands behind him, his arms draped over the back of the wooden chair back to hold him upright and to slow him down in case he decided to play linebacker again. "Look, buddy, you are heading straight to the electric chair if you don't cooperate. Answer our questions and we will make things easier for you. We can tell the judge you helped us and ask that he give you life instead."

The Kid looked square at him, face relaxed now. Still, he

did not utter a sound. Stringer lifted the phone book from the table again.

"Watch it this time," Branford cautioned him. "Remember, we can't leave a mark. Show up in court with bruises all over him and you can guess the headline on the front page of every paper in America. *INEPT COPS FAIL TO BEAT CONFESSION OUT OF KILLER.* That will turn him into a victim and us into the bad guys. Everyone will assume we caught the wrong guy and beat the snot out of some poor, innocent kid for no reason."

"Then take a couple swings at him yourself. It's about time I get a pinch-hitter."

Three raps on the door signaled the captain wished to speak to them.

"Wait right here," Branford said on his way to catch hell for their lack of progress.

"Let's call it a day." The captain shook his head. "This is going nowhere. A couple of days in lockup will loosen his tongue. I'll leave word to forget to bring him his meals. Hunger has a way of convincing a reluctant criminal to open up."

Much as they wanted a confession to wrap this case up, they realized the boss was right. Once the captain had himself been a detective, and had more experience interrogating prisoners under his belt than the two of them combined. There is more art than science in obtaining a confession. And they sure could use a break; neither had slept for two days.

Branford said outside, "Good work in there today."

"We need results, not just work. The guy's still a moot."

Ignoring it this time, he instead answered, "Your questions are top-notch. Most men would have folded by now."

"That guy is not most men. Nothing we do fazes him."

"We'll break him. Just keep doing what you're doing."

"Figures the good cop in our duo turns out to be a Pollyanna." Pleased at his dig, Stringer recalled how successfully he provoked a rise ribbing his partner about his mother last time, and right about then provoking a reaction of some sort from somebody was his one great need. "Your mother sure must be proud to have raised such a Babyface."

A cloud descended over Branford's visage. "What did you say?"

It was working. "Mine hoped for a good cop, too, but stuck with a mug like mine? She'll have to be satisfied with a son who's the bad cop."

Steam boiled out from those prominent round ears of his, the Branford bad cop bubbling to the surface. His face took on a purplish hue, then he turned away as his expression took on one of taciturn control. And he not so much as glanced back toward his partner as he hurried down the hall.

†

While The Kid did not love the beating, frustrating the cops proved more fun than he imagined.

Why had he been so arrogant, foolhardy enough to feed?

He had no one else to blame, because, after all, it had been his fault.

Why he descended into a coma-like sleep after feeding remained one of many unfathomable mysteries. A typical episode lasted between four and six hours, although a few times he'd passed out for twelve hours straight. The worst part, he missed the cops watching his house. Sloppy! His decades of experience made him quite observant of such things, but this time, anger and grief weakened him. Made him careless.

Not that he shied from a welcome a ride on Old Sparky. No human had ever deserved the death penalty more. A couple of years ago, part of him began fading away. The part he still liked. Killing no longer meant a thing—no trace of the bitter aftertaste it once left. When he watched the beautiful skin bubble and burn off Kat and Grace, smelled their flesh being incinerated, what had not faded shattered into a thousand unrecognizable fragments.

Leslie did not deserve what he did to her. He could not help it. He lost control. Worst of all, he damn well enjoyed figuring out how to sever the upper part of her body from the lower half. Dr. Hodel told him with exacting detail how to do it, but he could not bring himself to watch. In hindsight, he was glad he had chosen not to be there to see him destroy Elizabeth's delightful face. Had he witnessed that mad doctor carve that evil, clownish smile into her flesh, he might just have put a stop to it right there.

Goddamn Dr. Hodel! He should have returned to L.A. and chopped that sick bastard into pieces, instead.

The cops kept him confined to a private cell. While certain no tears would be shed over Kansas City's most hated murderer being shivved during his first night in a cell, it would give the police department a black eye and lead the public to assume the cops did it themselves.

The plaster cast on his leg caused him to shake his head. He had grown soft, become complacent. Enjoyed life—or whatever it was he had. There he was, with a harem of women willing to give themselves to him, and he felt sure with at least one of them, he was bound to figure out how to pass along his curse to her. His gift.

Instead, he stood by, watching them burn.

All because Joey chose to kill them the one way he was sure to have killed him had the pimp's effort been successful.

God loves fools and babies, just as surely as He hates vampires.

✝

Through the two-way mirror, John Doe stared from his seat at the familiar interrogation table, hands cuffed behind his back. This time he stared at the mirror, paying no attention to his own reflection, but as if made from plain glass. His eyes followed the two detectives' conversation, as though listening to their words. So uncanny was his eye movement back and forth when one stopped speaking or asked the other a question, it sent chills down their spines.

"Good work yesterday," the captain said, walking up as they finalized the day's interrogation plan.

Surely, he must be mocking them, Stringer thought. "He didn't say a thing; not a single word."

"Sometimes these take time," the captain answered. "This is one clever boy. Not as clever as he thinks he is, but smarter than the average Joe we face in the box. What I meant is you didn't leave a mark on him. Not a bruise or scratch. Well done."

"We've been running this back and forth; how would you approach a tight-lipped killer like him, Captain?"

"Change it up on him. Don't ask about the murder. Try to get him talking about something else. Anything else. Doesn't matter if you spend the whole day with him and never ask a single question about the murder. Just figure out how to get him to start talking. If you can crack that shell, we'll worry about getting the nut out later."

Armed with this new strategy built upon decades of experience, they strode back in with confidence, threw their legal pads on the table, and drew up chairs across from him.

"Hey, Kid, how was your night? Sleep well?"

"The first night in jail is always the hardest." Branford relished taunting him. "It isn't so much the noise, I don't think. You know what it is?"

When he did not answer right away, Stringer blew a smoke ring, then answered for him. "The smell. Am I right? Just guessing, because I've never spent the night in a jail."

"Doesn't matter how many times I've been in there," Branford added, "the stench hits me every time I walk in through those metal doors."

Nothing. The Kid leaned back and let his eyes wander. Taunting is so enjoyable.

Stringer asked, "Are we boring you?"

He answered with a little grimace.

"How 'bout we discuss something different today?" No reaction, so Branford continued, "My partner and I realize you didn't want to answer our questions. We get it. So, we thought you might enjoy talking about something else instead."

An interrogation of an empty room, with the prisoner relaxing on his cot back in his cell, would yield the same results with less effort expended. But they had come to expect this reaction.

Before beginning, they decided Branford would reprise his role as good cop, Stringer continuing his stint as bad cop. As such, good cop took the role of primary lead. "Tell us about the girls. Where are they? Their possessions are still there: hairbrushes, makeup, clothes, but we have found no sign of them anywhere."

Silence.

"Did you kill them, too?" bad cop asked.

"What are their names? Neighbors say one of them lived with you for a couple of years, the White girl. The Colored girl not as long, but she stayed in your house for since last year, right? Who were they, Kid?"

For the first time, he reacted to one of their questions. This one, he wanted to answer, yet remained in control. He said nothing.

"What did they do for you?"

"Look, we aren't interested in charging you as a pimp, Kid," Stringer said.

Sensing he might be close to giving up the silent act, Branford kept at it. "We can charge you with pandering if necessary, but right now, we just want your help to find those girls."

The Kid was not the only one to have mastered the art of using silence, so they let that question hang in the air for a couple of minutes. Only ticking from the big clock on the wall opposite the two-way mirror broke the painful silence.

Finally, unable to bear it any longer, Stringer stood and shouldered the phone book that remained in the room from the day before, the on-deck hitter in the batter's circle. "Did you kill them, too?"

"Might want to answer Detective Stringer," Branford

cautioned him, "because he's been itching to hit the books since last night. Gets a kick out of it."

When The Kid smiled in response, Stringer smacked him in the ear. Only a tap, really. Better to start slow, giving something to build up to as the morning progressed.

"See what you made him do? Tell us who the girls are and he'll cool off a bit."

More silence.

"Okay," Branford conceded, moving on. "We're going to level with you—we know who you are. Raul di Silva."

"You don't look much like a Raul." The mocking way Stringer emphasized the name made clear he didn't buy it. "What is that, Brazilian?"

"Does sound Portuguese, doesn't it?" Branford added, "Either that or Spanish."

"He look Spanish to you?"

"Nope, sure doesn't. He might be a good-looking guy, but he's no Latin lover."

"Hey, here's an idea," Stringer said. "Why don't you say something so we can recognize if you have a Spanish or Brazilian accent?"

A houseplant would provide better conversation.

Branford kept plugging away. "Here's the thing, Raul. We've been able to dig up lots of interesting things about you, Raul."

"Very interesting things," his partner added.

Turning to Stringer, he asked, "You know which fact I find most fascinating?"

"The part about him being dead?"

With a snap of his fingers that ended pointing at his partner, he said, "Bingo."

"That one got me, too."

"Turns out Raul di Silva is dead. Did you know that?"

If aware of his demise, he was not letting on. This guy would clean up in a poker game.

"Doing pretty good for a dead guy, too," Stringer added.

"Can still take a punch."

"According to the State of Louisiana, you died of polio in 1932. You were seven. This untimely death did not prevent you from buying that Auburn boattail in your garage a few years later. Now, here we are, sitting here talking to you, and it's what, 1949?"

"Yup, 1949," Stringer confirmed.

"Which leaves me with the question, who are you?"

"And why are you pretending to be a dead guy?"

For two hours, they kept up their routine. About an hour in, frustration led them to rely more heavily on Ma Bell's book than their banter. No matter what they tried, this nut proved impossible to crack. After lunch, they resumed, and by dinnertime, yellow confetti littered the floor. They wore out the phone book without producing a shred of results. The Kid —whoever he was—had the patience of Job combined with the chin of Rocky Marciano.

The detectives each choked down a patty melt at a diner down the block. Only one line of questions produced any visible reaction, so they decided to give it another shot. When they picked up where they left off after dinner, this time rather than sitting and appearing comfortable, Stringer stood while Branford leaned, half-seated, on the table next to the cuffed prisoner and resumed the questions that had touched a nerve.

"You will feel better if you get off your chest what you did with the girls. If they're dead, don't they deserve a decent burial? And if you killed them like you did Leslie—"

It happened so fast, neither had time to react. With the speed of a cat, The Kid sprung from the chair and drove his shoulder into Bradford's gut hard enough to send him sprawling across the floor. Stunning quickness, a flash of lightning unhindered by a cast and walking peg on one leg. Before he could reach his partner, Stringer, too, flew weightless as a rag doll into the wall on the opposite side of the interrogation room. The Kid had the strength of a tiger, leaving Branford gasping for air.

Outside the room, where a dozen cops had gathered to

watch until beginning a mad rush into the room to tackle him before he killed someone, what The Kid did next chilled the observers to the bone. In complete control and calm, he turned to the group scrambling behind the mirror and one side of his mouth curled up into a grin.

THE JAIL

"How do you do it?"

Branford gave his partner a quizzical gaze. "Do what?"

Clenched between his lips, a Chesterfield bounced with Stringer's words, chased by the steady flame of a Zippo. "Keep your cool grilling that creep? That smug grin of his, mocking us with the silent treatment. I'm choking back the urge to grab him by the throat and choke the life out of him!"

"Think killing him will put an end to the silent treatment?"

"It will put an end to my frustration." He blew out the first puff. "Might as well; the case will be closed, even if he takes his reasons for chopping her in half to the grave."

"Can't argue with that," Branford chuckled.

Three days. Three fruitless days wasted bouncing questions off a brick wall. Not only had the Kid refused to answer questions, but after spending his incarceration with him, they still were clueless about what sort of voice he had. It could go either way: a soft, high-pitch to match his youthful appearance, or the deeper voice common to men that tall. At this point, they would be thrilled if The Kid told them to go fuck themselves just for the satisfaction of hearing his vocal sound.

Branford had begun to agree with Stringer. The Kid was a moot. A meaningless waste of valuable time as well as one phone book which tore free from its bindings and ended up tossed into the trash.

"Is that ice in your veins, or don't you care if he never

sings?"

"Does it matter why he did it? Maybe he's hoping to start a new career as a magician, but can't quite get the hang of sawing the lady in the box in two. Look, the D.A. begs us to get a full confession to make his job easier, but what does it matter why he killed a girl, drained her dry of blood and cut her in half? People like him, their reasons never matter. Something's gone wrong with his brain, and the sooner you accept that, the easier it is to sleep at night."

"Yeah, you've got a point there. But it sticks in my craw." He spun clawed fingers, emphasizing his frustration.

"Don't let the diseased mind of the criminally insane get under your skin. We got the killer, so airtight he refuses even to open his mouth in his own defense. He may be craftier than the average knucklehead, but he knows whatever he says will only help us nail him."

"What about those other girls? Don't you care what happened to them?"

After a deep exhale, Branford said, "That's the part that is stuck in *my* craw. Are they dead? If so, where are their bodies? If they were alive, you'd assume they'd come forward. That old bat next door says the third one might be his sister, but who knows what's true with this creep?"

Calmed somewhat by his smoke, Stringer let loose a long blue cloud. His partner was smug as the placid veneer that crazed murderer hid behind, making this the perfect time to rile him up again. "Did your old lady raise you to let nothing get under your skin?"

Branford moved fast as a cat. Close to matching the prisoner when he lashed out at them. Two fists twisted the collars of Stringer's plaid blazer and drove him back against the wall. "I'm only going to say this once: next time you mention my mother, you get a knuckle sandwich. Got it?"

"Hey," his hands held up in surrender, "don't go bananas. I didn't mean anything by it."

He let loose with a shove against the wall, stared him in

the eye while smoothing the rumpled lapels, spun on his heels and left. Stringer looked around, hoping no one was nearby, just as Sergeant Gallagher approached from the opposite direction, shaking his head. "What?"

Giving him a sneer, the Sarge asked, "Didn't anyone tell you not to talk about Branford's mama?"

"What's with his mother?"

"No one knows the details, but we all know better than to mention his mother around him. Once he booked some fathead who then started mouthing off about her and ended up in county needing his face sewn back together for trial. Consider that a final warning."

Stringer never had been one to give heed to warnings.

†

In the hours before they shipped the suspect to the county jail, the Sheriff fielded calls from the police chief, the district attorney—even the mayor. All with the same message: no special favors for John Doe.

This was one of those situations where the general population of felons awaiting trial could do the city a huge favor by sparing the taxpayers the expensive spectacle of a trial. The fact that the D.A. expressed no interest in adding this notch to his belt was puzzling; maybe John Doe's refusal to defend himself made it seem an unfair fight. With his arraignment coming up, they loaded him into the jail's old converted school bus, which delivered him to the county jail. Unlike the passenger list of robbers and car thieves and one guy who emptied his revolver into the front of a house, too drunk to realize a total stranger lived there, John Doe arrived in shackles with ankle chains.

A new jail, built a dozen years before during the Depression as a WPA project, it consisted of a double stack of cells designed to hold either two or four prisoners each, with metal walkway running along the second-floor cells. A first-floor atrium opened up outside the cells to serve as an indoor recreation area. The most violent, dangerous criminals were housed on the second floor.

John Doe went upstairs.

One of the two guards escorting him slid open the barred door. "Wake up, Bubba; say hello to your new roommate."

Another guard unlocked the handcuffs and gave him a shove inside.

"Aw, geez, he looks like a choirboy."

"Consider yourself lucky; he's a celebrity. This one is the Red Dahlia killer."

"No, you don't say!" Mood brightened by this delightful news, Bubba sat up on his thin mattress to take him in. "Promises to be more interesting than the last guy."

"Don't count on it. He's a mute." The guard slammed the bars shut. "Have fun."

"Make yourself at home," the large man waved to the vacant cot. And he was large, the full extent of his bulk masked while seated, but his seated height and broad shoulders testified not all of his mass lay in his generous gut. "I'm J.W., but everyone calls me Bubba. What's your name?"

"Just call me Kid; everyone does."

"Alright, Kid. So tell me—are you like everyone else in here, innocent as a babe? Or did you do it?"

"Does it matter?"

"Yeah, I see your point. Someone's going to Ol' Sparky for that job. Guess you are the lucky one."

For a while, Bubba watched The Kid stretch out on his cot, staring at the bottom of the one above.

"The Red Dahlia, huh? That's some fucked-up stuff." He shook his head, but a smile hinted at admiration. "Nothing to compare to that. They just nabbed me for a misunderstanding with a few girls. Got a little carried away when one started screaming. She'll be fine, just gave her a fat lip. Hey, did she scream when you chopped her in half? Or was she already dead before that? There's a bet among the guys here on the upper block. Bookies split at 50/50 odds around here."

"You talk a lot."

"Well, if you have any better ideas, I'm all ears. Nothing much to do in this joint except chew the fat. Ever been in jail before?"

"No."

"Figures. What are you, about twenty, twenty-two? Nice way to start, I've got to admit. You've got style, Kid."

"Listen, it's been a long day." He lay back on the lumpy, stinking mattress, two inches thick and covered only by a thin, navy-blue woolen blanket.

"No need to be so rude about it. We're going to be locked up together for a while. We should try to get along."

"I didn't ask for a roommate," The Kid said.

"Well, you got one." On his feet, he looked even more imposing. Standing over The Kid's bed made clear he intended to decide when to nap and when to socialize. Somewhere down the block, someone screamed; not in pain, more a wail of some poor slob suffering from grievous agony.

The Kid pulled himself to his feet, facing the giant, who stood several inches above him and easily outweighed him by a hundred pounds. "We don't have to do this."

"Do what? We're just shooting the shit. Am I right?" He shoved The Kid's shoulder in a manner which might come across good-natured in other circumstances, but in here, an unmistakable display of dominance.

The Kid raised open his palms. "Don't touch, okay?"

"Oh, well, excuse me." He squeezed chubby cheeks between the cell bars to holler down the block, "Prima donna here does not like to be touched." Laughter and a couple of hoots responded.

"Just let it be, J.W."

"You've got a lot to learn about how things work inside." This time, his shove was unmistakable. The Kid responded by catching his wrist in his left hand, twisting so fast J.W. did not have a chance to respond. And he kept twisting until a sickening sound like a green tree branch splitting filled the cell, followed by a second.

J.W. screamed and swung a wild left fist in the general direction of The Kid's head.

It never made it.

"Guard? A little help. Cell fourteen needs a doctor!"

The standard procedure upon hearing a prisoner's cries for help was to ignore his bellowing, the major exception being a call for a doctor. After a prisoner bled out in January, a petty crook released a week later leaked to newspapers that the poor guy lay screaming for help all afternoon. Amid the ensuing uproar, the warden made clear this was never to happen again. Expecting to find the Red Dahlia killer already with a shank in his gut, this took less time than the guards expected from ol' Bubba.

The sight greeting them inside the cell sent a shock through the responding guards, though. Sprawled across the floor, J.W. lay surrounded by spattered blood and, other than his prone position on his massive belly, gave the impression of a turtle on its back. He was trying to roll over, an impossible task with his useless arms flopping like flippers. His left arm went off at an unusual angle in an expanding puddle of smeared blood.

"Back!" The first guard to arrive rapped a bar with his two-foot-long wooden nightstick; The Kid stepped away and placed his tin cup on the shelf over the sink. "What the hell happened?"

The Kid shrugged his shoulders. "I think he fell."

"Jesus, Bubba! Is that what happened?"

"Oh, my fucking arm!"

"I think he needs a doctor," The Kid helped out by diagnosing, smirking while leaned against the rear wall with arms crossed over his chest.

"Bubba, can you stand up?"

"Fuck you!"

"Somebody bring a stretcher, will ya? And a couple more guards; Bubba must weigh 350."

As shock set in, J.W.'s pale face grew quiet, but screamed like a little girl when they rolled him onto the stretcher, despite holding his non-dangling right arm still to turn him that way.

"Damn, Bubba, I think you broke both your wrists. That must have been some fall." As four guards hefted J.W. out of the cell, the first guard held his nightstick against The Kid's windpipe and pressed him against the brick wall. "We don't tolerate troublemakers around here, ya got that?"

"I'll try to remember that."

A gut punch he did not see coming doubled him over. "Don't try—do. And when you speak to me, you call me Boss."

"Boss—got it."

The bars slammed shut.

✝

The prison doctor arrived a half-hour later from his usual job as a family practitioner in town. After taking one look at J.W.'s shattered arms, he summoned an ambulance to take him to the hospital. There, X-rays revealed a spiral fracture of both bones in the right arm above the wrist. The left was not as lucky.

"Thirty-seven fragments, to my count," the prison doc told the surgeon who was called in.

At the light board, a quick count confirmed the number. "Probably will locate more once I get in there. Let's prep him for surgery right away; I'll do what I can to save the arm. What happened to him?"

"They say he fell."

"No fall caused these breaks. A spiral fracture like this requires twisting by some force—a powerful one in this case. The other?" The surgeon shook his head. "Not sure what can cause this. I've seen people hit by a Mack truck that didn't crush their bones this completely."

Although the severity of his injuries was obvious to the doctors, neither knew how badly two destroyed arms also mangled the state's prosecution. Over the years, J.W. had been a regular in the county lockup, a reliable repeat offender who long ago discovered an effective strategy to earn an early release. In fact, he had become somewhat of the prosecutor's secret weapon, the best jailhouse snitch anyone could remember having seen.

So, while the doctors were wiring bone fragments together in his arm, the warden and prosecutor were reviewing the roster of prisoners trying to identify anyone who might be impressed into service as John Doe's roommate, a crook trustworthy enough to rely on his account of the killer's every action and word. One who was not prone to falling preferred.

Unbeknownst to everyone, on his bunk, the prisoner sat with a grimace on his face as he sipped from his tin cup. It was a technique he learned years ago. It's rank taste expected, but in here, he had little choice in the matter. Bubba did not seem to notice when he slipped the cup under ripped flesh and let it fill with his blood. As predicted, the guards were too focused on the injured prisoner to notice a cup full of Bubba blood on the shelf.

THE LAWYER

With his arraignment set for the following the morning, the prosecution team debated the merits of bringing John Doe back to continue for another round late into the night. In the end, convinced of the futility, they decided their best option might be to wait him out. Maybe sticking him in a cell with another jailhouse snitch stood a greater chance of discovering what he was keeping secret in that hard, blond head of his.

To ensure fair justice is also timely, the Sixth Amendment to the U.S. Constitution requires a speedy trial, which means an accused has the right to his arraignment soon after arrest. As a testament to the professionalism of the detectives, when deputies escorted the prisoner into the crowded courtroom at nine sharp the following morning, not a visible mark appeared anywhere on his head or other parts of his body left exposed by his prison stripes. Even the beating the half-dozen cops who bum-rushed the interrogation room after he tossed Stringer and Branford left no bruises anywhere on his head or neck.

"All rise," the bailiff called as the judge entered, gray haired, thin, gait hunched over, the crowd standing for the judge to take his seat high over the courtroom to call the first case. "State of Missouri versus John Doe."

John Doe rose. "This is a capital case—murder in the first degree, kidnapping, criminal mutilation of a corpse..." A murmur arose from the packed audience, so the judge grabbed his gavel and pounded it eight or ten times. "There will be quiet in my courtroom! If I hear so much as a sneeze from anyone in the courtroom during this hearing, I will instruct the bailiff to take you out, and downstairs, you will be charged with contempt of court and thrown in jail."

"Now, it seems you have been busy while in jail, Mr. Doe—you are also charged with several counts of assault and battery on police officers. Before we proceed, I feel foolish referring to you as John Doe. What is your name?"

The defendant said nothing.

Addressing the prosecutor, the judge asked, "Jim, is this defendant a deaf-mute?"

"No, your Honor," the prosecutor rose to his feet. "We've spoken to several people who know him, none of whom mention any difficulty speaking or hearing."

"Do they mention a name?"

"People we spoke to call him The Kid. In some documents we have uncovered, his name is listed as Raul di Silva, but the person named Raul di Silva with the same birthdate he uses died in the early thirties. We believe, your Honor, this is an alias."

"Alright. John Doe. For now, I will call you that. How do you plead to these charges?"

Again, his silence continued.

"Do you have an attorney representing you? Jim, are you aware of any defense counsel?"

"No, your Honor, no one has entered an appearance."

After a moment of contemplation, in which the defendant continued his defiant silence, the judge rendered his decision. "Under our Constitution, a defendant is granted the right against self-incrimination. The Court will assume you hereby assert that right. Now, I have no intention of entering a plea of guilty on a capital case today, not on behalf of a defendant asserting his right against self-incrimination and not represented by competent counsel. We're going to enter a plea of not guilty." Handled otherwise guaranteed any conviction being overturned on appeal and retrial, and this judge only wanted to be the ringleader of this particular circus one time.

The judge addressed his clerk. "We need to appoint someone to represent him. Let's check his assets, see if he qualifies for the public defender. If not, get someone good. Try George or Sidney, someone like that. I'm not having this remanded back on appeal."

The Kid continued his steadfast silence, so the judge wrapped up the hearing by refusing to set bail and transferred John Doe back to the county jail, where he was to remain pending trial.

†

"Jesus Christ, Judge! I'm a sole practitioner. You know how much time a death penalty case takes—and that's when your client doesn't believe himself to be Helen Keller. I will need to set aside two months—minimum—to dedicate full-time to this one. Did you talk to Sidney Finkel about it? At least he's with a firm, with other lawyers to help out and bring in some money while he's tied up handling this case."

"Sidney passed, claiming he has a trial in Federal Court scheduled for next month, and there is no way out of it. It's probably bullshit," the judge added, "but I took him at his word."

"Then there is the fact that you are proposing I handle this *pro bono*. Two months minimum is nearly twenty percent of my annual salary swirling around the bowl, not to mention the appeal, because the papers have already convinced everyone in the jury pool that this mystery man is the Red Dahlia killer."

"I thought about that, too, George. He's living in a house on Quality Hill. Delightful house, worth $30,000 easy. They list the owner in the county records as William something or other. No one's ever heard of him. Owns the house free and clear, though. Odds are, William is your John Doe. So, slap a lien on the property. I'll approve it unless William shows up in my courtroom and can prove to me he is not your client. If you don't get paid, the house is yours. Give it to one of your kids, rent it out —hell, from what I hear, it's nice enough to live in yourself, if you don't mind living in the house where the Red Dahlia was likely sawed in two. You don't believe in ghosts, George, do you?"

"How long do I have to consider your request, your Honor?"

"Is 48 hours long enough for you to notify judges and have continuances granted on all your other pending cases?"

"You're killing me, Judge."

"George, you are going to love your new house! I'll look for your entry of appearance by Wednesday."

†

Near the main entrance, past two reinforced steel checkpoints, the county jail had several small rooms set aside as attorney rooms for meeting with incarcerated clients necessary to plan defenses or, more likely, plea agreements. Plain, cinderblock walls painted with two shades of green, a darker green on the lower half, pale to the ceiling, likely war surplus made available to local governments for pennies on the dollar after the Japanese surrendered. Inside, the furnishings comprising a wooden table and three chairs. Many counties had replaced the table and chairs with benches because wooden chairs make such fine weapons, but not Jackson County.

Two guards escorted John Doe in, his arms and legs cuffed and shackled. The two burliest guards they could round up had the honors. "Want we should leave him cuffed?"

"At least uncuff him."

"Are you sure?" the guard asked. "He put his cellmate into surgery five minutes after he arrived."

"In my experience, clients don't attack their lawyers; at least not *before* trial." The grim-faced attorney scowled.

"We'll be right outside; in case you need us."

Looking up from his papers, George warned them, "If I catch you eavesdropping, the judge will hear about it before dinnertime."

First, he gave his new court-appointed client a once-over. "George Bartow. Judge Reynolds appointed me as your counsel." Not surprisingly, John Doe gave a firm handshake. "Can I ask your name, since we're going to be working together?"

"Does it matter? What, are you surprised by my voice?"

"Everyone says you haven't uttered a word since your arrest, so I didn't expect you to speak to me."

"Well, you are my lawyer—they aren't."

"Can I inquire as to your name?"

"You can."

"Well?"

"Ask away. Questions I care to answer, I will."

"Look, this is not a game. They are hell-bent on sending you to the electric chair. From what I've gleaned from this file, they stand a damn good chance of doing so. Better than even odds. You knew the victim; knew her pimp, too. Your car was seen driving in the neighborhood hours before her body was discovered nearby. Inside your house, belongings and clothing of at least two missing women were found, but no trace of said women. It's all circumstantial, but unless you stop clowning around, it's plenty for you to fry."

"Has it occurred to you I might just want to try out Ol' Sparky?"

"Then you should have pleaded guilty."

"Where's the fun in that, George?"

"Your days of having fun are over..." George looked up, flustered. "What should I call you? Raul? William?"

"Everyone calls me Kid."

"I'm your goddamn lawyer, asshole, not some hustler in a back-alley craps game."

A corner of his mouth lifted into a pleasant grin. "I like you, George. A little tense, but no-nonsense. That's good. I prefer *Kid* to *Asshole*, but if that's the name you prefer, we can go with that."

George conceded defeat. "Okay, Kid, you win. Now, let's start with the missing girls the cops are talking about. Are there going to be other bodies?"

"Theirs won't be found."

"Oh, Jesus..."

"I did not kill them."

"Great. Let's start there. Who did?"

"Someone who's not around to bother anyone anymore."

George put down his fountain pen and stared at his client over the top rim of his glasses. "There are others? How many people have you killed?"

"I heard lawyers don't like to ask their clients questions about guilt or innocence. Something about removing some cards away from their deck."

"We cannot introduce evidence we know to be false, so we avoid asking too many questions which may jeopardize our ability to put on defenses."

"Then maybe we should discuss something else."

"Why all the secrecy, the refusal to speak a single word to detectives, refusing to even tell me your name?"

"I can tell you, but you won't believe me. I tend to be a pretty honest fellow, so if you don't believe me when I admit who I am, where is the trust then?" The attorney examined him with the skepticism of a bank teller handed a counterfeit twenty. "Is something wrong?"

"Well, from the sound of it, yes. Oh, you mean why I'm looking at you? Surprised the cops didn't work you over down at the station."

"Oh, they worked me over, alright."

"Well, you look good under the circumstances. None the worse for wear."

"One of my peculiarities; I don't bruise."

"But you didn't say a word?"

"I have trained myself in the discipline of self-control."

"Alright, listen, um, Kid: we need to come up with a defense. A plausible theory explaining how you are not guilty. An alibi, another suspect, that sort of exculpatory theory. Their case has holes in it—no eyewitnesses, no crime scene, no motive —I suspect others. But the city has spun itself into a frenzy and is screaming for your head."

"Yeah, the same happened out in L.A. two years ago with

Elizabeth Short."

"How do you know the circumstances in Los Angeles then?"

"Oh, I was there. Saw first-hand how crazy people were."

George did a face-palm, converting it into a way to rub his eyes. "Dare I ask?"

"No, I suppose that is another detail you are better off knowing zilch about. Ignorance is bliss."

"Alright, just so you know, you are not charged with the Black Dahlia murder, nor are you a suspect, best as I can tell. The cops have pegged you a copycat killer. And since I am not an attorney in California, I would not be involved if you are, so I am asking you, did you kill Elizabeth Short?"

"Technically, no."

"What does that mean, *technically no*?"

"This stays in the room with us, right? Attorney-client privilege?"

"Yes, I can never breathe a word about anything you confide to me without your consent."

"George Hodel killed her. Carved her up afterwards, too. That part I didn't like, not at all."

"How do you know this?"

"Well, I was there. That's where the *technically* comes into play."

"Kid, you may be onto something. If you inform the police of any relevant evidence about the Black Dahlia and this George..."

"Hodel. H O D E L. Funny, he has the same first name as you. Small world."

"It may be sufficient to pull the death penalty off the table if we can engineer a plea deal for this Hodel."

"No." He shook his head. "I'm not snitching on George Hodel. He may be a crackpot and high-class abortionist, and I think he probably killed some other girls out there, but he helped me out when I was in a jam. I wouldn't call him a friend, but I owe him, you know?"

"This is unbelievable!" Perhaps asking the guards to uncuff him was not his wisest decision of the morning. "Kid, this is your way out of death row! You need to take it."

"George, I'm going to let you in on a little secret: I have no intention of setting foot on death row. But for an idiot cop inadvertently tripping me down a flight of stairs, I would not be here today, wasting your valuable time with this nonsense. Just keep doing what you are doing, prepare this for trial, and we'll see what happens. My ankle feels almost back to normal, so soon as I can get this cast off my leg…"

"That happened less than a week ago. According to your medical records, it was a severe fracture of both bones in your leg. You are stuck in that cast until sometime in autumn."

"We'll see. Funny thing about people who don't bruise—we also tend to heal remarkably quickly. Can't really explain it—you probably will not believe me if I try."

THE HOLE

Under normal circumstances, the prison dining experience is among the more unpleasant aspects of jail life. Chief among the reasons is the reliable lousy quality of the cuisine. Not to be outdone, guards take full advantage of the opportunity, while prisoners are spooning up slop, to toss empty cells in search of contraband. Less widely recognized is the inherent danger of bringing together the entire prison population into one cramped room for a shared experience. An opportunity to establish and enforce the pecking order.

Powerful prisoners help themselves to the more palatable items from the trays of weaker prisoners: the elderly, cripples, those of small size, perverts and those who harm children. Meat and desserts are among the more popular stolen items, but it is purely a matter of taste. Large, intimidating criminals and those with connections outside take advantage of the chance to bully others and put down anyone willing to challenge them. Gangs form to offer protection; Irish gangs and Colored gangs and Jewish gangs. Outsiders and those at the bottom of the pecking order may have a rough go, following the inherent law that shit runs downhill.

Long ago, prison administrators learned the dangers of providing criminals with knives and dispensed with them, but forks make efficient weapons, too, if marginally less lethal. In experienced hands, metal trays can lethal effectiveness, and although no one maintains records of this particular statistic, many prisoners have died of an artfully broken chicken drumstick driven into the throat or gut. On those rare occasions when fried chicken is served, the fine art of splintering off the knuckle of bone at one end to leave a sharp tip is practiced in every finger licking prison across the nation.

These, however, were not ordinary circumstances.

The Red Dahlia so dominated headlines that other criminals lost any notoriety their crimes once bestowed upon them, now eclipsed by this new arrival. The Kid. Others found his butchery offensive, particularly when inflicted on such a pretty redhead. A few were antsy to meet this new star—and soon, before someone stuck a fork in his eye. And—his identity as a snitch a well-kept secret—J.W. was popular among the prisoners.

Heads turned the moment he entered, and a hush fell over the prison mess. His fame preceded him. Rumors spread with lightning speed in prison—wild exaggerations while, at the same time, underestimating who walked among them. Those who had not seen him paraded past the bars of their cells were eager to get their first impression of him. Every beady pair of eyes sized him up. A respectable specimen, to be sure, but judging by his size, not one to take apart a seasoned convict as capable as Bubba without breaking a sweat.

More a pretty boy, a notion which set alight a fair share of anticipatory grins and hearts aflutter.

"Here comes Hollywood now," someone shouted, breaking the silence to an approving roar of laughter. Few rituals offered entertainment enjoyable as labeling prisoners with their prison nicknames within these walls, and in an instant, everyone knew this one would stick.

"The Hollywood Kid," another voice called out, carving it in stone.

He took a place at the tail end of the chow line behind a tattooed prisoner, both taller and broader than him, who turned and faced him with arms crossed over his chest. When the line moved, the behemoth stood still, blocking his way.

"Excuse me," he said as he tried to go around, but the other prisoner side-stepped to bar his path.

"Where do you think you're going?"

"None of your business." So powerful was the shove that moved the inked bulk of the other prisoner out of his way that his head jerked forward as his body flew in the other direction, toward the wall of cinderblock painted a familiar green. No one could have expected such force from a man wiry as him, even if not hindered by a walking cast that limited him from realizing his full potential.

Around the mess hall, the sound of two hundred prisoners leaping to their feet came across as chairs crashing and screeching across the floor. Whistles blew as the blue suited guards sprang into action, bashing prisoners with nightsticks to restore order before this mushroomed into a full-scale riot. Someone knocked The Hollywood Kid to the concrete floor. Several others piled on, enough bodies to block most punches aimed toward him from sheer lack of swinging space.

It took the guards several interminable minutes to clear the pile and drag The Hollywood Kid to the hole. The punishment cell stood out in the yard. A hotbox, truth be told—concrete walls, a tin roof, no windows and one steel door.

There, he spent the remainder of his first day in jail.

It was far from the first time he'd been alone and in utter isolation. Before he adapted, learning to function among the world of humans while no longer being one of them, he spent years honing the skills necessary to hide his new nature from society while walking unobserved among them.

With only the example of his sister to guide him, he wondered how she learned her secrets while appearing so natural that even her own family never suspected a thing. This is what she planned to explain to him, the cryptic hints in her letters. Denied of her opportunity to explain to him before their father ripped out her heart and liver and burned them to ashes, which he then forced both him and his last surviving sister to drink. While burning Lena's organs accomplished the goal of killing her a second time, the ashes which were supposed to inoculate them failed—at least in his case.

The most troublesome part was learning how to view humans as prey. This skill he had to learn on his own.

†

A rat scurried along the empty bunk, believing darkness offered it protection.

As a man, his appreciation of irony never had a chance to reach full maturity. That came later. Perhaps, given more time, his taste might have developed, although he doubted it. After death, his tastes in most things remained unchanged. More refined, sure, but over the decades still quite similar. When he left Exeter, Rhode Island, as a small-town boy who awakened one day transformed into a deceased abomination, Eddie Brown understood how sheltered a life he led.

During the First World War, one of the most popular songs posed a question that resonated across America. He first heard it in a raucous, sweaty jazz club in Paris, and before his unit shipped back for the states, every band in every club was playing the ditty. For the doughboys, the lyrics captured an abiding fear churning deep inside each soldier even before he was ready to form it into a coherent notion, putting words to an unexpressed and indistinct emotion. Their sweethearts at home found the lighthearted tune and style encapsulated their own fears, second only to receiving the dreaded telegram expressing appropriate regret for the death of their beloved soldier—or worse, injuries leaving them horribly maimed.

> *How ya gonna keep them*
> *down on the farm,*
> *After they've seen Paree?*

To him, the lyrics brought a sense of nostalgia. Sure, Paris and the French and Belgian villages he visited were exotic, the women wonderfully wanton in their desperation. But while most ordinary farm boys experienced their first taste of an enticing, alien world on leave after the Germans surrendered, Eddie lived through it twenty-five years before.

His first taste of blood came in the guise of a dream. In reality, not a dream, of course, a mere illusion his sister created, one enabling him to accept the gift she imparted to him. His first taste of human blood, compelled by some instinct he still did not understand—that changed everything.

So when the boys sang the song when returning from leave, back in the trenches, he sang a unique altered version.

> *How ya gonna keep them*
> *down on the farm,*
> *After they've tasted blood?*

Once, he belted out those lyrics in a dive on the *Rive Gauche*, giving his buddies stitches because, in their ignorance, they misunderstood the meaning. They assumed he meant the taste for killing Germans, not a literal appetite.

Perhaps that day his genuine appreciation for irony was born.

The rat held so little blood, and of such a poor and distasteful quality, it acknowledged his growing sense of desperation. He flung its limp corpse between the bars of his cell.

His unique situation consisted of so many layers of irony, peeling them back entertained him for hours in the solitude of his cell.

Sure, the police arrested him as the Red Dahlia killer, but they had no inkling how many he had killed over the past six decades. He had no intention of correcting the failure of their imagination, of course, any more than he would correct their inability to grasp his motives for killing. They labeled him a madman, a psycho-killer, closer to Jack the Ripper than his true nature.

And they considered him a mere copycat, inspired by whoever killed Elizabeth Short.

If those fools had any idea!

They wasted all their energy trying to solve murders he never committed, some being murders which never took place. When it because obvious the phone book and a foot-long piece of garden hose they brought in was inadequate to convince him to talk, they started asking about the girls he picked up at the bus station.

The detectives returned to the jail most days, a fact he chose not to share with his lawyer because he might spoil his own source of entertainment by putting the kibosh on these jailhouse interrogations. Sometimes he spoke now, as the mood struck. The cops now focused their efforts on the whereabouts of the other girls. Only two were dead, neither by his hand. When he suggested they ask Frankie Four Fingers what happened to those girls, they brought the phone directory back to aid in the interrogations.

So, he shut the hell up again—how's that for irony?

Never mind the delicious irony in the very concept of the death penalty they were busy building a most solid case for imposing upon him. As a construct itself, the death penalty was as ironic as it comes. On the level of punishment, it worked just fine, although he wondered how frequently the wrong man ended up getting fried. It was, however, intended to serve a grander purpose, that of deterrence. The theory went that no one will commit murder if killing risks a ride on Ol' Sparky. Headlines in every newspaper around the country functioned as a daily reminder proving the foolishness of that theory.

Why did headlines never read *Death Penalty Inexplicably Fails to Discourage St. Joseph Man from Strangling Mother-in-Law*?

The greatest irony, of course, was the fact he brought all of this upon himself. Begged for it. For decades, he fled city after city, town after town once the heat was on. What does he do when he commits his highest-profile crime?

He supposed the answer lay in his growing sense of frustration, his self-destructiveness. His struggle between the desire to continue his deceased existence or to die once and for all.

Soon after the first war, fueled by Absinthe, some French philosophers coined the perfect term for it. Existentialism. He first stumbled upon the word in a philosophy class he enrolled in at UCLA on the GI bill. He wore the cover off a translation of Camus' *The Stranger* he bought at a subversive bookstore soon after he arrived in the City of Angels. Now he had become Meursault, jailed for murdering a pimp's girlfriend, which is how Meursault should have handled the situation in the book instead of killing the Arab. That hapless Arab never betrayed anyone.

Here, though, the stranger was The Kid, whose identity still stymied the police. As translated in the original British version, the book title is more *à propos*: *The Outsider*. In this context, it applied more directly to The Kid. Rather than the victim having no name, here the killer had no name. At least one unknown to all but him.

For decades, he considered introspection a dangerous indulgence. Now, he had little else to occupy his time. Was this perhaps the greatest irony of his sorry circumstances? Now, when more unmoored than at any point since that horrifying day he awakened inside his coffin, yearning for blood, his own recklessness forced him to think on it. To consider his life and the course of his death. To face shame for the first time. To face himself with honesty—and the monster he had become.

Now, Eddie Brown was a murderer, in jail awaiting trial and execution. A sentence he deserved—and yet doomed to fail.

THE GIRLS

The only thing the detectives learned once The Kid regained his powers of speech during their visits to the jail's interrogation room? The sound of his voice. Deep, one of those baritone voices with an inherent calming quality. The fact that the only questions he chose to answer were irrelevant and his answers to those irreverent frustrated the Hell out of them. The rest of the time, he sat in silence inside his little shell. And he took enormous pleasure in antagonizing them.

"Still trying to figure out how you do it?" Back at the station house, they conducted their daily autopsy on another interview that was DOA.

Branford turned toward his partner. "Put up with that clown's crap?"

As per their routine, now growing all too familiar, an unlit Chesterfield bounced with Stringer's words, as usual, away from the trusty flame of his brass Zippo. "He's so full of it, it's a wonder the whites of his eyes haven't turned brown."

"He wants to talk about those girls—you can read it on his face. It's killing him, but for some reason, he can't bring himself to tell us what he did with them. Who they are; *where* they are. What he did with them. Their fingerprints scattered all over that house, but none of those girls are on file. No arrests, no bodies in a morgue somewhere. If I didn't know better, I'd swear those witnesses are making them up, because it is like they never existed."

"But they did." Stringer completed his thought for him.

"Yeah, they did. Or still do—somewhere." He flipped a

pencil pinwheeling into the air, letting it land on the table. The lead, broken off upon impact, rolled off the edge onto the floor. "They can't fry this guy in the electric chair soon enough, yet the idea that he will take his secret to the grave keeps me from sleeping."

"Aw, that's sweet. You do care."

"Call me sentimental, but this is one loose end I refuse to let go."

Somehow, the lighter had caught up to the cigarette, allowing Stringer to fill the tiny room with a full exhale. "What do you suppose he was doing with them? They weren't prisoners. If he locked them in their rooms, nothing was keeping them from climbing out the window onto that big porch roof outside. Heck, my grandma could shimmy down from there."

That house was no prison. From the look of their rooms, it was lived in. Home. "There is something we're missing."

"Like what?"

"Well," Branford answered, "if I knew what it was, we wouldn't be missing it, would we?"

"Let's find out what it is, then."

Easier said than done. Without names, no photographs. Where to start? The typical missing person case starts with a name. A body, at least. A starting point, although far too many Jane Does never are given back their names. The city's Potter's Field holds far too many mysteries buried within.

"Makes me sick." Stringer's words, expelled as smoke, resembled Morse code drawn up in cartoonish smoke signals.

"What makes you sick?"

"The thought of a sicko like him having a house full of girls, imagining what he was doing to them. How does a guy like him do it?"

"He is handsome."

"He is a murderer. Don't tell me a bevy of pretty girls living under his roof never picked up on that little detail."

"Good."

The way Stringer looked at him suggested he suspected his

new partner might be crazy. "What is good about any of that?"

"It's good that you are with me. I haven't figured out how we're going to do it, but at least you haven't given up. We're going to solve this mystery of what he did to them. Dead or alive, let's track down who they are or were or whatever the case may be. If that jagoff doesn't start singing, we won't need Ol' Sparky—I'll kill him myself."

†

If a human being ever desired to spill to the police everything they knew, that person was Florence Peabody.

And as the killer's next-door neighbor, her position to observe was unrivaled. Branford and Stringer had a brief conversation with her weeks ago, but with the paucity of leads, they returned to pry more information from her, this time concerning the topic of those girls.

"One thing for sure—they were pretty little things. Even that Negro girl. Kept to themselves, they did. Polite when speaking with you, respectful—which, come to mention it, was the oddest part, considering the shenanigans taking place in that house."

"What was going on in that house?"

"Well, I'm sure you can imagine."

"The thing is, Mrs. Peabody," Branford cleared his throat, "what we can imagine is not important. The important part is what you observed with your own two eyes."

"Well, I didn't go spying on them through the windows, if that's your meaning."

In desperation to wrangle her toward something productive, Stringer asked, "Did you see the girls outside the house?"

"Oh yes. They were often out and about. When they saw you, they'd wave or say hi, that sort of thing."

"But they weren't held captive?"

"Heavens, no! Came and went free as they pleased.

Habitual shoppers—went all the time—and inevitably returned home lugging bags from the expensive stores, never the Five and Dime. They drove his car, the one that burned up."

"Do you know how it ended up catching fire like that?"

"Not a thing. Must have happened when I was down in St. Louis. My son and my grandchildren live there, so I visit them often. When I returned from my trip, the entire bunch were gone. That was two days before you showed up and arrested him. Can you imagine, all this time I was living next door to a murderer! If I had any notion those girls were in danger, I'd have certainly reported it to the police a year ago. The worst I ever imagined was the unmentionable sort of immoral behavior they were engaging in over there."

"In total, how many girls stayed there?"

"Oh, I don't know. Some arrived and then poof—you never saw them again. The pair I mentioned stuck around for a while. Then the new one came. The one he said was his sister."

Branford joined in, pressing for useful information. "Do you have reason to believe she was not his sister?"

"You mean, other than the constant parade of young floozies like her through the doors? No, I suppose not. They share a passing resemblance—slim, same blonde hair and all— but I never got a close look at her. She wasn't here long."

"Do you recall any personal information about them? Their names, where they were from, that sort of details," Branford asked.

"That girl who was here longest, her name was Kat. Not sure if she spelled it with a C or a K. That little Colored girl, she was Grace." Mrs. Peabody leaned forward, which they hoped might be some important detail she wanted to remain confidential. "She had light skin. I always had the impression she may be a mulatto."

"And the other girl was brunette?" The lady nodded, which gave Branford an idea. "If we asked you to sit down with our sketch artist, do you think you could describe the girls to him? At least the couple who stayed until recently?"

"One thing I remember is faces," she answered, then took a step closer. "Here's the strange thing—I've seen one of those girls around town."

"Which girl?"

"One who lived here way back when he started playing house over there. She must have been gone six months or more."

"Where did you see her?"

"Oh, I don't know. Around. Nowhere in particular. When we run into each other, she waves and says hello. Wait—I remember seeing her down at the phone company. I went down to pay my bill, and she was there in line waiting to pay hers, too."

At least narrowing the list to people who have telephones. A meeting with the police sketch artist might bear fruit. Something more useful than being one of the hundred thousand city residents who use a phone.

†

For some reason even he could not fathom, Stringer decided it was time to take another dig at his partner while lingering over in vice squad waiting for a pot of coffee to finish percolating. "You've been holding out on me."

"What are you talking about?"

He flashed an evil grin. "You've got a way with older women, you know that? That Peabody broad was putty in your hands. Or should I say, Silly Putty? Your mother must be so proud."

Without a word, Branford spun and landed a low blow just below Stringer's beltline. A few inches too high, it still packed enough venom to buckle the younger detective's knees and stagger him two steps backward to the wall, where he crumpled down into a pile. In his flash of blinding white pain, the other detective disappeared before he regained the senses required to take a look around.

Gallagher walked past, shaking his head, making no effort to conceal his glee. "Told ya not to mention his mother."

Struggling to his feet, still doubled over and sucking wind, Stringer managed to grunt, "Are you going to fill me in?"

"Nah. You're the detective; I'm just a desk sergeant."

By the time he caught up to his partner out front by his Hudson Super 6 unmarked car, he was able to walk upright again, though sliding down the wall had displaced his jacket, which he hadn't noticed, enhancing his still hunched over appearance.

"Okay, I get it. Not another peep out of me about your mother."

Branford took the wheel, silent as a stone. Only the occasional chatter on the police radio broke the monotony until they had parked in front of the four-story brick monolith of Central High School with its church-like steeple, where the sketch artist held down a day job as an art teacher. Staring straight ahead and making no move to get out, Stringer waited for the storm to break.

"Six years old," he said after a long silence.

When he volunteered nothing more, Stringer asked, "Who was six years old?"

"That's how old I was when my mother disappeared."

"Oh." This revelation struck with the raw force of another gut punch. "What do you mean, *disappeared*? She ran off?"

"That's what everyone said. Pop, my relatives, the kids in the neighborhood. *Run off with another man* is how Pop explained it. At the time, I didn't understand what it meant, but I never bought it. She wouldn't do that; not my Mama. Not without me." He paused for a moment, but his eyes continued boring into whatever brick in his direct line of sight he found so fascinating. "You see, I remember her threatening to leave during their fights, but when he wasn't around, she promised to take me with her. She knew exactly what kind of man he was."

"Look, partner, I shouldn't have stepped out of line like that."

"Mama lost a couple of babies after me, which irked my pop because he wanted an entire platoon of little Branfords.

Complained about it constantly. Accusing her of all sorts of things. Drinking pennyroyal tea—I was a clueless kid who did not understand what he meant by that for years. They'd fight and then make up. Many families in my neighborhood were the same, although most were bigger families."

"They had a fight this one night. Heard it up in my room. Heck, I was used to it by then, so I didn't think the last words I'd ever hear my Mama speak were accusing my father of whoring around. That I understood, and it infuriated me—at her, for speaking about Pop that way."

"That's rough, Scott," Stringer said, using his first name for the first time.

"You know, he never reported her as a missing person to the police. Just told everyone she'd run off. Back in those days, the police never interfered in people's marriages. Not without a body, and then only if the husband was drunk, threatening to kill her in public, waving a bloody butcher knife—something overt. No, she was gone, and no one cared where or with whom she supposedly ran off."

"Is that why you became a detective?"

"Beats the hell out of me," Branford answered, turning to his partner for the first time since he threw that punch, "although I never thought about it much. Didn't take me long on the job to figure out it's always the husband, right?" A hint of a wry grin appeared for an instant before fading away. "Well, not always. Sometimes it's a sick monster like our John Doe. Doesn't matter who did it, when you think about it. Or why. What matters is who she was."

"And who she left behind."

"Yeah, I suppose so."

"Look, I deserve a fat lip on top of that shot you gave me back at the station, so if you want to pop me again…"

"Think I'll hold off until the next time you say something stupid to bust your lip. Alright, we're burning daylight. Let's go see if we can rustle up the info we need to send our monster straight to the electric chair. And to find those girls."

HOLLYWOOD BABYLON

Deprivations spawned by a decade of Prohibition, the Depression following hot on its heels, then by four brutal years of warfare left deep, lasting scars. After being forced to commit horrible acts in order to survive, acts few dreamed possible in their darkest nightmares, the majority of the kids from the generation which grew up in the thirties then sent overseas to fight Hitler and Tojo.

Little wonder why American GIs proved so brutally lethal in combat.

War has a certain way of numbing the soul. Whether serving in the Pacific or Europe, no one could have expected the absolute evil or wholesale atrocities they witnessed and, indeed, took part in. Not limited to those seeing action at Anzio, Bastogne or Iwo Jima, the war held ample horrors for each of the millions of American boys sent off to fight. Enough for the kids who watched their buddies' heads blown off in battles too small to warrant mention in history books, the sailors forced to hose their bunkmates off decks after a kamikaze raid or the colored troops tasked with burying the mangled, decaying corpses of the slain.

Few faced punishment for rape or what otherwise is considered murder of civilians, particularly in Italy, Germany and Okinawa. Brothers, fathers and husbands of the slain or defiled then sought to exact revenge by vowing to kill these GIs who despoiled their women. Any GI would do. The act of revenge was more important than taking care to aim their pot-shot at the right guy. So great the threat, in some theaters troops only ventured outside the base in armed groups. Such pent-up energy and stress needed release. Most carried it home with them four years before, when the war ended and the soldiers returned stateside.

The vast majority dealt with their souvenirs of war by savoring tranquility, whether through drink or silence. Others, however, who struggled less effectively against trauma and guilt, ended up imprisoned with The Kid and in hundreds of other prisons across America. The ways they nurtured the demons carried back from combat varied as widely as the individuals harboring them.

One positive aspect of prison is the time it offers to ponder such esoterica. Alone because your cellmate is facing an indeterminate stay in hospital provided a perfect opportunity. Although he had not realized it when heeding the call, the wave of hedonism which spread like wildfire after the war is what drew him west.

Sure, he had to leave the East, his home for the last several decades. When the body count grew into dangerous numbers in one town, for years he simply packed up and shipped out again. With the East Coast played out, desperation of a very different sort sent him in search of… something.

The brightest lights cast the deepest shadows. Although the moniker Hollywood Babylon had yet to be crafted, the concept was already widespread by the forties. Behind Tinseltown's glittering klieg lights and glamor lay a darkness appealing to him.

"Hey, Red Dahlia!" The clanging of a wooden nightstick against his cell bars roused him back to the real world. Not knowing what to call him, "Hollywood" too distasteful, the screws had taken to using the popular name of the victim for his own, too. "You okay in there?"

Eddie opened his eyes. "Yeah, boss." For some inexplicable reason, guards preferred this term to "screws", even though it is a jailhouse acronym for *sorry son of a bitch* turned around backwards.

With an acknowledging nod, the screw continued his rounds, muttering, "For a minute, lying there, you looked dead."

If this guard only knew.

†

In theory, perhaps the most unlikely city in America to be the haunt of ghosts is Hollywood, California.

The City of Light—crawling with stars infinitely more dazzling, their mansions brand-spanking new. What was once the Hurd Farm began its transformation a few years before World War I, accelerating faster than a jet fighter over the thirty-one years since. Maybe rivaled in unlikeliness only by Levittown, that new-fangled Long Island community where affordable houses for returning veterans were springing up like toadstools after a long rainy spell, at the astonishing rate of thirty new homes per day. One thing ghosts must require is time to inhabit brand new buildings. Centuries.

At least, that is the popular perception even The Kid once shared. Recent decades, though, allowed him the clarity required to see deeper. Where moviegoers saw sunny L.A. exteriors, bright white beaches and stage lighting sufficient to melt skin, all that brilliance cast the shadows he perceived. Smelled it—in fact, he sensed it with every fiber of his being.

In just three decades, tragedy, death and heartbreak were more concentrated in Hollywood's few square miles than anywhere else in America. Only bloodstained battlefields in Europe and the Pacific or Hitler's death camps concentrated more misery and evil than along the boulevard of broken dreams and seeping into the hills above it. Perhaps that infection is what drew him there.

Murder, suicide and mysterious death ended uncounted lives—stars and those aspiring to be, along with many who failed. The sheer volume of unsolved deaths raised more than a few eyebrows, and the LAPD practice of covering up the actual causes of deaths at the request of studio heads was common knowledge. Dozens of beautiful starlets and other innocent young girls arrived seeking fame, only to die at the hands of various actors and Hollywood moguls. Even Fatty Arbuckle killed a starlet and waltzed away scot-free, thanks to generous bribery payments for witnesses willing to commit perjury. Those scandals and tragic stories attracted him at a deep, dark, subconscious level.

Ghosts he sensed haunting the hotels and mansions were the closest thing to other immortals he knew. If only he could do more than sense them surrounding him.

First, he rented a room on Sunset Boulevard. It seemed prosaic, as did the place he later chose as a more permanent home, a Spanish-style bungalow at the infamous Garden of Allah. Built for scandalous silent film actress Alla Nazimova, the sexy star of *Camille* and many other films, who converted the Hayvenhurst estate into a hotel when after the twilight of her career in pictures by erecting two dozen villas on the premises. After remodeling the lower floor of her mansion into a bar and restaurant and relocating to her apartments upstairs, Alla continued residing there until she died just two months after the Germans surrendered.

Every step he took around the property, The Kid could sense her presence there with him.

Tales of the debauchery unfolding in these bungalows and the stars who lived and died there—despite or, perhaps, enticed by its reputation—ensured the Gardens' infamy. Everyone from Harpo Marx to Rachmaninoff and F. Scott Fitzgerald made the Gardens their homes in its heyday. Although it had lost some of its former panache, stars and those who had fallen still resided under its red tile roofs when The Kid took up residence in Villa 8 midway through 1946. Villa 8 had once been Bogart's home and, when he was away, his buddy Errol Flynn stayed there.

Lying on his cot, The Kid's mind drifted in and out of his reminiscences. What sizzle the Garden may have lost over time, it more than compensated for with decadence by the time he arrived. When he lived there, it remained a safe retreat for writers, photographers and more than a few actors, although by those days, more likely former stars brought back to earth by the morality clauses written into their studio contracts.

Back then, he was not yet known as The Kid. In Hollywood, he still went by his given first name. Eddie.

How many starlets, hopefuls and former starlets had fed Eddie's needs there? How many had died? Two? Three? Strange how he lost count. There in Villa 8 is where he truly began losing himself, and perhaps that is why memories of the more unpleasant parts faded until little but shadows and wispy images were all that remained.

Credit Alla and her dissolute Gardens, for there he cultivated acquaintances who introduced him to Hollywood's elite and powerful. Among the rich and famous and deviant, he found acceptance. Soon, he became a regular fixture at parties thrown by Hollywood royalty. That is how he met Dr. George Hodel.

†

"Are you in pictures?" It is a question Eddie fields at these sorts of parties, few with answers more fraught with peril. The handsome young men at these parties are either actors, hopefuls or the homosexual lovers of some industry bigwig. He is none of those. The host of this soiree, a famous producer and almost as famous Sodomite, is one of the few producers Eddie holds in genuine high regard, but he does not want anyone to consider him another backlot boy toy.

The dish asking on this occasion is a tall brunette with eyes a remarkable icy blue. Pretty—a fact of which she is well aware—although clueless that she is neither pretty nor slender enough to attract that lightning luck of stardom. Her black dress hides it well, while also displaying her cleavage to its fullest advantage.

"No, I'm just a vampire."

Those alluring eyes sparkle. "Oh, that sounds kinky!" Despite her candor, there is a sense of shyness about her. She resembles a little girl who has lost her mother somewhere among a surging crowd.

It is not his first attempt at being so cheekily honest, and her response is typical. "And you? Are you a 'waitress' like everyone else?"

"Pretty much."

"Your eyes are enchanting," his fingers stroke her cheek, moving slow down to her chin, which he lifts an inch. "I'm Eddie."

"How fun! My name starts with an E, too—I'm Elizabeth. Where are you from? Do I detect a fellow Yankee accent?"

"Rhode Island. Don't tell me—yours is Massachusetts?"

"Medford, born and raised; although I've lived everywhere. Miami, Atlanta… Hollywood. Can I offer you a smoke?" She dangles a Lucky Strike in her mouth while offering him one.

"No, thanks." He takes from her hand a matchbook featuring a leggy redhead and lights her cigarette, the unfiltered other tip already bearing the stains of blood red lipstick.

She blows the smoke up, over his head. "A classy gentleman."

"A classy lady." He smiles, knowing she is hooked.

From the moment he arrived, he knew this bacchanalia is destined to result in bloodshed. Even by the high standards of parties thrown in the hills overlooking the strip, this one is wild. The couple walks past the pool, where a naked girl is splashing toward a man in a suit standing just beyond the spray's reach. Elizabeth turns away, then points. "Is that Lana Turner?"

A pretty blonde has her tongue down the throat of a kid no older than twenty. "I believe so."

On the patio, another topless girl sits on the cushy lap of a man with gray hair; she looks all of thirteen and has his full attention, oblivious to the two men swapping spit in a love seat not six feet away. As Eddie holds open the door to the house, the sound of moaning attracts his attention. There, against the trunk of an eucalyptus tree, a woman wearing a yellow dress has her legs wrapped around the waist of a man whose pants are around his ankles, his bare ass scrunching each time he thrusts up into her. Her eyes are closed, as if shutting her lids tight bestows invisibility from two hundred party guests.

An hour later, back out at the pool now, Elizabeth's long, black curls conceal an incision behind her ear. Her already pallid complexion has turned a ghastly white. With her raven mane and a fresh layer of bright red lipstick, she can pass as Snow White's older, faster sister. Eddie lights another Lucky Strike for her as a doll-like older man with a dark curly hair comes up and wraps his arm around her waist. Dressed in an impeccable double-breasted Navy suit, with a pinched face and bushy mustache. His eyes convey the intelligence of a viper.

"There you are." His nose bulldozes aside hair to kiss her on the neck, in dangerous proximity to the new laceration. "Are you planning to introduce me to your friend?"

"Eddie—I don't know your last name! Meet Dr. George Hodel."

The doctor holds out his hand for Eddie to shake. In a party awash with decadent society, something makes this man stand out among the lesser degenerates.

"Raynaud's?"

"Excuse me?"

Still gripping Eddie's hand, he turns it to examine. "Raynaud's phenomenon. Odd, your hand is cold, yet showing no signs of discoloration."

Doctors make Eddie nervous, so he retrieves his hand from the doctor's grip. "Maybe so. I don't trust doctors much."

For a moment, beady anthracite eyes examine him, then a slight smile comes across oddly feminine lips. "No, I suppose you don't. How very perceptive of you."

The doctor's hand slides down to Elizabeth's generous bottom and begins fondling it as she blows a smoke ring as though nothing is unusual. The two men warily eye each other.

Before the doctor leaves with Elizabeth to take her home or wherever he takes her, he hands Eddie a card.

George H. Hodel, MD
5121 Franklin Avenue
Los Angeles

"Drop by anytime. My home is a haven where like-minded people can gather for intellectual and sensual stimulation. I have a feeling you will find yourself at home there."

†

Like-minded. What had that odd doctor meant by that curious choice of words?

For several days, Eddie could not shake those words from his mind. The doctor did not strike him as the kind to use imprecise, careless speech. Was Hodel a vampire, too? One with an ability to identify others of his kind? When he kissed that girl's neck, had he seen the gash Eddie fed from? Or had he meant something as innocuous as another man interested in his party date?

†

One evening, he resolves to discover the truth.

Cars line the curb in front of Sowden House where the Yellow Cab pulls to a stop. Same as most evenings. This place is something off a horror movie set, more temple to the Mayan sun god than house, with a geometric pyramid towering over the front door and a huge, multi-pane window designed to catch the sunset on a winter's evening, creating the illusion of a second sun. No other windows face the front, to avoid detracting from this modern homage to Kinich Ahau. A monstrosity designed by Frank Lloyd Wright twenty years before, which Dr. Hodel purchased just over a year ago.

In his visits, which become frequent, he learns of Dr.

Hodel's fascination with Scotch, Cuban cigars and beautiful women, not necessarily in that order. Women always wander through this house, and not just the starlets whose careers he salvages with clandestine abortions. Although subject to a lengthy jail sentence for this service, calling it a secret is a charade. Everyone knew.

"The police do not trouble me," is one of the doctor's favorite jokes. In fact, Eddie met the police chief here last week, and the mayor stopped by once with the police commissioner in tow.

Dorero—Mrs. Hodel—does not seem to mind all the women any more than the doctor minds frequent visits by Dorero's ex-husband, John Huston, director of *The Maltese Falcon* and working on his current project, *The Treasure of the Sierra Madre*. This intriguing title prompted intense speculation at Hodel's parties whether Bogie might this time discover something more valuable than a hunk of lead. Instead of answering, her current and former husbands spend many evenings arguing about surrealistic art like old buddies, which, Eddie supposes, they are.

"Hi, Eddie; come in." He recognizes the girl answering the door, but cannot remember her name. Last time he saw her, she was wearing clothes, but this night she has only a white silk wrap around her waist as a makeshift skirt. Her breasts sway, and if she is concerned they may distract motorists passing on the street, she does not let on.

"I'm sorry, I don't think I got your name."

"Dorothy, as in…"

"Surrender Dorothy."

Her breasts sway marvelously as she shakes his hand. "Cute. Most people ask me to sing *Over the Rainbow*."

"How were your parents to know when they named you, what, twenty years ago?"

"Close—nineteen. I was almost Judy Garland's age when the movie came out and ruined my life. George was asking for you earlier. Acting all serious, too. He's not himself tonight."

"Better go find him, then. Nice to formally meet you."

Dr. Hodel is in his office, down the hall on the right. When Eddie opens the door after knocking, the doctor jumps to his feet, appearing agitated. "Where have you been? Come in; shut the door."

"Is everything alright?"

"No, nothing's at all right. Sit, please." The doctor paces about while Eddie sinks into a comfortable green leather chair on the opposite side of the desk. "I've had some suspicions about you since we met. One of the sundry benefits of being a medical doctor with an IQ of 187, not much escapes my notice."

"Is this what you meant about us being like-minded, doctor?"

"Yes, it is. My powers of observation are unsurpassed, although if I am correct, yours are perhaps particularly acute. Unnaturally so, some might say."

"Very astute. Do tell, exactly what do you suspect me of?"

"Have you, shall we say, unique tastes?"

Eddie swallows hard. "Do we share such unusual tastes?"

"To a certain degree. Different, perhaps, although we both enjoy tastes most consider unsavory. Mine are of a more— how shall I put this—carnal nature, less epicurean than yours. Cravings no less impossible to control."

Hope drains from his body, shoulders drooping with disappointment. "So you do not share my affliction?"

"A taste for blood? No. Well, yes, but a unique taste. One I have struggled to contain. Not a hunger, nor need. Mine is more a desire. Is my assessment correct?"

"It is."

"Don't worry, I am a physician. Consider it doctor-patient privilege. You may speak freely, and sharing a mortal secret shall protect us both."

"Protect us? From what?"

He leads Eddie to the guest room next door, through a hidden connecting door, avoiding any need to step into the hallway.

A surreal painting hangs on the wall depicting a nude woman or, perhaps, two. Other than the bedsheets, every piece of furniture is black. Except for the chrome everywhere. Various types of restraints, whips, gags, and articles of torture hang from the other three walls. On the bed, a dark-haired woman lies strapped by wrists and ankles, her face bloody and unrecognizable.

"You know her, of course."

"I do?"

"Elizabeth. That night, when you disappeared with her at that party? Well, I assumed you were helping yourself to her body. You were, albeit in a different manner than I expected. A puncture to her posterior auricular artery? And so expertly done! Since you aren't a physician, I wondered what possessed you to do it. Later, when Elizabeth denied the existence of such a wound, let's just say it aroused my suspicions. I have noticed the same incision to other women; these similar wounds occurring only after your visits. And limited to guests who have been the object of your flirtations. Under my roof. Like you are sending me a message."

"Your words at the party… I wondered if you, too, might be like me."

"Must you consume it to survive?"

"Yes."

"And your age? Is it advanced beyond your years?"

"I was born in 1868."

"Remarkable. No, more than that. Marvelous! True immortality combined with eternal youth. And all due to consuming human blood. Yet, you don't kill those from whom you feed?"

"It is best not to leave evidence in such an obvious form."

"Excellent!" His fingers form an A that prop against his thick mustache, perhaps intending to hide his grin. "I envy you. Sure, doctors accrue certain benefits during life, but immortality is denied all but a select few. Hippocrates. Galen. Samuel Mudd. The rest of us are doomed to obscurity the moment our mortal lives slip away."

"But the doctor who discovers the secret of immortality?"

"He, too, shall achieve immortality, even if he cannot harness it for himself. But that is for another day. Should you consent, I wish to study you. Hopefully, you and I together will discover the secrets of vampirism. For now, though, I have another idea. Curiously, these are concepts which mesh together nicely."

"How's that?"

He waves an open hand, palm up, in Elizabeth's direction. "She shall be our canvas, our test subject. First, you will feed from her, and I will begin my study of you with this first, most primal act. Then Elizabeth will become my canvas, from which I will obtain my first measure of immortality."

"What do you mean, your canvas?"

"Leave that to me. Something held long in my dearest dreams but, until tonight, have not dared consider a reality. You see, this never was supposed to culminate in a tawdry fashion. I harbored no ambition to hurt her; not this severely, at least. She ran off to San Diego for a while without revealing her plans to me. It seems I lost my head in a moment of indiscretion, and now…"

"She is alive. You can save her."

"Perhaps. But her face—unfortunately, this will leave disfiguring scars. Worse, she will remember, which I cannot allow. Once she reveals to the world my mistreatment of her? Well, it will be over. Everything. My career, my freedom, certainly my reputation and, not least, our study of what makes you who you are. Before it has even begun."

"So, you want me to kill her? For you."

"Yes."

"And then you will use her for some project, as some sort of canvas?"

"Precisely. Our canvas, to be exact. I will measure how efficiently you extract her blood, then I will transform this beautiful body you see before us into a timeless work of art which will transcend time."

He is mad, of course, but Eddie does not know. Not yet. Indeed, marketing his discrete, illegal services has made him a very wealthy man, and for decades, Eddie has yearned to uncover why he was afflicted with this blessing. This curse. He, too, has succumbed to his own form of madness. One commonality across many forms of insanity is that the insane cannot recognize their own madness.

But they can readily identify its manifestation in others.

BABYLON FALLS

In theory, breaking out of jail should be a piece of cake. Blood red velvet cake. After all, perhaps no prisoner has ever been better equipped with the perfect set of tools to pull it off. While his enhanced physical abilities gave him certain advantages, these abilities were inadequate to propel a leap over the fence and its coils of concertina strung along the top. A hail of bullets as he scaled that fence may not kill him, but it sure as hell would hurt, perhaps enough to knock him to the ground and foil the whole thing.

Fortune shined upon him, for his tool kit was both deep and well-diversified.

Any possibility of escape relied upon his in-cell lockdown coming to an end.

"Hi, boss." The biggest, toughest screw drew that day's duty, checking each cell to cut down on the usual digging, fighting, buggery and hangings.

"Morning, prisoner."

From way in the corner of the cell, leaning against the wall with stiff hands crossed across his chest, the Hollywood Kid posed no threat. All he needed was a little direct eye contact. "Boss, how can I get these restrictions off my back?"

"Pretty sure you are staying on full lockdown until your trial."

There it was. A request comical enough to cause the guard to take a gander at the crook cocky enough to ask it. And when he did, Eddie had him.

"Are you sure about that?"

†

Killing Elizabeth Short had been easier still. Unconscious, bound, each limb tied to a different corner of the chromed brass bedpost, each factor sufficient to make for his easiest blood feast ever.

Altogether, it feels disgusting as one of those ranches where they send aged zoo animals when they grow old, weak and lethargic, so rich guys can pay top dollar for the sheer joy of shooting these beautiful creatures while they graze inside a peaceful, fenced pasture. Acclimated to humans by then and therefore unwary. And then have the nerve to call it "big game hunting".

Her blood tastes of alcohol and some chemical tang he suspects is drugs. Seconol, he guesses. Why those don't affect him is but one of many mysteries. Too diluted, perhaps, but the blood of a drunk never makes him drunk, and all narcotics do is act as a distasteful, pungent spice.

Absent the thrill of the chase, draining this helpless woman's blood feels exactly like what it is. Murder. Murder for hire, some might say. As he drinks her tainted blood and the lust fills him, those doubts fall away. Back when he still cared, when vestiges of a heart remained, he only killed when necessary. Now? Simply the learned wisdom to not leave a trail of corpses in his wake discourages him from killing. It just does not matter. Even this poor girl beaten half to death by some sick doctor, perhaps raped or maybe desperate enough to have rented him her body for the night, she cannot bring his soul back to life.

It is hard to tell when an unconscious person is dying. Harder still when you don't give a damn.

Dr. Hodel watches, taking notes the whole time. From time to time, he checks her pulse, her breathing. The rest of the time, he watches with catlike focus. Per the doctor's orders, he feeds from an existing wound, one on the left side of her chest, from which blood flows freely. Precious little pressure left in her veins, but that may be due to her weakness from the start.

When her body surrenders the last few drops, he stops.

"Time of death, 10:47 p.m." Then, Dr. Hodel giggles. "Sorry, old habits and all."

With the back of his hand, Eddie wipes his face and checks for smears, removing her traces from his face.

"Tell me, what are you feeling? Does feeding bring on any particular sensation?"

"I feel alive. More than that. Aroused."

"Do you mean sexually?"

"Yes, but it's more than that. Greater than any sexual satisfaction."

"Very interesting—I did not expect that."

"What did you expect?"

"A wild animal. More shark than Casanova." A few pats on the back from the doctor. "You did great. Truly, a fascinating experiment."

"Don't call me an experiment!" The wall shudders as Eddie slams the doctor against it, hard enough to send a cascade of plaster chips falling around his feet. "This is my life."

Both hands raised in mock surrender, Hodel says, "Sorry. No offense. You knew what this was when you agreed to it." When the hand releases its grip from his throat, after straightening his tie, he asks, "This sudden agitation—does this occur often?"

"It's recent. Over the last few years."

"Good." He slaps his vampire subject on his shoulder. "Together, we *will* solve this, one of science's great mysteries. Power over life and death. The girl, she was going to die, anyway. She had to. She was a drunk and a whore; no more, no less. Not even a particularly good lay. Now you made her life worth something. She will not become immortal herself, will she?"

"No."

"How does sparking the transformation into a… specimen like you occur?"

Her body still lay in the open. In life, her complexion had

been ghostly pallid, but now, other than blood spatter from the whipping the doctor dished out, the white sheets she lays upon have more color. "I don't know. So far, I have failed in my efforts to turn anyone."

"First things first. Once we figure out what makes you tick, then we can try to figure out the method of transmission. Hang onto your hat—we are in for a fascinating journey. But before departing on our journey, now that your role is complete, it is time for me to play my part."

The doctor performs a number of tests, which Eddie assumes are the tests modern physicians give to normal patients in their annual physical. Tests of the blood, of course: pulse, a drawn sample, the pressure cuff. The stethoscope, his heart of great interest to the doctor. Measurements of height, weight, and body proportions. Reflexes, vision, hearing. The last doctor to examine him was Doc Metcalf, back in Exeter, more than a half-century ago. Enormous changes to medical exams occurred during the last sixty years.

"What do you have planned? This canvas you mentioned."

"All in due time, well worth the wait," the doctor says. "It will be something, that I can promise you. Something exceptional and revolutionary, so remarkable it will live long after you and I are gone." Another chuckle. "Well, long after me, at least."

Whatever this mystery might be, he suspects the worst. Books bound in human leather or stretched onto a frame with a sensational new work by Picasso painted on her skin, hung in a place of pride in his home, or maybe gracing a wall in the Museum of Modern Art. "Be sure and tell me when you finish your masterpiece."

A wicked grin transforms his face, his eyes penetrate. The very portrait of a mad scientist. "Should all go as planned, notification shall be quite unnecessary."

†

Three weeks in prison until a taste of freedom, his first decent chance to get the lay of the land. That first day, he explored half the joint, and nothing jumped out as helpful for an escape. Other prisoners kept their distance while maintaining a close watch on his every move. Larger and more secure than he expected, he discovered no useful gaps in the perimeter, verifying his first impression.

After a while, a gang seven strong blocked his way through the rec area. "Watch your back, Red Dahlia," one with arms covered in prison tattoos warned.

"Hey, I'm not looking for trouble, boys. If you want to find me, you know where I live."

"Fucking sissy boy—you don't look so tough."

So many days had passed since he fed, even the foul stench of their blood smelled appetizing. "Who wants to test how tough I am?"

Overhead, on the catwalk, a guard carrying a three-foot stick an inch thick called down, "Prisoners, stand back. I'm only warning you this one time. Murphy, send some more boys in here, will ya?"

With the goons' attention raised, all a fight would accomplish was the screws locking him back inside his cell. Trial scheduled to begin in two weeks cast his window of opportunity in stone, and he still was clueless how to pull off an escape. Any escape plan required freedom to move inside, so to avoid further punishment, tail tucked between his legs, he backed away from the gang and returned to his cell.

With any luck, someone will be fool enough to try it there. He needed to feed.

†

Almost a week passed. Five or six days—Eddie did not keep count.

At Dr. Hodel's request, he did not pay a visit during this time. "Not until it is complete," the doctor said in his peculiar manner, pregnant with unspoken detail. What he meant by canvas troubled Eddie. In his mind, he took it literally—the doctor using her skin stretched over a frame for one of his artist friends to paint a masterpiece on. A portrait of Elizabeth? No, not even George Hodel was capable of so brazen an atrocity.

Instead, the image forming in Eddie's mind was of a literal canvas of another sort. George visualized himself as a budding artist, taking lessons from some of his artist friends. And must be using this time honing his skills by decorating her body with bright colored oils. Garish dragons brushed onto her skin or her breasts painted as the sun and moon? The possibilities are endless, so he pushed those thoughts from his mind.

†

One thing no one could accuse Dr. Hodel of is a tendency for exaggeration. Eddie needed no one to tell him when the doctor revealed his masterpiece to the world.

The first day, the Black Dahlia splashed across the front pages. From there, the story mushroomed. The most sensational news event since the Air Force forced the Japs to surrender by turning a couple of cities into radioactive dust. An A-bomb of a different sort. The papers did not report Elizabeth's name at first, but even before naming her, he harbored no doubt.

Once the story breaks, waiting around to see what happens next makes no sense at all. Before the genius who immortalized Elizabeth by coining the name "Black Dahlia" experiences his moment of inspiration, Eddie packs up and, keeping close to the speed limit, heads north. Police are likely to pay closer attention to cars leaving on the road to Las Vegas than people traveling up the Pacific Coast Highway, which makes the choice a simple one.

Elizabeth was a frequent visitor to Dr. Hodel's house. People saw her there. Only a matter of time until they track her to that neo-Mayan temple as a human sacrifice, and he didn't trust that mad scientist to keep quiet once they had him.

Once the initial shock wears off, as he drives north on the scenic roadway along the coast, the doctor's sheer audacity begins to take hold. Admiration soon gives way to anger at his amateurism.

Breathless reports follow him up the highway. So desperate are people to hear every gory detail that radio stations nix their usual music in favor of constant updates on the grisly crime. Details pour out by the hour. She was cut in half. Posed. Not dumped where they found her, Hodel placed her on display. He carved her up, some stories reporting a gruesome smile cut into her pretty face, from ear to ear. And her body had been drained of blood. Every drop, they say, although Eddie doubts the accuracy of that last part. Some must remain pooled inside, although he has no conception what effect cutting her in half at the waist might have on the traces of blood left in her torso and legs when the heart stopped beating.

Dr. Hodel must have measured the amount of blood remaining in her body as one of his scientific experiments.

"Dumb, dumb, dumb!" His hands smack the wheel in beat with the words. For a man claiming to be a genius, his foolish audacity boggles the mind. Either that or his crime was sheer genius, unlike any murder ever before seen. "I'll be damned—the son of a bitch did it exactly as he said!"

An act of genius or pure madness. Only time will tell. If they catch him, he's a damn fool. But, in the unlikely event he succeeds and gets away with it, he had to hand it to the guy. This is one murder no one will ever forget.

†

Another Black Dahlia seemed a grand idea at the time.

Not entirely planned, but the inspiration came after a period of dark rumination. Without the debasing mutilations of the woman's face, of course. Those were nothing but crass acts of barbarity. Had Elizabeth done something which set George Hodel upon an orgy of inhumanity even Eddie found impossible to comprehend? Hodel's genius, though, was the barbarous maiming of her face and body. This is what guaranteed Elizabeth's immortality as The Black Dahlia—and thus George's, as well. The madman and architect of such pure evil, with the capacity to destroy a pretty girl's face and body so completely. So irredeemably.

Cracks began to etch paths across Eddie's skin. First his lips, then the webbing between his fingers. His face felt like sandpaper and his hands were worse. He detected the scent of death emanating from his pores. He was not dying in the strictest sense.

It happened before. Early in 1918, to be exact, soon after his arrival in France. In truth, it began on the troop ship, but he took no notice his symptoms right away. Funny how when signing up to defend your country, you never stop to consider how long it takes a ship to cross the Atlantic—or how the only souls aboard this ship will be your comrades in arms. Men. Trained to kill, every one of them.

It was a rough sail at this time of year. The Atlantic seas raging. Below decks, in the troop holds, the stench of smoldering tobacco and vomit permeated the air. Some men never get over seasickness. Under strict rules prohibiting the soldiers from the top deck, out in the open air, where unrelenting waves might wash one overboard or a careless flick of a lighter to ignite a cigarette might be all a German U-boat needed to aim a salvo of deadly torpedoes.

Eddie never was one to follow rules intended for mortal men.

Because of the rough seas and a nasty storm, the crossing took ten days. On the seventh day, in sheer desperation, Eddie made his way topside. It was a calm night. He waited for the change of watch, hidden in a 5-inch gun emplacement. The sailor relieved of his watch never saw Eddie as he made his way back toward his quarters filled with the prospect of several hours' sleep before dawn. His body made a slight splash in the icy waters of the North Atlantic, which only Eddie heard. When he never made it back, the crew assumed the poor swabby must have fallen overboard, a rare but not unheard-of accident. Not on these rough seas. No one gave it much thought.

Two deep cracks split his upper lip, with another fissure growing on the lower. Deep and painful, these crevices would have bled more if significant quantities still flowed through his veins. A similar one tore through the small webbing between two fingers, although this one was far less painful. They nagged at him, though, less for the pain than the signs of vulnerability. The fate of a vampire denied an opportunity to feed was impossible to predict. During his wartime deprivations in France, it never progressed this far, but back then, he did not suffer this long without a proper feeding.

Breaking out of prison could be no more difficult. Right?

THE FINAL OBSTACLE

In the end, nothing ever goes as smoothly as planned.

"Hey, boss—come here for a second. You need to see something."

He only had to wait for the guard to establish eye contact. A big guy, flush with enough blood to feed him two or three times over, he left him lying in the empty cot and waltzed out, wearing his uniform. On the floor lay the crumbled plaster fragments of a walking leg cast. If any of the prisoners he passed noticed anything out of the ordinary, they kept their traps shut. The prison code. Same thing at the entrance to the cell block, where the screw on duty obediently ignored the bulky uniform cinched tight with a belt.

So far, so good.

At the main entrance, two guards killed time chatting with the duty guard at the check-in desk. Did he have the capacity to simultaneously mesmerize three men?

"No, seriously, Arlene is a real dish—one of those covered dishes they serve in mansions, with a silver cover over it so you can't touch."

"Maybe *you* can't touch her, but leave it to ol' Billy Boy here. I'll teach you a few tricks."

The guard at the desk spoke through his barred window. "Five dollars says she won't let you lay one finger on her."

"Five bucks, eh?" Billy Boy seemed willing to take the bait.

The other guard remained doubtful. "How are we supposed to know? Take his word for it?"

"Hey, would I lie to you?"

"Like you lie to your wife about working late?"

All three shared a laugh at that bit of comedy gold. "Okay, you got me. But I'll be a stand-up guy with youse guys."

Choosing between trusting these guards to tell the truth over five dollars or a prisoner, Eddie may have chosen to believe a convicted felon. The crucial difference seemed to be the screws were free to leave and spend their five dollars cheating on their wives tonight, while the prisoners relied only upon their memories of such infidelities.

When ultimately deciding they, too, did not find Billy Boy credible enough to risk five dollars on his ability to get under Arlene's silver tray, they went about their rounds and left the one guard by himself. Sensing his opportunity, Eddie strode up, looked him square in the eyes and asked the screw to buzz him out.

Outside, he twirled the guard's nightstick by his side as he strolled with a real swagger down the long walk to the gate.

It was too easy, and that gnawed at him as he approached the gate, the one final obstacle between himself and freedom.

"A little early for your shift to be over, ain't it?"

"My lucky day, I guess."

The guard checked the oversize clock in the guard shack, the source of official times on the log sheet. "Seventeen after?"

He looked everywhere but at Eddie's eyes—his badge, his belt, the length of his pants. Nothing fit quite right, an unavoidable fact due to this week's duty assignments posting the fat screw in the block this shift. In back, the belt cinched in the pants a good three inches, and his shoulders strained the shirt. When the guard got to his shoes, he knew those scuffed black and white wing tips did not belong to a prison worker, and his eyes shot up to the face.

"Who are you? Wait—I recognize you…"

Unlike the interior guard posts, this one had no bars. Great for Eddie, who reached through the window and dragged the screw through without allowing him a chance to react. Big, strong and ornery, though, this guard made up for being ambushed with a vigorous lunge out the window once his feet found purchase on the frame. The bulky guard landed upon him, scoring a punch before turning toward the main entrance.

"We've got a…" Eddie's punch landed before he could shout *breakout*, but he managed to block enough of the blow that it failed to inflict much harm. The man swung wildly, arms a windmill in a hurricane. Frenzied, unaimed punches, most blocked but raining down so fast, they succeeded in preventing Eddie from mounting any offense of his own. After several tries, he got control of the man's arms, holding them at bay. He pulled the screw forward, toward him, and the guard focused so intently on the struggle he did not call out.

Inches away from his face, Eddie bashed his forehead into the guard's nose hard enough to break it and stun the man. Eddie tossed him before the blood began dripping onto his stolen uniform, reversed the position, and landed several punches of his own before he caught himself and held back. Eddie knew how easily his strength could snuff out a fragile human life.

Chest rising and falling from the effort, the guard lay still with blood flowing over his face. Tempting, but he had no time to kill. In his younger days, he lacked the discipline necessary to walk away from a helpless meal.

The guard stuffed back through his window and sprawled safe on the floor of the guard shack, Eddie found the electronic release switch, marked in big red letters, and flicked it to OPEN.

A metallic clunk signaled the gate unlocking. He did not wait to take his steps out into freedom.

Funny how willing random people are to stop and give a lift to a man in uniform. A holdover from the war, no doubt, when helping a soldier or sailor to their destination was every American's patriotic duty. Within five minutes of walking through the gate to all appearances a free man, Eddie sped down the road in his new Chevy. The car's former owner did him a favor, for which he repaid the good Samaritan by making sure he was still breathing when he left him in a roadside ditch.

Just keeping the pedal to the metal might have been

the better plan, depending how quickly they discovered the guard. Fresh air—untainted by sweat and excrement and that undefinable musty smell of desperation—never smelled so good. After such recklessness, actions which might be considered suicidal if taken by a mortal human being, he swung to another extreme.

Better safe than sorry, he ditched the car and the ill-fitting prison guard uniform in favor of some clothes swapped off someone's backyard clothes line. Then his post-feeding fatigue grew so great that he slept in some bushes like a hobo until the moon had set, when he awakened.

The Kid was dead. So were John Doe and Raul di Silva and the other aliases which served him so well. They no longer existed. Dead, the same as he was. More dead than him, because those names were gone forever.

Now, for the first time in years, he was once more Eddie Brown.

For a while, he lay there, nothing running through his brain other than wondering whether anyone in town bothered to install burglar alarms in a men's clothing store.

THE RIDE

One thing the Singleton family shared was a love of music. Whether two or three got together or the whole extended family met for a holiday, before long someone sat down at the piano or launched into a song, which the entire bunch joined in with their voices or accompanying instruments.

In fact, music is the only reason for Camilla Singleton to exist at all. Her parents met during the Depression when her mother left home at sixteen to take a gig as a singer with a jazz band. They did well, too, traveling around, following what money they could find. After a couple of years, she married the band's young trumpet player. Within a year, she had to quit when Camilla came along, returning to her parents' home to give birth while her new husband stayed with the band, sending money home to support his new family and returning to visit whenever the schedule allowed.

Later, when their daughter was still a toddler, she rejoined the band. The little girl's first eight years spent on the road, where she listened from behind stage every night as her parents performed. Her mother's voice was the most beautiful she ever heard. The war upended that, and her father joined the Navy before they extinguished the flames at Pearl Harbor. Rather than fighting, though, the Navy spotted his talent early on and assigned him to one of the Navy bands that traveled between port cities in the Pacific Theater entertaining sailors, Marines and sometimes Australian or British troops, too. Men of such immense talent were too valuable to risk in front-line combat.

Despite knowing she lacked the pipes God had blessed her

mother with, Camilla hoped to follow in her mother's tradition, too. That Saturday night, they sang a series of duets, joined as a sing-along by half the family members present. Must have been thirty people there, many who brought their guitars or saxophones or other instruments to form the usual impromptu Singleton family band.

As often happened, this one threatened to go well past midnight. They were all pretty tipsy, aside from Camilla and her younger cousins. Since she was the last sober person with a driver's license standing, around 11:00, Camilla rounded up the other kids, piled them into her parents' Oldsmobile and began dropping them off at their houses. Most lived within a couple of miles of Uncle Louis' house, where that night's festivities again lasted late into the evening. Since receiving her driver's license on her sixteenth birthday, she had already followed the same routine a half-dozen times.

Only her cousin Mildred lived far from the neighborhood, close to the Troost Dividing Wall in a new house near the factory where her husband worked, so she saved their three-year-old son Melvin for last, as always.

The kid slept the entire way home.

After carrying the sleeping toddler to the house and tucking him into bed, Camilla returned to her car for the quick drive home. She checked her watch. After midnight already. It was a cloudy night, so only streetlights provided any light. Only one block east of Troost Avenue, being this close to the White side of town always made her nervous. Any colored man, woman or child crossing to the west side of Troost could expect police to stop them within seconds, and cops were famous for paying close attention a block or two east to make sure the Wall held secure.

A man strolled in her direction up the sidewalk. A white man. He should not have surprised her, so close to the dividing line. White folks did not face the same scrutiny when they crossed the street. Still, it unnerved her, running into a white man here so deep on a Saturday night. At least he was alone.

Every Singleton family member had their own tale to tell—a white stranger over here raised the hair on the back of her neck. One of her uncles had survived to tell the tale of the Tulsa riot thirty years ago, so she eyed this man with a healthy dose of caution.

"Evening, ma'am." He tipped his fedora, and she relaxed at his polite gesture.

"Good evening."

"Say, is that your car?"

Oh, no—here we go. "It belongs to my parents, sir. All the paperwork is inside."

"Good. Is this where your parents live?"

"No, sir, we live over on Flora. I'm just dropping off my cousin."

"Why is someone so young dropping off your cousin at this hour?"

Not another soul visible anywhere up or down the deserted street. His questions raised her hackles, but he was so out of place, he might be an undercover cop. Or worse. With any luck, a neighbor keeping similar ungodly hours will drive by and keep an eye on her. "He's three, and his parents are out late with my parents. I drive the children home when they run late, like they are tonight."

When nervous, Camilla had an annoying tendency to babble on and on. Well aware of her tendency, yet her knowledge alone did not help her stop once the nerves kicked in like they were right now. Every bone in her body screamed to shut up, tell this guy a polite goodnight and drive off fast as their little car would go.

The man moved closer, the streetlight close behind him casting his face in shadow under the brim of his fedora. "Mind if I ask you a question?"

"It's late, and I must be going..."

"That's just it—I find myself in need of a ride. I'm not from this part of town myself, and haven't spotted a cab in a while. Do you know where the nearest bus stop is?"

"I'm afraid not. Maybe over by Troost Avenue? The street car runs there. It's one block over," she pointed to the west. The man turned, so the streetlight lit his eyes of icy blue. Blue-eyed devils, her Uncle Vincent called them, yet, now that she could see his eyes, an eerie sense of calm came over her. She should have been afraid like she was a moment before, and yet, glistening in the light, those eyes radiated an odd intensity, pulling her into him with curiosity she could not explain.

"Maybe you can give me a lift? Don't worry, I won't bite."

One mistake she knew never to commit was to give a man a ride, let alone a white stranger. Drilled into her for years, by her parents, aunts and uncles: never get into a car alone with any male, even one she knew. Her female relatives were fiercely adamant about this rule. Her parents raised her right, to be a "nice" girl. So when she answered, her words startled her. "Sure, I can take you."

Why did she say that? Because he seemed so nice and harmless. A gentleman. Handsome, too, for a white guy. Elegant men are the most dangerous species.

Like a true gentleman, he held open her door, closing it after she pulled her mid-calf-length skirt in to keep it from being shut in the door, and walked across the front of the car to the passenger side. He took his seat next to her and closed the door.

"Where are we going?" she asked while guiding the car away from the curb.

"Head north."

"Toward the river?"

He turned and smiled. "Is that a problem?"

"No, I thought you were heading west, is all."

"Nice night for a scenic drive, isn't it?"

Such vague instructions should terrify, and she knew it. Had the part of her mind which urged caution and common sense switched off, leaving the portion that loves adventure in control? The same urges which sometimes encouraged her to skip school or play a rash prank on one of her classmates. Another sensation welled up inside, one which had increased in power over the last year or so, which her mother warned her about in talks behind closed doors.

The last time she was alone with an adult man escaped her memory. Since elementary school, if then. And never with a white man.

It was this lust which confused her the most. Other than Frank Sinatra or Errol Flynn, she could not recall a white man stirring such animal emotion inside her. Her body tingled under his gaze.

"What's your name?"

"Camilla; pronounced like Pamela, but it's spelled with an I, so everyone calls me Cam-ILL-a." *Stop babbling! What is wrong with me?* "What's yours?"

"Eddie. Eddie Brown." He held out his hand, which she took despite her father teaching her to keep both hands on the steering wheel at all times. His fingers slipped around her small hand, enveloping it in a firm grip, yet with skin supple as her own. How long had he wandered outside in the cool evening air for his paws to become so frosty this time of year?

"Camilla," he repeated, pronouncing it the correct way. "I like it. Beautiful, just as your name should be."

A chilled bead of sweat ran down her temple—on her left side, thank goodness, blocked from his view. Strange, because the pleasant temperature was tepid that summer night. She thanked him, then held her tongue, since it had proven impossible to control.

"Turn here," he instructed, and without questioning, turned on the left turn signal onto Cherry Street, heading into the white side of town.

THE CRASH

"Where are we going?"

"Don't worry about that."

"Well, how am I supposed to drive to your destination without you even cluing me in the direction we are heading?"

"Calm down. Just focus on the driving; I won't get you lost."

"Are we going toward St. Joe?"

By this time, they had left the city heading north, past scattered houses punctuated by clusters of small businesses and gas stations toward where they gave way to farms and bait shops. One bright service station sign, mounted low to the road, shone through the windshield, illuminating their clothes and faces.

"Keep your eyes on the road," he warned, too late.

Her eyes scanned him, examining his face but also searching for signs of a weapon. A pistol or knife. If he had anything, it was nothing larger than a pocketknife. Passing the sign cast them back in dark shadow.

"I thought so."

"Thought what?"

"I know who you are." Soon as her regrettable words spilled out, she realized her mistake. By admitting she recognized him, she turned herself from a person offering a hitchhiker a ride into a witness. A liability.

"Does that frighten you?"

"The Red Dahlia killer is in my car, and you ask if I'm scared?" Incredulous, she asked in a voice normally reserved for reprimanding a child caught doing something stupid. "Are you going to kill me?"

"Why would I kill you?"

"I knew it—you are. You're going to cut me in half and dump my naked body along the road somewhere, aren't you?"

In a calm, measured voice, he answered, "I am not going to hurt you. Quite the opposite, in fact. Besides, right now you are driving, which makes this a remarkably poor time to kill you."

"What is the opposite of killing me? That makes no sense." Although arguing with an escaped murderer might not be high on her list of bright ideas, Camilla was not one to give up without a fight. Her mother always called her a lioness, and no lioness was going to drive into the dark countryside with a killer beside her doing nothing about it.

"I'll explain everything to you when we stop. I give you my word, I have no plans to hurt you… or kill you."

"Is that what you told her?"

"Good point. I didn't, but I understand how trusting me may be difficult."

"Kidnapping someone is not the best way to establish trust." He struggled against a grin at her valid point, and focused out the windshield in an effort to hide it, but the glow from a passing Sinclair gas station sign fell upon him just then. "Does it amuse you to scare the crap out of a girl still in high school?"

"No. You're right. And you have a fantastic sense of humor even in a situation like this. I like you, Camilla; even if I wanted to hurt you—which I didn't—I'd never do so now."

"Did you like her, too?"

"Leslie? Once. That was before her pimp murdered two women I cared about. Burned them alive attempting to kill me. When she heard about it, Leslie laughed. Laughed! One of them was no more than a couple of years older than you. In fact, you remind me of her, which is why you are safe with me."

"So it was personal? Revenge? That's not what the papers say."

"The papers don't know nothing," he said, reverting to his

manner of speaking back on the farm when he was a boy.

"What about the pimp?"

"Oh, he won't be hurting anyone else."

"Did you kill him, too?"

"Are you a detective?" Again he smiled. "You can probably coax more information out of me than they did with rubber hoses."

"Well? Did you?"

"No, he's hiding from me. But after I go to ground for a few weeks, he'll show his ugly mug—and so will I."

A killer threatening to kill again had the effect of terminating the conversation. But silence was too painful, so she gave it another go, this time by broaching a different topic. "Was she funny?"

Her questions were scattershot, understandable with the pressure on her, kidnapped by the most famous murderer in years. "Was who funny?"

"Your friend; the one I remind you of. Is that why I remind you of her?"

"No, she didn't have a strong sense of humor. Not sarcastic like you, at least. She was smart and pretty and about your size. Looked a lot like you, too. If someone told me you were relatives —cousins or something—I'd not doubt it for a second."

Visible surprise changed her expression. "A Colored girl?"

"Yes, does that surprise you?"

"A little. Not nearly as much as being kidnapped by the Red Dahlia killer. What was she to you?"

"It's hard to explain."

"Was she your boo?"

"My what?"

"Your sweetheart?"

"Boo; I haven't heard that one before. I guess she was my sweetheart, although probably not the way you think of it."

"Is that why…"

"Enough questions for now. Concentrate on your driving."

It only lasted a couple of minutes. The painful quiet,

driving down this lonely road with a murderer sitting next to her saying nothing while who knows what thoughts were spinning through his brain. That was worse than speaking to him. "Aren't you afraid?"

"Me? Afraid of what?"

"The electric chair? They will capture you—you know, they always do. They'll shoot you on sight. Probably shoot me, too, while they're at it. *Oops, we shot a Colored girl while stopping the most wanted man in Missouri.* Maybe I'll just drive into a tree to escape."

"Won't do any good, crashing into a tree."

"Why not? I smack the tree, you fly through the windscreen and I just scamper off into the wood where you'll never find me."

"Trust me, you don't want to try that. And a car wreck does not worry me at all."

"It's better than letting you chop me to pieces."

"You just say whatever's on your mind, don't you?"

"Of course you'd say it won't work. That's reverse psychology. You *are* afraid."

"Camilla, don't even think about crashing the car. It might kill you, but it won't hurt me."

"What, you can predict the future?"

"I wish. What I know is you will be hurt, maybe killed. And for what? You are safe with me and it won't hurt me, anyway."

Her fingers tightened into a death-grip on the steering wheel. What she must not allow him to witness was her body shaking. "How can you be so sure you won't be hurt if it will kill me? You aren't making any sense again."

"There are things you don't know. Once we get where we are going, I'll explain everything to you. Now you will never believe it."

"Try me."

This time, her guts and humor brought a chuckle out of him. Admirable qualities, and she remained so calm under stress. This girl was one in a million. "Time for all the details soon. We're getting close. For now, let's just say when I arrived at jail, a prisoner twice my size tried to rough me up; he ended up with two broken arms. Not a scratch on me, though. The same will happen if you crash the car, only who knows how badly the crash will injure you? All you need to realize is I seem to be protected from harm."

Right away, he realized how carelessly he spoke. Trees whizzed by, and out here, the distances between houses increased with every mile. Of course, that is why she is so chatty, trying to trick him into slipping up the way he just had. For the first time in half an hour, her pretty face twisted into an expression he recognized. The same one she had when she began driving.

Her features contorted into pure fear.

"Oh my God—you're mad, aren't you? You're a lunatic!"

"Camilla, why don't you pull over?"

"You're going to kill me, aren't you?"

"Stop the car!"

"Why don't you just admit the truth, rather than toying with me like a cat who jumps on a helpless bird?"

"Camilla, please stop the car!"

She had been sticking to the speed limit, per instructions, staying below 40 as the road became darker and curvier the farther the distance from town. Hearing this madness, she mashed the gas pedal, the engine roaring to life in response. The feeble power in the old pre-war engine of this ten-year-old Oldsmobile paled alongside those improvements developed to defeat the Germans during the war. Still, the car began picking up speed.

Eddie's pleas for her to pull the car over were becoming insistent when she jerked the wheel. The headlights fell square on a tall pine tree growing close to the edge of the road. In a split second, the beam separated into two lights that disappeared around either side of the tree an instant before the Olds plowed straight into it.

Camilla had almost been right. His head smashed the

windshield, and he ended up with the upper half of his body splayed across the hot, twisted steel of a smashed hood, jutting upward into the sky at a steep angle. When he moved, searing pain shot through his head and chest, and he wondered how debilitating the pain would be if he were human.

Crumpled beside him, laying sideways across the front seat, Camilla was very much human. Glass tumbled from his scalp as he began to crawl back inside the car, and he brushed more shards off his head. Because of her position—head near the center and one limp arm lying across to the passenger door—he twisted around to kneel on the floorboard.

"Camilla, can you hear me?"

She did not respond and even his exceptional vision failed to cut through the backwoods darkness to see much of anything, so he touched her chest, his gentle fingers following the curve of her rib cage. It rose and fell—halting and weak, but regular. He felt her side, her arms, the left side of her face. The smell was strong now. The scent of blood. Virgin blood. So strong, he knew her bleeding from somewhere on her body was profuse. He gently lifted her head, his fingers touching something warm and wet.

The next town so distant that few cars drove about at this late hour. At least ten minutes passed since the last one. The sweet, delicious scent of the fresh, untainted blood of a beautiful virgin was too tempting to ignore, but inside the pitch-black wreckage of the car, he could not see from where it flowed.

It took three jolts from his shoulder, each more forceful than the one preceding, to free the door. Each time he slammed his body against the metal sent pain shooting down his chest, and he wondered how many ribs he shattered in the wreck.

Crickets and tree frogs had resumed their chirping by the time he dragged her from the car by her upper arms to avoid hurting her more than she had done to herself. Starlight revealed a gash above her hairline, the source of most of her blood. Minor cuts glass gouged into the right side of her face produced a bare trickle.

And how sweet and warm her blood tasted! Its thick texture went smooth down his throat. A feeble moan escaped, but out here, gave no cause for alarm. Drinking deep, consumed by bloodlust, he savored his first taste of virgin blood since Kat and Grace were murdered. Now moaning without a care, his hand caressed the undamaged left side of her face with a lover's touch. With her draped across his lap as she was, a passing motorist might mistake them for a lover kissing the forehead of his beloved. His boo.

Somewhere in the deep recesses of his mind, he knew he lacked the control to stop before every drop of her precious blood was inside him. He began mourning her already, but he no longer had three girls enthralled to him to feed from, and weeks had passed since he had a proper meal. A shame, but these things happen.

Besides, if she died, all this rare and precious blood would go to waste if he did not drain her before clotting set in.

This simple rationalization of avoiding waste worked well enough on his mind, addled as it was by bloodlust. The spot where her gash opened her flesh to him, high on her forehead above the hairline, allowed a few thick, long strands of hair into his mouth, tickling back into his throat as he drank from her. Aroused and enraptured as he was, this tickle irritated him to stop long enough to extricate these hairs.

A beam illuminated trees lining the far side of the road. Pausing to listen, the sound of an engine rose above the chirping nighttime forest creatures. Loud enough for him to have heard before, but taken as he was by this delightful girl's life force, he dropped his guard for a brief moment of enjoyment. He cursed his inattention as the headlights swung into view around the bend their own car never reached thanks to the tree's intervention.

The driver spotted him with Camilla's head still cradled in his lap, as the engine revving down and a red glow brightening on the trees behind the car made clear.

He was stopping.

The back of one hand wiping across his face, their car bright in his high beams, Eddie waved at the slowing vehicle as if to signal *everything's okay*. Of course, it was anything but okay, which the driver, now rolling to a stop, crossing to their side of the highway aiming his lights on the gory accident scene, could not miss.

With an annoying squeal, louder in the forest than elsewhere, the pickup truck jerked to a halt, its light too bright in his eyes. One hand shielded his sensitive vision. A second passed, two, the door still closed and white light blasting him from less than ten feet away, rendering impossible any effort to make out the driver inside. A pre-war Studebaker Express Coupe pickup truck, the chrome lines of its high, narrow, grille coming to a sharp point and enormous close-eyed headlights on either side of the exposed radiator and fender-mounted spare tire a decade out of style, a relic from an older age.

The door latch clicked and opened. The driver spat tobacco juice on the ground as he slid off the seat and his boots crunched upon gravel.

"Are ya hurt?"

At that moment, the folly of wiping blood from his face became clear, as a trickle from one of the cuts in his head, replenished with Camilla's nectar, ran down his forehead.

"Oh, I'm fine."

"Need some help?"

Camilla lay motionless in the headlights. Sending him away or refusing offered assistance would strike as even more suspicious than the scene greeting the man. He looked to be an ordinary sort, middle-aged, with a sizable gut held in by overalls. A farmer, not terribly unlike who he once had been.

"The girl is hurt." It sounded foolish as his words spilled out, for even though he licked the blood off her face a minute before, even a fool could not miss her bloodstained blouse and still body. In fact, she already looked dead.

"Did you hit that little Picaninny?"

"It was an accident. I swerved trying to avoid her…"

"Don't worry," the man chuckled, "Her bad luck is our good luck. Dead girls don't say no, am I right?"

If only he knew. "So, this stays just between us?"

"Hey, I ain't gonna say nothing. Sure not turning a man like you in for runnin' down a niggra. Not even a pretty Negress like this one. Shame, though; she is a fine specimen, you've got to admit."

"What did you call her?"

"Pretty. Not that they are my taste. Pretty for a niggra, I mean."

"I thought that's what you called her. That girl just helped me when no one else would. And now you are going to help her."

Confusion clouded the farmer's doughy face for that brief second before Eddie's pocketknife slashed through his neck. Damnfool redneck did not even notice him opening it—taken, as he was, by his own pathetic lustful thoughts. Saucer eyes shifted from the blade—glistening red in his headlights—then back to Eddie. Too small to cut all the way through, but the pocket knife plunged plenty deep enough to sever the jugular vein, so his silence was only due to shock.

He turned toward his old Studebaker and tried to run, but his feet went all wonky. He only made it a few steps before his legs flopped instead of stepped, the toe of his boot dug into a root leading from the pine tree and he landed graceless on the gravel along the roadside.

Laid out in the headlight beam, those eyes only grew larger and pupils dilated when Eddie rolled the man over and sucked from the gaping wound in his neck.

After Camilla's pure, redolent essence, this man's had a spoiled, tainted taste. Reminiscent of Bubba's. But given the choice of him or her, he sated himself on inferior blood to preserve enough blood in her veins for her to survive. This fat boy had enough in him to last a month. It pleased him that the horrified man received no pleasure. It must have something to do with the trance. He didn't bother charming him, using speed rather than his ability to mesmerize.

Soon, the man fell limp on the dusty gravel. Eddie let out a belch.

He hurried to Camilla's side.

Whatever it was in his saliva that controlled blood loss—allowing it to flow, then stemming the flow when he stopped feeding—it worked to stop her bleeding, he noticed as he carried her around the front of the truck toward the passenger door. From inside her car, he retrieved her purse and any loose possessions he could find. After dragging the bloodless corpse near enough to the crashed car to convince a backcountry coroner the farmer had died in a freak auto crash, he cranked up the Studebaker's engine and tugged the heavy steering wheel around in a U-turn.

In seconds, only crickets and frogs broke the silence of the night.

†

A dark drop splattered on her cheek. In all the excitement, he had forgotten his own wounds. Now filled not only with her blood but the dead farmer's, as well, a gash somewhere on his head flowed freely.

Again feeling her chest, her weak, labored breath raised and fell.

"Damn it!" His gluttony and initial apathy allowed him to drain too much of her life. Blood he did not need, as it turned out.

Pulled over a mile or so down the empty road, far enough from the wrecked car and dead redneck to throw anyone off, he stopped to check the injured girl. In the cramped cab of this primitive truck, the only space available forced him to lay her head on his lap. Another drop splattered on her cheek.

After laying her head on the seat with care, he knelt on the running board and bowed his head low over her as in prayer. But this was no prayer. He pressed his own head wound to her lips, which were parted, allowing his blood to flow into her.

Unconscious as she was, he had no way to force her to

drink, nor could she choose to do so, but his blood flowed into her mouth. It was all he could do.

Then she coughed, a wet sound through pooled blood. Choked, more accurately—choking on blood. Only a few times, and he remained still, his hand caressing her. "Come on, drink, Camilla. Feed from me."

Down deep inside, a familiar sensation took hold. The pleasure of the blood. Somehow, a mystical connection established between them as she swallowed his offer to her. Bound them together. What he did not quite understand he nonetheless relished, not only for the warm ecstasy growing inside, for he knew consuming him meant she accepted from him his own life.

THE CABIN

Fog and pain seeped into the edges of her perception.

Next came the rose-tinted light of early morning, colored by a fog of confusion over where she was or how she got there. Her hands budged mere inches before stopping—that's when she noticed rope binding her to the posts of a strange bed in a room she had never seen in her life.

It took every ounce of self-control in her possession to keep her wits about her as she searched the room for a familiar sight, something to trigger her memory and ease the muddiness of her still-disordered mind. A thin sheet covered her to mid-chest, but her dress was missing. In its place, she saw only a man's white sleeveless undershirt against her ebony skin.

Memories seeped in, filling in some of the gaps. What foolish gullibility allowed her to trust this blue-eyed devil? Danger and fear. That came back, too. And she remembered a pervasive sensation of calm that convinced her to give him a ride.

Pain welled up, worse in her bones and in a circle around her chest, from her breasts in the center out toward her collarbone and belly.

At least he had not tied down her feet; she kicked the sheet off, discovering herself wearing only panties along with this undershirt she had never before seen.

Her arms refused to budge, and all she accomplished by tugging was to aggravate the intense pain in her ribs and to rub her wrists raw, so she stilled herself and took a deep breath to take stock.

Like a wave hitting, she recalled images of a tree rushing toward her and driving straight into it because the handsome, blue-eyed devil admitted to her that he was an escaped prisoner. None other than the man who murdered the Red Dahlia and butchered her…

The door opened, and there he was. "Oh, you're awake."

"Why am I tied up?"

He sat on the edge of the bed, down by her knees. "Well, we can't have you running off, not dressed like this, can we?"

"Where are my clothes? What did you do to me? Did you take advantage of me?"

"Slow down. I did not take advantage of you. Well, maybe took liberties, but not in the way you imagine."

"That's why you tied me up like this?"

"Don't you remember trying to kill me? To kill us both? I told you I wasn't going to hurt you, and you damn near killed yourself!"

"It's not my habit to believe what murderers tell me."

"See what honesty gets me? Now you are all busted up, tied to a bed. Your dress is pretty much ruined, by the way. I tried scrubbing it, but it's stained with blood and road grime."

"So, what are you planning to do? Kill me? Or does your plan involve raping me a few more times first?"

"Okay, first, I didn't rape you. Second, I promised not to kill you, and meant it. Too bad you missed the entire part of last night where I saved you—I'm pretty sure that redneck would have done both to you if I hadn't stopped him."

"What redneck are you talking about?"

"You missed the most exciting part of the evening. Do you remember driving into a tree at fifty miles an hour? That part was pretty exciting, too."

"So, you tied me to your bed—what have you planned for me?"

"Well, I was coming in to check on you. You are pretty banged up. Now that you're awake, tell me how this feels."

The moment his fingers pressed on her chest sent a

shock of exquisite pain through her, from the point of pressure right to the core. Unable to help herself, she screamed.

"Pretty sure they are broken. There's a bruise the shape of the steering wheel over your chest and your…" His hands moved over his own chest, the spots where breasts were on hers. "It's going to hurt like hell for a while. How's your head? You bashed it in real good."

Tears flowed down her temples from just the slightest touch on her chest. Under normal circumstances, her high pain threshold might have given her the strength to not cry like a baby, but she had never been tied half-naked to a stranger's bed with broken ribs before. These were the least normal circumstances she had ever faced. "It's not too bad."

"Just be glad you can't see it. The gash is about," he leaned forward to check, "three, almost four inches. Right down to the bone, too. Don't worry, it's above the hairline, so no one will see it once you heal up. I gave you something to begin the healing. These little ones on your cheek, I don't think they'll leave scars."

Without warning, he bent down and kissed high on her cheek, right below her eye. She jerked her head to the left, away from him. "No, don't! Please, don't do that to me!"

"Calm down. The crash scratched your cheek right there; you don't want ugly scars on that pretty face, do you?"

An unusual, intense shade of blue, those eyes, she found herself thinking. Why that notion wormed into her brain when this lunatic had her tied to his bed in the middle of God only knows where and was trying to kiss her, she could not imagine. Watching from the corners of narrowed eyes, she tried to pull away. But when he again bent down, she tilted her head to the side, cool as a cucumber, offering her right cheek to his lips. After kissing several times, he kissed her forehead, too. Up in her hair.

Do all white guys kiss like this, she wondered? His butterfly tongue flicked through her hair and what must be the gash he mentioned, although it did not hurt at all. In fact, it felt kind of amazing. Her body tingled, particularly in her nipples and down very low, below the painful part of her belly. Weary eyelids grew too heavy to hold open, and that was the last thing she remembered.

†

"So, if I untie you and let you get up, can I trust you?"

"What do you picture me able to do?"

"Who knows? Grab a knife from the kitchen drawer and stab me? Run away and notify the police who I am and where I'm holed up? I get the distinct impression you are a highly intelligent woman, so plenty of clever ideas might pop into that pretty head of yours."

That made her smile. "Woman? How old do you think I am?"

"Nineteen? Twenty, maybe?"

"Hah!"

When she did not volunteer more, his expression clouded realizing she must be younger, a revelation which seemed to cause genuine concern. "Oh. You are so mature," he said, glancing down at her body.

He must have enjoyed taking off her dress and examining her body, which made her wonder why he bothered to dress her in one of his undershirts. Time had come to bargain with this madman, before boredom sent his twisted mind wandering in dangerous directions. "Will you let me go if I promise to never utter a single word about what happened? I'll just say I bashed my head in the wreck and remember nothing."

His head shook. "No can do. For now, you must stay here."

"Why? Seriously—and I'm not just promising this and will do the opposite the minute you are out of sight—not one word to a soul."

"Well, police must have stumbled onto your car by now, and I did not have a chance to clean up that redneck, so they probably assume you did it…"

"Oh, my God! You killed him?"

"Trust me—had you been awake, you would have been just fine with it. He had this crazy notion we tag team rape you while you were out cold. Well, he figured you were dead, which, from the looks of it, posed an insignificant obstacle for his romantic intentions with you."

"Sweet Jesus! And you killed him for that?"

"Well, that and he called you some names. There you were, hurt, bloody, and all he could think of was screwing a pretty Colored girl before your corpse stiffened. He didn't say Colored, either; he used a couple of other terms for you."

"I've heard them before."

"Does it ever make you so angry you wish you could kill someone for calling you those names, if only you could get away with it?"

"All the time. That's the difference between you and me." Narrowed eyes glared at him. "I don't kill them."

"There are other differences between us."

"Obviously."

"Yeah, and not the ones you are thinking of."

"What do you assume I am thinking?"

"Well, differences besides, I'm Caucasian or a man or a…"

"Cold-blooded murderer?"

"I have bad news: they assume you are a killer. His body lying right next to your crashed car? And out here, in this county?" He leaned over and untied the rope around her right wrist. "I don't believe they will worry about who you claim killed that guy. You're safer here with me."

"You murdered the Red Dahlia!"

"Would you rather take your chances with the Klan out there? Because they are looking for you. They know whose car is with that dead cracker. Think any other details matter?"

"The cops are looking for you, too."

"Here's the good news: we have plenty of food in this cabin to last months. There's a hunting rifle downstairs and these woods are chock full of game." He undid the other rope, and she rubbed her wrists before scooching up to half-sit against the headboard. "Don't get any foolish ideas about the gun."

THE RABBIT

Change has a leisurely pace.

A tree grows year after year, but other than the new leaves each spring which, in turn, die come autumn, its incremental growth passes unnoticed. Only when comparing the living tree to old photographs of the tree which once was, taken decades before, do its imperceptible changes become obvious. Without photographic documentation of its history, no one recalls exactly when the tree first shows signs of growing misshapen, unbalanced.

When that tree matures, no one remembers that once another tree grew too close. This encroaching tree forces into the other, and when the intruder dies or is felled for firewood, only the scar remains, its shape forever imprinted on the form of a lopsided oak.

When he lost his principles is the wrong question. Not lost in their entirety, time and loss had the effect of warping him over the more than a half century since his becoming. Deceased almost sixty years, his scars were less obvious to see but no less profound.

At some point, he stopped reflecting upon himself as he had in decades past. Being deceased does not mean freedom from pain or his own distinctly pernicious form of torment. The lifestyle of a lone vagabond, forced upon him by this curse, was not easy for him.

Once upon a time, Eddie lived in a large, close-knit family on an honest farm in a simple town. Although one sister died as a toddler, the other three survived until he was a grown man. His parents raised the family as best that they could, even while death stalked them. First, it took his mother. Then his eldest sister, two years older than him. His middle sister died mere months before he did, just when his illness faded while he convalesced in the high, dry air of Colorado Springs, halfway across the country from his surviving family.

Lena died before he returned. At the time, everyone considered her the latest victim in the unfolding Brown family tragedy. Soon after his return from Colorado, though, all that changed. On St. Patrick's Day, his father—in concert with the town's leading citizens—exhumed his mother's and sisters' bodies and changed everything. Two months after Lena died, they found her still alive, of sorts. Not quite alive, yet not dead.

How merciful, at least, that the last vampire killed during the New England Vampire Panic is remembered as Mercy Brown. In life, Lena never used the first name made infamous upon her second death.

Of course, the last vampire as recorded by history—killed as the violent, concluding spasm of hysteria which infected the American Northeast—was not, in reality, the last vampire. Like so much else about his family curse, a myriad of details remained shrouded in the mists of history. Did Lena kill their mother and elder sister as she killed Eddie? Or were all three victims of another, unknown vampire, with only Lena defeating death? Before he, too, arose from the dead, of course.

Belief in that second option kept him sane, or some semblance of it. Burial underground trapped his mother and sister, he preferred to believe, and being buried for two years is the reason they did not survive. Lena, stored above ground in a crypt until the winter's frozen earth thawed, could therefore survive. The analogy was incomplete, however, as his eldest sister, Mary Olive, also died in winter and remained in the crypt until spring, yet she did not turn.

Sanity, of course, is a relative term. Can the deceased be either sane or insane? Forced to feed upon human blood for his survival warps the mind. During life, Eddie never hurt a fly.

How he loathed killing and de-feathering a chicken for dinner, but in death relied upon draining the life force from the bodies of others. Learning the secrets of taking just enough for his needs while leaving his victims alive required some practice, as did trusting that somehow the memories of his predation faded from those he left alive.

For decades, contemplating these and other questions tore away his sanity and humanity. Left with no one to teach him nor a companion to share this curse with, inflicted their own excruciating variety of scars. Before she died, Lena made clear to him she intended for them to experience this new form of life together. Any chance of doing so ended when he consumed the ashen remains of her heart and liver. Destroying her organs killed her but failed to cure him as intended, dooming him to an eternity of solitude among the living.

The last vampire.

Lena fed from him in dreams, or what upon wakening he believed to have been dreams. A predator making his solitary way in the world cannot afford such luxuries.

What eluded him was her secret. How had she transformed him into an undead monster craving for human blood? One who required it for his very survival? Did she possess secret knowledge that eluded him over the 57 years since? Or was this his punishment for participating in her demise? Had consuming her organs taken from him the power to bring someone along with him? A partial cure that rendered his curse far more insidious?

Camilla stepped through the door from the bedroom, wrapped in her sheet. Held in place with one hand above her breast, she asked, "Where is my dress?"

"It's ruined. The blood proved impossible to get out."

"I don't care if my blood is dripping a trail behind me—it will still be better than running around in my underwear."

"Sorry; of course. It is hanging out back. Should be dry by now. I'll bring it in."

"I can get it myself."

"Probably not a good idea without shoes. One of yours fell off, either in your car during the wreck or along the road. If you'll turn over these eggs in a second, I'll go fetch your dress."

"You lost my shoe? I'm stuck in the middle of some forest with only one shoe?"

"Next time, don't crash into a tree in the middle of a forest and I might be able to gather essentials we need before we scurry off into the dark night." He knew it rang of a trick to discourage her from trying to venture out on her own, knowing any trek through the woods was itself treacherous for a city girl, let alone trying to make an escape barefoot.

This girl was different. He liked her. Such poise, so full of piss and vinegar. Anyone else hearing the Red Dahlia killer had kidnapped them would cower in a corner crapping themselves, yet here she was, giving him the business. Pretty, too. No, pretty doesn't begin to cover it. A knockout. Her beauty first attracted him, even before he caught her scent on the street. Blood of the innocent, the beautiful and the young is the sweetest. The powerful aroma of her virginity he detected from half a block away.

Along with their blood, he takes a portion of that person's life essence. When he preys on any available person—older, the criminal, the homely—it shows on his face and through changes in his behavior. Once he learned this lesson, he adapted his feeding when possible, although it was a diet difficult to stick to.

Her dress fluttered in the breeze on a wooden clothes hanger dangling from a low branch on a small maple tree out back. Blood clings to fabric, making stains difficult to remove, and hers had already set by the time he carried her here. For around the house it had to do, but before taking her anywhere, she needed a presentable outfit. He took time to scan the trees; you never can be too careful.

The scent of her honied blood was still strong on her dress. Years ago, he set a rule to never prey upon kids. Not just the heightened risk of eagle-eyed parents watching over their brood or the fact that they simply lacked a sufficient volume of blood in their little bodies. He loathed killing, and the little running through their veins runs out so fast. Killing kids somehow feels worse than murdering adults, even those only a few years older. He decided against asking this girl's specific age.

While continuing to scan the woods surrounding the cabin for any sign of movement, any unusual sound or smell, he breathed in deep the country air. No unpleasant aroma of deputies scouring the woods would drown out the scent of the crimson stain on the fabric. He pressed the conical bulge where her right breast fit in, stained with her fragrant essence, to his face, and inhaled deep to savor her aroma. Her age mattered not, whether technically a kid by math alone, but by no other measure.

Keeping her here and taking only a small amount of her blood each day would keep her alive indefinitely. If he could keep her fed.

When he returned inside, he handed her the dress. "I did my best. We'll get you something else to wear; until then, this is all we have."

"Thank you," she said. This girl was good! Perhaps this was her strategy—willing to give as good as she got, but ingratiating herself as a survival strategy.

Two guns hung from pegs over the mantle, a double-barrel shotgun and an ancient, bolt-action hunting rifle. He chose the shotgun, breaking it in the center and filling each barrel with shells from his pocket; two boxes of ammo he had hidden on an upper shelf in a kitchen cabinet while she was still out.

For the first time since awakening, her face showed fear. More than fear, pure terror, controlled best she could manage. "What are you going to do...?"

The shotgun clunked, shattering the momentary silence inside the isolated little cabin. "Before long, you'll be hungry. The woods are full of animals. Deer footprints and rabbit pellets are everywhere. This will make some noise, so I want my shot to count—something more filling than squirrel. There's a down slope which may lead to a pond, if we're lucky—do you like goose?"

"I… I've never had goose."

"Wish me luck, then. It's delicious."

He wondered what goose blood tastes like.

✝

A vantage point through two hundred yards of forest afforded him a full view of the cabin. There he lay, motionless. Waiting. As long as she did not attempt to run off in one shoe down the dirt path following tire tracks back to a road, his time was unlimited. Dozens of cottontails scampered through the underbrush, and he resolved to make some snares later, the kind he made decades ago when he was her age.

Two hours passed. Three. One skill the dead can master is lying still. Chipmunks and birds came so close he could have grabbed them with his hand. If only animal blood satisfied his craving. To a certain extent, it did, and in emergencies he had subsided off the blood of everything from raccoons to rats, but it had an effect similar to chewing ice. It may be something in the stomach, but it only curbed hunger by volume, leaving his need unfulfilled.

The canopy of pine and oak and sweet gum offered near complete shade, but a patch of sunlight crept close, so he slid out of its path, his movement so slow it was imperceptible.

A jackrabbit cautiously approached. It sensed his presence, but seemed unable to identify what he was or the proper course of action when confronted with a dead body blocking the path to its burrow.

THE HEART

"Did you find your unmentionables?" Blood had pooled inside the right cup of her bra and by the time he removed it from her body at the cabin, the liquid had dried to a viscous brown that clung like glue to her skin. He had to peel it off her, leaving ruined fabric stained a dark red, impervious to scrubbing. He laid it out for her alongside her dress.

"Yes. How much did I bleed?"

"It's a deep gash."

"It needs stitches. I looked in the mirror."

"We can't take you to a doctor—you know that."

"I found a sewing kit."

"Camilla, I can't."

"It will leave an ugly scar."

"Hair will hide it; it's above your hairline."

A tear rolled down her cheek, perhaps understanding that scars only matter if she was to ever leave this forest alive. He hated the thought of closing this ready source of his blood, but her faith that she might survive this ordeal is the one thing he must never crush. Later, he'd open another wound somewhere on her body to feed from.

"I'll stitch you up, but we'll need to get you to a proper doctor soon." That brought the slightest hint of a smile to her full lips. "Why didn't you run off while I was hunting?"

"With you out there somewhere carrying that gun?"

"Staying put is better than dying?"

"Give me another option."

"If I wanted you dead, they would have found you in your

car at dawn." With her smarts, she figured that out already.

"What do you want from me? Hold me in this little love shack and take advantage of me?"

"Could have done that last night, too."

"Maybe it's no fun for you if I'm out cold."

"You're probably right about that."

"See, the way I figure, you need to lie low until the heat is off enough for you to cut me up into your latest piece of art to dump in someone's yard."

How wrong she was struck him funny, so he chuckled. "That's what you figure, huh?"

"It's true, isn't it? I've heard of men keeping girls for months in a cabin like this where no one will come looking for them. The whole time doing terrible things to them."

"Then I'll chop you up?" Her head nodded in sober acknowledgement, and she somehow prevented the tears filling her eyes from streaming down her face.

"Remember my promise not to harm you? Have I given you any reason not to trust me?"

"Besides the kidnapping part?"

"See, that's why I have no interest in hurting a hair on your head. I like you, kid. You're really swell."

"You talk like my father—who says swell anymore?"

†

Nearly every night since she had been there in the cabin with this killer, the most wonderful, tormenting dreams visited upon her during the darkness.

The same each night, it seemed. Odd, since back home, she never remembered dreams. She dreamed of her kidnapper. Instead of a vicious killer holding her hostage, though, he came to her as her lover. His icy touch on her body lit tremendous tingling inside, in places she felt but could not name. The murderer held her while tender lips kissed her. On her lips. Her eyelids, her neck.

If someone had predicted she would dream of a white man touching and kissing her, so intimate and delicious, she would have called them crazy to their face. Those dreams left her breathless, dizzy and with a profound sensation of fulfillment beyond any experience in her life. In those moments when he embraced her, she yearned for him with a need approaching hunger.

Nonsensical as it seemed in her waking hours, she desired those dreams, the only pleasant interlude she experienced during her captivity. Her mind told her it was her way of controlling him or maybe releasing the stress of being held captive by a criminal deep in a county well-renowned for its population of Klansmen.

Something more, though. Since she first tasted puberty, similar thoughts crept into her desires. Never enchanting, forbidden fantasies involving a white man. Sometimes, at home in her own bed before she fell asleep, she imagined herself in some movie she had seen, yet never could imagine herself hugging and kissing the white leading men. Although she hated to admit it, the killer was handsome as most movie stars, in a boyish way. This is what her mother warned her about.

"Watch out for the handsome bad boys," she said.

And she had. The best way to avoid falling victim to their charms had been to deny herself. Rather than dream of boys, her waking dreams focused on attending college. Spelman was her dream school, a college for ambitious Black women like herself. Friends tormented her for her relentless focus, but it served her well. Kept her out of the sort of trouble so many girls stumbled into.

Until this white killer kidnapped her. Now with her guard down and trapped in a dismal, hopeless situation, why did this terrible man—white and the worst of the worst—fill her with such warmth and illicit desire as she waited for sleep's embrace —and his?

†

By moonlight, blood appeared black draining from the deer hung upside down. He drank a little because unable to feed fully off her—not with that tiny body holding such a small volume of blood. Just enough to take the edge off.

The skin made a ripping sound as he opened the torso from pelvis to ribs, then the entrails sloshed formless onto a tarpaulin underneath. The hide peeled off like a glove; since you never know when deer skin may come in handy, he set it aside. Old habits die hard. When he was young, he lifted deer this size over his shoulders; now, he hefted it with ease in one hand. The only place to keep it safe from scavengers stealing their fill was inside, so he lugged it into the pitch-dark house.

It hit him about the same time he saw the flash. He dropped the deer carcass on the floor as pain wracked his chest. The noise overwhelmed his sensitive ears, contained as it was inside the room like this, and left in its wake only a ringing ache. It took several seconds to realize she had shot him.

In the dark, Camilla struggled with the bolt, trying to ram another shell into the chamber. The impact doubled him over and staggered him back a step, but he recognized her frantic efforts to ready the gun to fire again and needed to act fast to stop her.

Her face registered the shock of his fist grabbing the barrel when, a rapid heartbeat before, he staggered across the moonlit doorway. Although she put up a valiant fight, taking the gun from her was no trouble at all. Tossing it aside, his hand wrapped around her smooth, slim neck and slammed her against the wall a few feet behind her firing position. Her bare feet lifted off the floor, where they flailed in the air a few times before kicking out at him. Aimed at his crotch, her foot instead hit his thigh—hard, but failing to inflict damage.

In her dark, glistening eyes reflected an icy blue glow coming from his, only inches away. "Why? Do you want me dead?"

Harmless fists bounced off his face and shoulders, then

one hit the bullet hole an inch away from his sternum. Another shock of pain forced a grunt from him, and his fingers tightened around her precious throat. She was screaming something, but the bell tolling in his ears drowned out any words.

His fingers relaxed. Her feet landed on the floor. "You can't kill me!"

"Why not?" He more read her lips than heard her voice.

"Because you cannot. Damn it, that hurts!" Camilla slid down the wall, pulling her knees against her chest as he fired a lantern and ripped open his shirt to assess the damage. Not that it mattered, but did arouse his curiosity.

If he was alive, this bullet would have inflicted a fatal wound. It must have at least grazed his heart or the surrounding jumble of arteries. In him, though, low on blood as he was, only a trickle ran down his chest. He turned to her, holding open his shirt. "Are you satisfied?"

She was screaming again. This looked to be a different scream, although above the ringing in his ears, it sounded the same. "What are you?"

"Angry. And hurt!" When he reached for her wrists, she waved them back and forth like a boxer in a clinch, but her best efforts failed to prevent him from catching up to them, lifting her to her feet and marching her down the hall to her bedroom, where he tossed her toward the bed. She collapsed on it, rolling over to keep an eye on the impossible threat of her still-living captor.

"I'm sorry—I'm so sorry," she kept repeating, knowing how feeble she must sound, how horribly she had failed and, instead, kicked over something immeasurably worse than a hornet's nest. How he remained alive must be almost as terrifying for her as what her failure meant. This man or whatever he was is a killer, and she accomplished nothing more than infuriating him with a stupid, meaningless gesture.

He shut the door and turned the key to lock her in tight.

†

Time really can stand still. Not those fleeting moments of trauma or embarrassment or a child waiting an endless Christmas Eve for Santa to arrive. Simply stops, when time ceases to have any meaning. An hour might pass, or a day. If a week had passed, it would not surprise her. Only light and dark filtering through the window offered any conception, but neither felt real.

Is this how a death row prisoner experiences time? Now that the Lonely Hearts Killers' public trial was over, no longer splashed over the front pages and they rotted on death row, for the first time, she understood. She sentenced herself to death row, complete with the realization how plodding is the passage of time without hope.

Someone long ago painted the window closed. She spent endless hours picking away dried paint, but some must have dripped down inside the frame, freezing it in place. An urge to kick out the window, to throw something through it, grew inside her until it strained the limits of her self-control. Only fear of what he would do to her if caught gave her the willpower to stifle such foolish thoughts.

At night, during daylight, whether picking flakes of paint from the gaps in the windowsill or curled in a pathetic, quivering ball on the mattress, the image of that hole in the center of his chest replayed before her, real as if she still aimed the rifle at his torso. That too-sparse river of blood, less than from a kid with a skinned knee, straight from a horror movie. If not for the undeniable facts her own eyes witnessed, so close and clear, it was impossible.

But it was true. She shot this—whatever he is. From close range, and all it accomplished was knocking him back a couple of steps. Straight through the heart, and now he was outside, lying in wait. A thought terrifying enough to render sleep impossible. In fact, after sunset, her nerves were so rattled that the sound of a breeze or an owl hooting made her jump and set her heart racing all over again.

At some point, in the eerie, dead silence of the house, another thought intruded. What if her shot killed him?

Why else the silence? The bullet must have grazed his heart, nicked his aorta or one of those other blood vessels surrounding it. A tiny nick, a slow bleeder, allowing him to toss her in here before crawling off to die. That had to be it. A simple, scientific answer. Somewhere in this house he lay dead, and she was too cowardly to leave this room to see her handiwork.

If true, although less terrifying, this likelihood offered little hope. A black girl shooting a white man in a county like this stood zero chance. If anyone discovered his body and then found her wandering down one of these lonely roads in the middle of the forest, death row was foolish optimism. More likely, a lynch mob would string her up after forcing her to endure unimaginable shame, indignity, and torture.

Better for her if he survived.

The realization, when it crossed her mind, shocked her. But it was true. So far, he had not raped her. Even shooting him did not provoke a beating from him. Strange as it seemed, she stood a better chance with the man who carved up the Red Dahlia, kidnapped her and survived a bullet to the heart. The man or whatever he is.

Waves of goosebumps swept across the surface of her skin as the significance of this reality sank in. *Please, God, awaken me from this horrible nightmare.*

✝

Immortality is not indestructibility.

Similar as the concepts may be, they are not synonymous. This he knew even before becoming immortal, having witnessed another immortal being destroyed.

Gunshots may not kill him, but bullets do their damage. And although his pain tolerance had risen to insane heights, a hole through his chest—complete with more shattered ribs and an exit wound between his shoulder blades the size of a half dollar—hurt like hell.

For two days, he did little more than lie in bed, allowing his body to rejuvenate. Different ribs needed to regenerate than those he broke days before, when his chest took the full force of the car smashing into a tree, bones themselves not yet healed. Much of the time he slept while his body used all available energy to regrow crumbled bone, ripped skin and who knows what all in between.

It was dark when he awoke, feeling somewhat refreshed and able to move without too much agony. Stretching an arm across his chest elicited a painful grimace, so he decided against doing that again. More acutely than the pain, he had hunger.

Two white saucers surrounding large, ebony centers greeted him as he peered inside her bedroom door. With knees pulled tight to her chest and both arms hugging her shins, she said not a word. All his energy focused on her eyes. For a moment, they returned to their usual lovely almond shape before drooping. Just like when someone is hypnotized in movies, her chin sank. In films, though, the hypnotized never curled themselves into a terrified ball like she did. Her forehead dropped with a small thud to her knees.

Laid out on her side along the bed, pulling her hair aside revealed the spot. He made a small incision below her ear. His preferred spot for those he chose to keep with him, behind an ear, thus out of sight in the mirror, hidden behind hair from others' prying eyes. Directly over a blood vessel. The same spot from where he drank Elizabeth Short's blood. Neither as large nor as powerful as the carotid artery it branched from, the posterior auricular artery provided the perfect spot for leisurely, repeated feedings.

Nestled with her back against his chest, her warmth also offered some measure of relief to his still-gaping wound. Soon as her sweet, virginal blood flowed over his tongue and down his throat. Intense pleasure welled up in him, wiping away any traces of pain, even before the healing effects of the blood took hold.

Soon Camilla began moaning, as well. Her body responded to the touch of his hand, caressing it as he pulled hers against his. A deep, soulful moan escaped from her lips as her back arched sensuously against him. Any remaining traces of pain drifted off, overwhelmed by the intensity of the pleasure her life essence gave.

When leaving, he covered her with a sheet, so when she awakened, if she remembered anything at all, it would be only fragments of a wondrous, forbidden dream.

THE AWAKENING

Dawn had broken. Wiping sleep from her eyes, she realized she had drifted off.

Anger welled up over her utter failure to keep her guard up, but how long did she manage to stay awake? Two days? Three? Everything felt like some vivid, terrifying nightmare, one obliterating the lines between what was real and what existed only in her fragile mind.

Of course, nothing since that night when she shot him was real. It could not be.

Outside, a Blue Jay squawked angrily, answered by another fussing at it from further away. She stretched and, as she did, another fragment of her dream came back. Her kidnapper coming to visit. Soon as she saw him enter the room, they were together in bed, his hands caressing her in the most wonderful ways, his lips covering her face and neck with the sweetest kisses imaginable. Her body shuddering with pleasure so intense she could only assume it was that climax the more worldly girls spoke of in hushed, breathless tones.

Still dressed, she realized a sheet covered her as her mind awakened, but her head aimed the wrong direction in the bed, where her feet were when she slept here, with her feet up near the wall where the pillow should be. From this unnatural position, the door visible only by cranking her neck. Her head jerked in that direction.

The door was wide open.

Ever so slowly, she peered around the corner. Nothing in either direction. Aside from chirping songbirds outside, inside the cabin was quiet as a crypt. He wished for her to come to him. If still angry for shooting him, or shooting at him or whatever in fact happened, he could have done anything to her while asleep —the additional message an open door conveyed clear as day.

Barefoot, she crept across the worn wooden floor, steps so light and tentative, toes ready to jerk up at the slightest hint of a squeak.

There he was, sitting in the main room, reading a book. Her heart—beating fast as a Gene Krupa drum solo—froze in a sudden wave of fear and, for a second, she could swear it stopped altogether. For a painfully long time, he continued reading. Without looking from the page, he spoke. "There is nothing to be afraid of."

"What are you?"

A bookmark trapped between closed pages, he set the book aside. "Sit down—we need to talk."

"Answer me. For days I've done nothing but sit in that room trying to convince myself I'm losing my mind. Now tell me what you are, because I shot you in the heart and now you're sitting there reading a book like nothing happened."

"Please, sit down—I'll explain everything."

Why had he lost her shoe? Those she needed for when she made her break. Trying her best to act casual, she stepped toward the door to his right. "How are you not dead?"

"Camilla, it's a long story. An interesting one, I assure you. If you sit down, I'll try to explain. Please, I promise not to hurt you."

How can he be this calm with her heart thumping fast as a jackhammer? Something in his eyes, glowing cerulean by the morning light, convinced her to trust him. Just to play it safe, she pulled a kitchen chair close to the door, keeping her eyes glued to him the entire time. "Alright, tell it to me straight. Did I shoot you?"

"Oh, you shot me. Hurt like hell at first, but it's getting better."

"Some kind of misfire? A defective bullet? Old, wet

gunpowder or something?”

“Camilla, my dear, this will be hard to understand, but there was nothing wrong with the bullet, and you caught me square in the chest.”

“Then why aren’t you dead?” she again demanded. “How are we sitting here discussing this?”

“See, that’s the thing—I am dead.”

“If you think I’m going to sit here listening to you mock me like that, you’ve got another think coming.” As she shifted to stand, he held up a hand, motioning for her to stop. First, he unbuttoned his shirt, pulling it open wide enough to expose the wound. Gasping, her knees failed, and she fell back into the seat.

Neither a wound nor a scab, the place where she saw a hole rent in his flesh, now covered with delicate pink skin like an old burn scar. Minor though, about as big around as the tip of her pinkie. Once, she saw the nasty scars cigarettes leave in skin, and his looked just like that.

He must have been aware this teeny scar did not satisfy her, so he stood, removed his shirt, and turned around to reveal a larger mark on his back that must have been an inch and a half across. Like the scar on his chest, raw, pinkish skin covered an area broad as a half-dollar, its center concave. Incomplete.

“Went clean through.” As he turned to give her a better view, his muscles rippled. Toned like an athlete, she had never seen a grown white man without his shirt. Skin much paler than she ever could have imagined, almost translucent. His beauty transfixed her, despite the sickening hole she shot through him.

“How? How has it healed up so fast?”

With a hunch of his shoulders, he answered, “Not sure. That’s how it’s been since, you know, I died.”

“Stop saying that! How can you be dead and standing there talking to me, showing off your Charles Atlas muscles like that?”

“Beats the hell out of me.” Not bothering with his shirt, he sat down again, leaning forward with elbows on his knees. “What do you know about vampires?”

“Oh, no! Hell no!” Arms waved in front of her face, palms

out, shaking her head with vigor. "Do not treat me like a fool!"

Now on one knee before her, like a man proposing marriage, he enclosed her hands in his. They were frigid, cooler than the temperature in the room. "This is the truth, Camilla."

"So, you drink blood, like Count Dracula? Okay, turn into a bat—maybe then I'll believe you."

"It isn't like the movies. Well, some of it is; not the part about bats, though."

"Which parts are true?"

"The blood. I need blood to survive…"

"Oh, damn! That's why you didn't want to stitch me up—you've been drinking my blood, haven't you?"

"I need it to survive, as you needed the strength it gave you to pull through after you nearly killed yourself. I can't explain better than that; there is so much I don't understand, myself."

"What do you mean, gave me strength?"

"To save your life, I had to share with you some of my blood."

Her expression flickered back and forth from confusion to horror as her fragile mind attempted to make sense of what he told her. "Are you trying to tell me I drank some of your blood?"

"Just enough to keep you alive, although I am afraid it may have been too much."

"Were those dreams when you came to me?"

"Not really."

"Then what does that make me? Am I a vampire, too? Or am I like that guy Dracula has, the servant who is under his spell?"

"Neither. It doesn't work that way, although I can influence you, almost like hypnotism. But outside your dreams, I have chosen not to control your thoughts, Camilla. You see, it has been a very long time since I have felt anything resembling compassion or caring in my cold, dead heart, but for reasons I can't fathom, I like you. There you have it: I have a crush on the girl who shot me through the heart."

"So, I'm not a vampire like you?"

"No, I haven't… I don't know how to make anyone like me."

"And although you have this mysterious power to turn me into your zombie slave girl, you don't want to? You expect me to believe that garbage? Why am I sitting here listening to this crap?"

"Let me prove it to you."

"How? Can you make me do something against my will?"

"Explain why you gave me a ride that night?"

"I felt bad for you, is all—a white boy lost in an unfamiliar part of town late, after midnight."

"Do you even believe what you are saying?"

Arms clenched over her chest, naively unaware of the enticing way it pushed her breasts up, she said, "Go ahead, prove it! Make me do something—sing a song or dance around like your damn puppet on a string."

Head shaking, he answered, "Singing won't work; it must be something you won't otherwise do, or else you'll convince yourself it was just a carnival trick."

"Try me."

His eyes, smoldering blue, scanned her up and down, from the dangling leg, the one crossed over the other with its foot twitching, up to her dark almond eyes. "Do you want me to see your body naked?"

"Of course not! I'm only—what kind of girl do you think I am? I'll have you know, I have the highest moral character."

"Yes, I know—you're a virgin. I can tell."

Although this certainty surprised her, it was no more impressive than the sideshow barker guessing her weight. After days spent together, you pick up things. "Most girls my age are."

"Oh, you might be surprised. Most not by their own choice, I suppose, but I knew the moment I saw you. Look at me." His eyes locked upon hers; her cheeks burned and turned red. "Now, take your dress off."

Then, the strangest thing happened. She reached behind, coaxing down the zipper far as the pain in her ribs allowed, then stood to pull it the rest of the way. This dress, though, was hard to reach even without bruises and broken ribs, the tiny brass pull hard to grasp. She turned, facing away from him, and he rose to unzip it the full length. A quick move had her arms out, and the dress fell to the floor around her legs.

Made of two layers, smooth cotton under a woolen outer layer, this dress needed no slip. She felt no embarrassment standing before him wearing only her bloomers and ruined, blood-stained bra, so she did nothing to cover herself.

"Need help with the bra?"

"No," she reached back, "I think I can get it."

With a clicking sound, the hooks freed, the straps over her shoulders grew slack. Cool fingers, the same temperature as morning air in the room, touched her cheek, lifting her chin to direct her attention back to his eyes. "Don't."

Spell broken, aware of her state of disrobement and filled with shame, her hands flew up to hold her bra in place an instant before it slipped off her shoulders to join the dress on the floor. "Oh, my God!"

"Now do you believe me?"

"I... I..."

"Turn around." Chilly hands turned her by the shoulders and re-hooked her brassiere. Then he jerked her back to face him. "Now, drink my blood."

"What?" Again, his hand caressed her face with astounding gentleness. The lover's hand from her dreams.

"Drink from me, so you can become like me."

His thumb dug into the pink skin where her bullet tore into him days before, drawing a trickle of blood down that skin the color of fine china. At first, she hesitated. His hand urged her, though, and his eyes pleaded with her to drink from him. Her soft, full lips closed around the hole she made and a sweet, metallic taste filled her mouth. As she swallowed, her body tingled all over, although stronger in her breasts and down inside the pit of her stomach, spreading down between her legs.

His blood electric, thick and alive; her tongue on his hairless chest felt nothing but silky skin. Her hand pulled his back toward her, and she drew deeply because she yearned for his blood. Why? This she did not try to understand.

He touched her, too, in ways that, if any of the boys from school tried with her, would have earned a vicious slap and the evil eye in class for weeks. He, though—she allowed to touch her any way he wanted, for she wanted it, too. When he tried to push her away, she sucked harder, nose pressing into his pectoral muscle, tongue lashing at the tiny hole as it would his lips, if he kissed her. But he was strong, stronger than her, and the suction released with a smacking sound.

Her eyes, crazed now with an unknown passion, saw her saliva on his skin, her tongue still reaching out although too far away as he forced her back.

"Hey, hey—that's enough."

Again, the spell broken, flames fading inside the small portions of her body hidden by her undergarments, her flushed cheeks burning, spilling down her neck to her chest.

"What did you...? Oh, my God, am I...? What have you done to me?"

"Well, I've proven a few things, I hope."

"Am I like you now? A vampire?"

"Perhaps. Only time will tell. I must say, I cannot remember anyone so eager to taste my blood, so there is hope."

Camilla hated the idea that he had made her drink his blood—enjoyed drinking from his body—almost as much as she loved the dark, powerful sensations it gave her to do so. Her body still tingled, but not for the same reason, aware now of her vulnerable nakedness. His fingers brushed the skin of her chest above her bra.

"It's so beautiful."

"What is," she asked.

"Your skin. The color, so rich. Mine is so blah by comparison." He stared into her lovely eyes. "Do you realize how beautiful you are?"

"You're kind of beautiful, too," she answered, "for a murderer."

He laughed, which gave her a welcome sense of relief, because she did not understand what drove her to say that, and joined in when she realized he took it well.

†

What had he done to her?

For the past two nights when he came to her, he did not manifest as a dream. Wide awake, she welcomed him to her bed, relished his kisses and the cool feel of his skin against hers. Until then, she knew nothing of a gash to her neck near her ear, where he fed from her. It neither hurt nor itched—it had no sensation at all, at least before his lips closed over it, his nose nestled between her ear and neck and sucked her blood from her.

His lips, his suckling of her, brought the purest bliss, exciting the whole of her body, her soul, or those fragments left of it, beyond anything her dreams or imagination allowed. He never attempted to entice sex from her, though she spent her days envisaging little else, wishing he would. Because she gladly gave herself to him in any way he wanted. He desired her, too. Men cannot hide that from a woman—not with their bodies pressed together, writhing in the sort of intimacy they shared.

Each day, she resolved to ask why he did not take her virginity from her, too. And each day, she found herself unable to ask him. He touched her in the most wondrous ways, but left this last remnant of her innocence fully intact and in agony.

Nor did he remove every stitch of her clothing. One night, she took off the undershirt she still slept in, to feel his skin against hers, and that skin on skin only served to further inflame her passions—and his. A woman can tell, even though— in the strictest terms—he had not made her a woman.

Although it was still summertime, somehow she came down with a chest cold. For the last couple of days, coughing racked her body and left her spent and weak. Perpetually tired and desiring nothing more than to sleep all day. The way he kept her awake all night, like lovers in that first bloom of love, although he refused to make her his lover, no wonder she slept all day!

As she grew weaker, his moods darkened with it. He said nothing, nor did she ask, because people in love do not ask their lover's secrets. A lover must freely share all their secrets with the other.

"We must leave," he said as she lay naked upon him. It must have been near sunrise.

"Why? Where will we go?"

"We cannot survive only sharing blood with each other. I must take fresh blood and give it to you."

"Do I have to kill someone?"

"No, you aren't ready. For now, you will take from me. I will feed from someone."

"Will you kill them?"

"Killing is usually unnecessary. Sometimes it is unavoidable. I will try not to kill for you."

"Good. I don't think I want to kill anyone."

A humorless smile crossed his luscious lips, pink with her blood. "I hope that does not change."

"Do you enjoy killing?"

"Sometimes. It wasn't always that way."

A question, held back for some time, burst out. "Is my blood different?"

This time, his smile was genuine. "Oh, yes."

"How is white blood different from colored blood?"

"Colored blood? The only color blood comes in is red. There is no such thing as white blood or black blood. The only black blood I've ever tasted was in Europe. They make wonderful sausage from it in Spain and in Scandinavia. No, there is another reason your blood is different."

"Then what is different about mine?"

"You are a virgin. Nothing on earth is as sweet as the blood of a virgin."

She rolled off him, onto her back, staring at the ceiling. "Oh, is that why...?"

"That is one reason. There are others."

"Is that why you like me? Because I am a virgin?"

"That is why I enjoy your blood so much. Without your untainted blood, I would hold the same feelings for you. It only makes your blood different, not you."

His hand caressed her stomach, finger tickling inside her belly button, chilling her to the core in a most delightful way. "You want me to unburden you of that, too?"

"I want to possess you in every way—and for you to possess me every way you can imagine." Again, she rolled over him, embracing him with a deep, passionate kiss. Hard to believe she barely had kissed a boy only a few weeks ago, and now kissing was no longer enough for her. "Where will we go?"

"Where do you want to go?"

A giggle escaped. "I can decide?"

"Why not? Where do you suppose the most delicious people live?"

THE DEARLY DEPARTED

Mostly, they drove at night. Although sunlight posed no risk of causing him to burst into flame if some fell on him through one of the small, kidney-shaped windows, his fair skin burned so easily only an hour of morning sunlight falling on his arm and he'd turn into a lobster.

More importantly, a white man and a colored girl driving together were sure to invite attention—the very dangerous attention they needed to avoid. The Klan still controlled much of the countryside, and after passing through several counties, they realized they risked traveling where mixed couples could not travel in safety. With most states having anti-miscegenation laws on their books, but neither sure which states those were, they had to assume those laws applied everywhere they went.

Eddie stopped a to swap license tags on the stolen Studebaker pickup to stymie cops from linking the truck to its previous owner, the exsanguinated redneck. Besides, local tags attract less attention, so soon as they crossed a state line, he began a new search for plates to swipe.

Over the years, Eddie had mastered the art of avoiding attention. He made a subconscious study of the skill. If not, he possessed a natural bearing and presence that announced his arrival the moment he entered a room. But he learned and honed the skill of drifting down a street without heads turning or women paying particular attention.

Camilla was a different story. Few girls or grown women had beauty comparable to hers, with a svelte, shapely figure to match. Despite her innate ability to turn heads, like others of her race, she found it to her advantage to sometimes disappear into the background. One of their first stops was a small-town department store, where Eddie picked her out a fresh new dress.

"Pick something cute," she instructed, waiting in the truck since, in these small towns, you never can tell the welcome a colored shopper might receive. He returned with two bags, one containing a pair of new shoes.

To her chagrin, he chose the plainest dress available in her size. "Remind me never to let you buy clothes for me—this is without question the ugliest thing I have ever seen."

She hated it, an excellent sign. "Good. We sure don't want you standing out in a crowd, do we?"

In another town, he purchased new undergarments in the sizes she requested. These were less plain.

Once underway again, she held up a lacy, black bra to catch the glow of a passing streetlamp. "There may be hope for you, yet."

Camilla's beautiful voice filled the miles with song, her love of singing along with the radio made for welcome entertainment as they made their way down dark, deserted roadways. In the hours before dawn, miles often passed without seeing another vehicle. They liked that.

Their choice of destination fell to little more than a guess. In very few places were mixed couples welcome. Large cities offered more opportunity to disappear into the masses and unlimited opportunities to feed. New York a logical choice, perhaps too much so. Distance mattered—the further, the better. Neither had ever been to Denver.

The lure of the mountains drew them west.

Most nights, meals consisted of PBJ sandwiches and a handful of chips from the large tin that sat in the pickup bed, too large to fit in front with them. Since they drove at night, restaurants were never open when hunger struck. And who needed an ugly confrontation in some greasy spoon? Better to eat on the tailgate at an old gas station sitting abandoned since the Depression than to draw unnecessary attention to themselves. Eddie sometimes stopped for something to eat later on—some fried chicken or pickled eggs from a gas station.

He hungered for something more.

Aimless drives down country roads or through strange cities in the middle hours is no way to hunt. At night, cities sleep, their streets vacant. Rare were signs of life other than the occasional odd car sharing the road, let alone a pedestrian he could snatch up. The small cab offered no room; two filled it too well to squeeze in a kicking, screaming victim with them.

Inside the old pickup, easy conversation flowed as they burned up the miles. Light topics, punctuated by bursts of laughter, her singing and the occasional comforting silence. One topic they avoided discussing was the connection Camilla's second feeding created between them. Unlike her second, the first time, while comatose, had involved no conscious decision on her part. But when she willingly partook of his blood, that act forged a mysterious, almost mystical bond. Since then, each time they shared blood, deepened this bond in much the way making love binds young lovers to each other.

Not that Camilla would appreciate this analogy, so Eddie kept that one to himself. No need to discuss a readily apparent truth. Anyone around them together might see it, too, believing the couple to be in the early throes of puppy love. Which, in some ways, was true. But nobody witnessed this couple together. This was only between them.

"I'm sorry," she told him.

"For what?"

"Shooting you." The moment of silence following her apology hung for a moment until he started laughing. "I mean it," she said before she, too, joined in the laughter.

"Sorry for laughing at your heartfelt emotion, but I wonder how many women have spoken those words to their guy? And although I appreciate it, if you think about it, I probably deserved it. I suppose I owe you an apology for kidnapping and all." His hand found hers in the dark and squeezed it.

"Seems to me we're square after, you know, shooting you in the heart."

Well after midnight, their headlights played across a small cluster of picnic tables someone had placed on the shoulder of the two-lane road.

He slowed the car. "Looks like that restaurant has a few open tables."

"We haven't eaten at a proper table in days."

Stars spread out across the sky above them and, to the north and south, fields of crops spread toward the horizon. An outcropping of rocks shaded by day under several sturdy oaks showed why farmers never plowed this patch under with the surrounding land. In daylight, some enterprising farmer sold meals to passing motorists, who outnumbered those who shared the road this time of night.

While Camilla spread strawberry jam on several slices of bread, she watched Eddie slather his with a generous layer of peanut butter. "Aren't you tired of these yet?"

"Do you have any idea how exotic peanut butter was when I was a kid? They considered it a health food. Served it at sanitariums."

Her head tilted to one side. "How old are you?"

"Old." A two-sandwich stack and handful of chips on open napkins made a filling, if plain, dinner. He changed the topic. "At least this is a pleasant spot."

"Beautiful. Such a clear night."

Eddie was on his second sandwich when headlights pierced the night off in the distance. Before anything other than two brilliant dots of light came into view, the sound made clear a truck approached. A few hundred yards away, the engine began spooling down. As it rolled to a stop behind their pickup, painted red letters on a yellow and black shield identified it. Falstaff

Brewing Co., St. Louis, MO.

"Well, ain't this a pretty picture?" The driver walked up behind Camilla, who did not turn to acknowledge him. "Turn around; let me take a gander."

"We're just eating, buddy. We don't want no trouble," Eddie said.

"Oh, I see—that's why you bring Aunt Jemima out here in the middle of the night? Afraid the old lady might spy who you're stepping out with if you stay in town?"

Neither responded, hoping he might grow bored if he failed to get a rise out of them. It didn't work.

The trucker left the headlights burning, casting enough light to illuminate the picnic area well, and he worked around to the side, with intent interest in Camilla. Burly as a prizefighter with a cauliflower ear hinting at a pugilistic past and the arrogance of a man accustomed to provoking others at his whim. "She's a pretty shine, I'll give you that. Let me get a look atchya." Instead, she turned her face away.

Bored by his inability to stir them up, he sauntered over to the nearest oak, unzipped his fly, and proceeded to douse the trunk with a loud, steady stream of piss. "Ah. Feels good—I've been holding that in since Centerville. I suppose you've seen plenty of white pecker, so I figured you won't mind none." Before he zipped up his pants, he turned back toward them. "How old is she, fourteen? Git 'em while they're young, that's what I always say. More important with the jigaboos, I suppose. They say they're share-croppers from an early age, so who knows what she'll be spreading with that sweet cooter in a few years, am I right?"

Eddie had heard enough. "Alright, you've taken care of business. How 'bout you move along, pal?"

"Oh, I see—peckerwood here wants to spend some alone-time with his sweet little nigra girl. Maybe you're planning to poke her right here on the table? Think maybe I'll stick around to watch that show."

Camilla grabbed Eddie's wrist as he started to stand. "Don't let him get under your skin."

He ignored her. "Time to take a powder, wiseguy."

"What, and leave this darky dreamboat all for you?"

By this point, Eddie stood one pace away from him. "I said beat it."

This teamster looked able to handle himself in a fight. Bigger than Eddie and at least as tall, he posed an intimidating figure unaccustomed to being bossed around. And obviously deriving great, perverse pleasure from tormenting this couple, correctly surmising they were lovers. He drew himself up to full height. "Or what?"

"Don't ask questions you don't want answered."

The driver pulled open his loose, unbuttoned shirt to reveal a hammerless revolver shoved into his pants, the dark grip standing out against the background of a soiled undershirt. Guns have a way of making assholes even more obnoxious. "Keep talking and I'll let you have it."

"Gee, thanks, I've always wanted one of those. What is it, a .32?"

"A .38, funny boy." He pulled it out and had to step backward to give enough space to point it in Eddie's face without accidentally pistol-whipping him.

"What are you planning to do with that pea-shooter?"

"You mean, other than shut up a pretty-boy nigger lover?"

"Hey—I have a better idea." It happened so fast the teamster had no time to react. His gun failed to track Eddie as he moved like a flash from in front of him to alongside. In one swift motion, Eddie pushed the snub-nosed barrel up and back, twisting the pistol from his grip before he had a chance to pull the trigger.

"What the..." A sharp, ear-splitting crack ripped the serene countryside, the bullet tearing through the tissues of the trucker's neck, doing quite an effective job of silencing him. The far side, away from the road, exploded in a liquid red puff, his knees buckled and his body crumpled lifeless as a rag doll.

Such extreme violence wholly unexpected from the man

she, moments before, had been sharing a quaint, romantic dinner, Camilla shrieked in horror.

Blood spurted up several inches with each heartbeat as the man's light-colored eyes turned back and forth, pupils dilated wide. Looming over him, Eddie tossed the gun out of his reach, bent down and smiled, watching those eyes search for answers he was never to receive. "Did you really expect me to let a piece of shit like you insult a fine lady like her?"

His fingers explored through blood and ripped flesh to cover the gaping wounds on each side of his neck. "Oh, and I have some dreadful news for you—getting shot is far from the worst calamity that will befall you tonight."

"Let's get outta here," Camilla pleaded with him.

"You okay, Honey?"

"Yeah, fine. It's just—oh, sweet Lord Jesus—I've never seen anyone murdered before."

"Then keep an eye on the road; let me know if anyone's coming. Can you do that for me?"

"Uh-huh," she nodded, eyes still wide from shock. While this may have been the first murder she witnessed, it was not the first he committed in front of her. When he killed another man in strikingly similar circumstances, she lay near death, although he later spared her the details.

Nor had she witnessed Eddie feeding from a helpless corpse. Down low, on his knees, he lifted the finger plugging the entrance wound and wrapped his mouth around it, but not before warm blood sprayed all over his face. The trucker's eyes, wild before, now went frantic, and he gurgled some unintelligible noises that required no words to comprehend. Perhaps the bullet had clipped his vertebrae, because his body lay still while a vampire sucked down his life blood.

In less than a minute, the gurgling stopped, followed by the cheerful sound of chirping crickets again filling the night. When the heart stops, the flow of circulation ceases with it, but pooled blood remains in the veins and arteries. This bullet a direct hit which severed the jugular vein, a vessel large enough to have plenty still to drain. It took more effort now, requiring suction to draw the liquid that the heart only moments before so helpfully pumped to him.

And then, when suction failed to draw more, he wiped his face on the man's shirt and lifted him with ease off the ground. In seconds, the corpse was again seated behind the beer truck's steering wheel

Long-haul truckers often carry a spare five-gallon can of gas—just in case—and this guy was one of them. After a thorough dousing of both cab and body with gasoline, Eddie asked, "Do you have a match?"

"I don't smoke—my daddy would wear out my ass with a belt if I did."

"Check the Studebaker; it reeked of tobacco when I first took it." A minute later, she returned with a box containing a few matches, which he lit together and tossed onto the dead trucker's lap. In an instant, the cab erupted into an inferno.

The first few miles passed in silence. He could only imagine how lurid witnessing a traumatic death had been to her. Camilla was a true innocent and no one should have to experience such horrors, so to calm her, he had to break the icy silence. "They won't be looking for us. He died in a fire."

"He didn't die in a fire—you shot him in the throat and drank his blood."

"And fire will ensure no one uncovers any of those tidbits. If they do figure it out, it will take days sifting through ashes, and we'll be in Denver by the time they do." Glancing over, she was staring at him, the whites of her eyes reflecting every bit of light at him. "Sorry you had to see that."

"He did sort of deserve it, didn't he?"

That drew a grin. "Guys like him? They deserve worse. Too bad he didn't give me much time to plan."

"Is that what it's like?"

"Not usually. In fact, he's the first person I've shot. Well, shot for food."

"You've shot other people?"

"What do you take me for? I signed up for the army. Why do you look so surprised? I'm a red-blooded, patriotic American. Served under Blackjack Pershing."

"Pershing? Wasn't he in…?"

"The First War? Yeah. I told you I was old."

They did not pass another car on the road until slowing for a speed trap on the outskirts of a crossroads town twenty miles down the road.

THE SIREN

Some beautiful sights are foolproof. One so tempting no passing motorist or their passenger can pass up the opportunity to gawk. Some are certain to be lured to stop.

A few towns back, she coerced Eddie into buying her the delicate purple and white gingham dress that called out to her in the morning light from the window of a department store on Main Street. Their good fortune, the store had it in her size, so he could buy it skipping a trip to the fitting room reserved for white customers. When Eddie lifted the trucker's wallet was but one of his many mysteries, but it was fat with cash—more than enough to finance their trip and a few luxury items, to boot.

After he returned with the dress in a fancy bag, she directed him to stop at a store with a familiar sign on the window, and emerged with a bag stuffed with her favorite makeup and shampoo. Per her instructions, he also bought a copy of the *Green Book*.

Armed with that travel guide, after one more night of driving, they located a hotel where he did not need to sneak her into his room to hide the fact a Colored girl was sleeping on their lily-white sheets. Behind heavy curtains, raindrops battered the window as he drank from her and she consumed him from the bullet hole she fired through his chest, ripped open again for her. The warmth his blood gave spread through her veins, growing more intense each time she drank of him. So did the climaxes feeding aroused from her.

"Is this what it feels like?" she asked. "For a man and a woman..."

Unable to bring herself to say such things in front of him, despite the intimacies they shared, he answered for her. "Similar, but making love is not this powerful—or as wonderful."

"Did that truck driver feel this way?"

"Oh, I hope not!" He laughed. "The first time is never as wild—I suspect the act of sharing arouses its pleasure."

"Is that why you came sneaking in to feed from me in my sleep?"

"One of the reasons."

Underneath the heavy layer of clouds that left the ground soaked after a drizzling day, the sun appeared as an orange ball in a gap only a hair wider than the glowing orb itself between cloud line and horizon. The effect was dramatic, setting the clouds aflame with reds, purples, and orange. Underneath it all, wearing her pretty new dress, Camilla looked far better than she felt. Strange how this illness sapped her strength and left her coughing, yet, at the same time, the mirror confirmed what Eddie kept telling her. With each passing day, she became more beautiful.

After feeding each other and a deep, dreamless sleep lasting all day, they got underway shortly before sunset. An hour later, along a narrow, paved country road, Camilla leaned against the fender. Behind her, a rod propped open the hood. A car appeared from the twilight without its headlights, but as it got closer, the lights flicked on.

"Hey, sweetie, need some help?" The passenger inquired through the window. The driver leaned across to catch a full view out the opposite side.

"No, thank you. I appreciate your generous offer, but everything is okay."

"Are you sure? We can run you into town."

The driver helpfully called over the man in the passenger seat beside him, "We know the guy who owns the Esso station. He's got a tow truck. He goes home at dinnertime, but he'll sure come out here to help you."

"You gentlemen are so nice." She kept her distance but bent down to appear friendly and entertain them with the view, "but he got a lift into town and should be back soon."

In all her life, she had never encountered white men acting so friendly toward a colored stranger. Rather than being comforted, it terrified her. What did they intend if she got into that car with them?

"Oh, your daddy got a lift into town?"

"Not my papa, my boss. *Stay with the car and make sure nobody messes with it*, he told me." A glance to her watch. "Should be back any minute. You might want to make yourselves scarce when he does—he can be ornery if he suspects you are trying to steal his truck."

"Oh, okay..." The driver did not let his buddy finish, hitting the gas the moment it became clear she was not going for a ride with them.

Forty-five minutes later, she wondered if they had chosen the wrong road as twilight faded without another vehicle coming into view. Eddie preferred sticking to back roads for the very reason; there they avoided prying eyes, but right about now, some prying eyes would be nice. Only one set per vehicle, though.

Then, two owl-eyed headlights came into view on the horizon, heading their direction. In a minute or two, those lights would fall upon her, so she primped her hair and adjusted her dress, making sure resting one foot on the flared fender lifted her leg high enough to reveal plenty of knee.

Soon enough light cast her shadow long and slender, far down the shoulder. An open hand served as a visor to see the approaching vehicle as it slowed. A handsome, expensive car. What is a Lincoln doing driving through lonely woods where they were?

"Hello there, Brown Sugar!" He looked older than her father's age by at least ten years, with the Brylcreamed hair and pastel blue suit of a preacher. A Bible on the dashboard added to her suspicion. "Having car trouble?"

"Oh, I don't know what to do about it, sir! You're the first person who passed by in forever."

"Traveling cross-country as I do, having some idea how a car works is a necessity. I'm an evangelist, you see. Pastor Boyd Dove is the name."

She made sure to bend deep, from the waist, elbows resting on the sill of the open passenger window, a modern, electronic marvel which lowered without cranking by hand. Lustful eyes panned down the front of her dress, not low-cut but loose enough to lure him when bent over like this. "Why Pastor, you are the answer to my prayers!"

"Women across God's kingdom have had the same reaction, Darling. Let me pull over and we'll see if we can get your engine running as nicely as mine is."

As he walked toward her truck, she held her hands behind her and turned her body to and fro in a coy dance, flirtatious yet like an innocent girl.

"Oh, you are a pretty little thing. Let me get a look at you." One finger spun, signaling for her to turn around for his inspection, so she did. "Oh, you are put together very well. Very nice, indeed! I think we will get along quite splendid. Do me a favor and give me another turn like that last one, my dear."

"Why, thank you, sir." She obliged him with another look at her ass and legs.

As he circled back into her vision, a dark streak from behind a tree growing alongside the shoulder darted toward him. Eddie's approach so silent, she didn't hear a sound. Neither did Pastor Boyd Dove. Only when the knife slit open his neck did he have any notion a Siren had lured him onto the rocks.

Blood sprayed his shoulder and down the front of the powder blue coat, but Eddie held a hand across his face to aim it away from him. Some sprayed so close to Camilla that she jumped back, protecting her pretty new dress. The hand slipped down off his forehead to cover the two-inch gash as he dragged the preacher on the heels of shiny alligator shoes, out of sight behind the parked Studebaker.

"Preacher, I don't know if you are a praying man, but if you are, make your peace now."

Rev. Dove glanced up at the man who had just killed him. At only two inches, the gash to his neck missed his throat and vocal cords by at least a distance of the cut's width, so he still had the physical capacity of speech. Funny thing, dying—some find peace while facing the afterlife, their God or Valhalla, the hope of reincarnation. Others experience fear so all-consuming that words fail them.

The reverend's mouth moved, but no sound came out. *Please*, his lips formed as Camilla held out the milk bottle they cleaned in their room. Blood spurted against glass the instant his hand let off the pressure.

Please. No.

"Anything to confess, preacher man? Last chance."

From his car radio, still playing loud enough to hear in the stillness, Bing Crosby sang *Some Enchanted Evening* as his life blood filled one quart bottle after another. By the third, his flow slowed to a trickle and his eyes fell still, staring up toward the Heaven he was never to see any closer. Had he any comprehension that Eddie devoured more still from his neck with the girl looking on?

The Lincoln's powerful engine roared to life with the throaty growl of that MGM lion, holding as much promise as after the previews and newsreel when the lion announced the start of the main feature. And with one tap of his toes, all that power surged, and the engine roared. Gravel thunked like hail, kicked up into the wheel well by tires spinning for a second until they caught and thrust them toward the macadam.

"Nice." Camilla rolled her eyes and pressed a button on the dash. A deep baritone voice and haunting male chorus filled the air. "Oh, I love this song! His voice is so deep. Yippee-aye-a, Yippee-aye-oh..."

As she sang along, Eddie joined in for the last line of the chorus, an octave above Vaughn Monroe on the radio. "Ghost Rider in the Sky!"

Neither knew the full lyrics, so they filled in the rest with humming, but when the chorus rolled around again, they belted it out as the road burned up beneath the tires. Behind them, a glow in the mirror grew brighter despite the rapidly gaining distance.

As Vaughn Monroe's rich, rumbling voice faded out, Eddie said, "I've never owned a Lincoln before."

"Technically, you don't own this one."

"Possession is nine-tenths of the law."

"Hey, my lips are sealed. Rides much better than that old Studebaker."

"Better than my Auburn boattail, too."

For several seconds, the nagging cough that had been coming on for days prevented Camilla from responding. "You have an Auburn?"

"Well, it's probably gone forever. Maybe we'll keep this one."

"Do you reckon they will assume the Rev. Dove murdered that guy who owned the Studebaker?"

"Ooh, I didn't think about that—wouldn't that be fun? If they can figure out who the charred corpse is."

"Maybe better if they don't. We gave them a mystery killer back in Nebraska and nobody will be looking for the Reverend's Lincoln."

The Bible on the dashboard caught his eye. "Praise the Lord! Hey, have you ever considered acting as a profession? You had me convinced."

Behind them, the sky lit up as the gas tank ignited, but no one saw it. The only potential witnesses not stone dead for miles around were not looking back, focused instead on the journey lying ahead.

†

The rising glow on the eastern horizon lightened the view from the rear-view mirror when they came to the hotel in a former frontier town neither of them had heard of. Their chosen destination for the night, straight out of the *Green Book.*

For a small, no-name town, at two stories, the hotel's size surprised them. Here, in the middle of nowhere southern Nebraska, where their circuitous route led them, they expected little more than another roadside cinder block motel or, more likely, the old-fashioned bungalows, once the rage, which went out of style before the war. In fact, dating from the 1800s, in its heyday, this establishment must once have been quite the fashionable destination.

Turned oak columns lined a still-grand entryway, separating a seating area where guests sipped coffee while reading the morning paper from the entranceway. Later, the whole right side doubled as a bar. Fifty feet back, a burnished copper and maple registration counter stood at the center, flanked by a carpeted stairway and elevator. It matched the fancy mirrored bar in the front corner.

The vibe of this place was so palpable it virtually reached out and grabbed you by the throat the minute you pass through antique double doors of oak and beveled glass, much like stepping inside a haunted house. It had the luster of a grand building once fallen on hard times, only to be resurrected to eclipse its former glory. Every surface in the expansive lobby gleamed spotless.

Curious faces looked up from their papers or their china cups, a ripple that spread across the lounge in a wave. Other than his, each questioning face tracking his every move was dark.

A couple carrying suitcases walked past, just checked out. If Eddie rode an elephant through the lobby, their expressions would have been no less incredulous.

"Lookie at that," the man said.

"Bringing that yellow-ass man in here like that," the woman said, her inflection a mixture of question and distaste.

Dignified and formal in bearing, double-breasted suit with buttons reflecting golden in the overhead light, the clerk watched them approach the counter. "Yes, ma'am?"

"We would like a room," she answered.

The clerk regarded the blue-eyed man standing beside her, from waist to blond hair, and if the counter did not block the view of his bottom half, no doubt would have scanned down to his shoes. Then, pointedly focusing his attention back to Camilla, asked, "For how many?"

"Two."

"One bed or two?"

"Two," Eddie said.

At the same time, she answered, "One."

The clerk slid the registry to her and took a key from the wall. After examining the key like he had never seen it before, returned it and picked out another one, instead.

"Don't mind them," she said as they walked up the stairs toward room 217.

"What was that about?"

"They think you are colored."

"Me?"

"Don't act so surprised. Haven't you ever met a blonde-haired colored person before?"

"Compared to me, everyone else is colored. Sometimes I feel so pale, everyone looks glowing pink or tan by comparison."

"They assume you are light-complexioned. A single drop of blood makes you Black."

"In that case, I have gallons more than a single drop running through me. Funny."

"What's funny?"

"Well, I was born White, but I drank myself Black after death."

She smacked him on the arm. "It's not funny—don't make me laugh about it!"

"It is pretty funny."

"You don't understand. There is a hierarchy. In our community, some light-skinned colored people look down on those who are dark, and some dark people look down on lighter ones as not true Black folks. So they are wondering why a dark-skinned girl is with a man they assume is passing."

"So we aren't allowed in white hotels and they don't want us at the hotels in the *Green Book*, either?"

"At least they allow you to stay here."

"What if they discovered my colored blood is by choice, not an accident of birth I had no control over?" They had arrived at the room. He slipped in the key and opened the door.

†

A Mercury dime clinked into the coin slot and Eddie retrieved a newspaper before holding open the door for Camilla. A hazel-eyed hostess looked down and made a tsk-tsk sound while shaking her head.

"Table for two, please."

The hostess replied, "She can eat in the kitchen, not the dining room."

"Excuse me?"

"We don't serve Coloreds in the dining room."

"According to the *Green Book*, you do." Two blocks from their hotel, they selected this diner on the route back to the highway.

"Under new management. Can't you see the sign?"

"Table for two," he repeated, and her face relaxed, her eyes suddenly glassy.

"Follow me."

Less than a minute after taking their seats, the owner waddled out, a fat man in white covered by a greasy cook's apron flanking him. "We cannot—oh, dear. Did our hostess not inform you we run a white-only establishment?"

"She told me. What will you have, Honey?"

She answered, "Why don't we just go?"

"Because we are hungry and are going to eat a delicious breakfast. Isn't that right, sir?"

"You can eat whatever you want, as long as she eats hers in the kitchen with the staff."

"Are you offering her a job?"

Visibly flustered, the manager's chunky face betrayed an internal struggle to decide whether this customer was playing the fool or if he was dealing with an actual moron. "No, that's not —we don't serve negroes in the dining room."

A family at the next table looked on with approval at such superb entertainment. "Please, such language. There are children here." Too fast for the eye to see, Eddie had the owner's tie firmly in his grip and yanked it down, stopping the man's chin two inches from the table. With his free hand, he pulled the short end of the tie until the owner's face turned purple as an eggplant. The chef took a step, but stopped when Eddie said, "And you stay back, Curly, or I'll pull this so tight your boss' head might pop clean off."

The owner croaked, "What can we get you?"

"Pancakes. You too, Dear?" When she nodded, he continued. "Two stacks. A side of bacon, coffee. And I can see the griddle from here, so if anyone spits on our food, we will see it. I'm sure nobody wants anyone's face pressed on that hot griddle, do they? Of course, if we find so much as a hair in one of our flapjacks, your fat jowls and that of anyone who comes within spitting distance of our food will stay on that griddle until they turn darker than her skin. Have I made myself clear?"

"Very clear, sir."

He straightened out the trembling man's tie when he let go. "Don't test me. The smell of burning human flesh? Most people find it nauseating. Don't let's find out if any of your customers share that opinion."

"I will supervise the chef personally," the owner assured him, since his fat jowls were on the line.

While they waited, Eddie flipped through the main section while Camilla read the local news. "Hmph."

"What is it?" she asked.

He held up a small headline on page 3 for her to see. *L.A. Doctor Accused Of Molesting Daughter, Aborting Grandchild.* "I know them."

"Who do you know?"

"Dr. Hodel and Tamar, his daughter. They had me out to their house all the time. He has parties with all the Hollywood types, nearly every night."

"Did you meet any stars?"

"Oh, sure, too many to remember. His wife, Dorero? She was married to John Huston, and he's always there. I suspect they're still sleeping together, not that Dr. Hodel cares. He's slept with half the young stars you see on screen."

She gasped, mouth forming an O. "Are you sure?"

"Positive. Rather openly—saw it myself, with my own two eyes. Never seen so many naked women as I saw at his parties! All this about Tamar, though? That's a shocker. She's a real sweetheart. That's too bad."

"Do you believe he did it?"

"Nothing that man did should surprise me, I suppose. Dr. Hodel, he's..." he leaned forward to whisper, "he suspects the truth. About me. Knows, really."

"Aren't you afraid he'll tell someone?"

"Not with what I know about him. Trust me—it's much worse than this story here."

"Your pancakes, sir," the waitress said.

"Serve the lady first. Don't worry, I won't tell the Grand Dragon you did. I can keep a secret."

THE PAST AND THE FUTURE

"Why did you do that to her? To the Red Dahlia?"

Narrow slits of blue, black and white glare at her, head slowing moving forward in what is most decidedly not a friendly gesture. "Why does that concern you? Do you believe every woman I feed from ends up as she did?"

She nodded like a chastened grade school student. This was the first time he had been curt with her, until then either answering questions honestly or dodging them with a sly smile or a joke to remind her of her place. Then again, she must have been burying these questions inside her since before she decided crashing head-on into a pine tree was the best option available to her. This one, though, got under his skin.

Another day's drive closer to Denver should have been relieving, but she felt awful—exhausted and coughing constantly. And feeling sick always made her cranky. Missing her home and family did not help.

"Is that all you believe you are to me?"

Her head swiveled from side to side so slowly it appeared an illusion. "But sometimes I do wonder."

"After beginning the process with you? Is that really what you believe?"

"Sometimes it is hard to know how you think. Like now, for example."

"What do you mean, *like now*?"

"Talking about her brings out all sorts of anger." Her intonation almost made it sound like a question.

"It angers me you believe I tried to make a prostitute my companion in immortality. Granted, a beautiful whore, but still a whore."

"A virgin is better?"

"A pure heart is better. Sure, blood of virgins has a certain richness, but do you have any idea what immortality is?" He was standing by then, speaking with his hands and body like he never did, still obviously unsettled.

"Then what? Are you going to tell me you fell in love, and a person cannot help who they fall in love with?"

"I am not a person."

"Does that mean you cannot love?"

"Love is fleeting emotion. It can last a lifetime, but can it last ten lifetimes? A hundred? For most, love dies in a heartbeat."

"So, what do you see in me? Is it more than love?"

A handful of hair at her neck pulled her face as close to his as her diminutive height allowed. "Until you have become like me, you will never understand genuine desire or the clarity of seeing a person for who they truly are."

"Maybe you just enjoy the prospect of spending the next ten lifetimes staying in *Green Book* hotels and hearing people call you a nigger-lover."

His face relaxed until a hint of a smile emerged. Then he laughed and kissed her. Not some sweet make-up kiss for yelling at her, but a kiss of unrestrained passion. "That is why."

By then, she felt totally confused. "You're already an outcast!"

"That's what draws me, your way of seeing through the bullshit. And the fact that you are funnier than you realize you are is a fine trait."

"Then it's true?"

"No one has understood me since..."

"Since when?"

"My family died."

"When was that?"

"Fifty years ago, some longer. I could not face them after returning from the dead, so I ran. Sometimes I wonder if they realized they buried an empty coffin, knew I escaped and left before they did to me what they did to the one who made me."

"What did they do?"

"They killed her."

"But aren't vampires immortal?"

"In most instances. But if our bodies are destroyed in certain ways, it kills us."

She pulled him close. "Turns out bullets aren't one of those ways."

"Who knew shooting me in the heart might bind us together?"

"What about silver bullets?"

"Good question. I've only been shot once."

"Hmm. That gives me an idea." She unbuttoned his shirt, seductively working down until exposing the still unhealed bullet hole.

"Tell me of your desire."

"I want you. I need you."

"What are you willing to sacrifice for me?"

Her answer more breathed than spoken as she pressed her virgin body against his. "Anything."

"Kill for me?"

"I killed for you that night—well, lured someone for you to kill."

They kissed, this time longer. He pulled the zipper down to where it ended at the lovely curve where her back became her hips. "Next time, it will be your turn to kill."

Her tongue lapped at his bloodless wound, trying to coax it out of him, but only when he drove his thumbnail in did the crimson stain her lips and the taste began to fuel her desire. Her dress hit the floor, and he laid her back across the bed, her lips suckling his chest all the way down.

Several climaxes later and nearly sated, she lay atop his

body. His skin felt alive against hers, even if it was not. Her hand traced the source of her fulfillment before wandering around his chest. Across his chest ran a two-inch scar, ending halfway through his left nipple. "I never noticed this before."

"We've never been in such a brightly lit room."

"What happened?"

"This is where I fed the one who made me. Well, one of the places."

"Can I feed from you there, too?"

"Someday," he answered as his hand ran down her back to the curve of her bottom and his chest became her pillow.

†

"What were you like—you know, before?"

"Before I died? A farm boy. Pretty boring, to tell the truth, but an ordinary, honest life. The farm was in our family for generations, so we all worked it. In the spring we planted, tended the crops all summer, harvested the fruit, then in the fall came the big harvest. My parents insisted their kids all get an education, so we all graduated high school, too."

"Farmers come in various shapes and sizes, but are not all alike, are they?"

"Well, in that case, similar to what I am now, I suppose. That's what I tell myself, if ignoring an obvious difference. Other than a few fistfights, I never harmed anyone. I was married."

"Oh, really? Tell me about her."

"She was the most beautiful girl in Washington County. Some say my kid sister was, but I don't really count her. Golden hair with eyes a little lighter than mine. Tall, but aside from that, her figure was similar to yours… only paler. For a while, I was the luckiest man in the county, maybe all Rhode Island, before I left her a widow in her early twenties."

Questions long bottled up inside flowed out until the sun rose high in the sky. Questions about him—about them. But they were not the only questions gnawing at her.

"What do you suppose I will be like when I transform?"

"Well, let's hope you will be the marvelous creature you are now."

THE GIRL

Even as she fell deeper into her illness each day, Camilla also fell deeper in love.

No, love is not the proper word for it, but what other word suffices? Lust? Obsession? The possibility that he was controlling her with that power of his—that doubt she pushed from her mind.

Her mother would kill her if she knew how her proud Negro girl let a white man put his hands all over her body, how she kisses him with the passion they sing about in those songs. How she touches him. Daddy would kill him.

What would they do if they saw their darling baby girl drink blood from his chest?

It might make them feel better knowing that wound she drank from she inflicted upon him herself. A bullet she fired, and that her aim had been true. The knowledge that she was with a man who cannot be harmed, impervious to a bullet through his heart? Another prospect she did not allow her brain to consider.

Most nights, they slept in the roomy and comfortable rear seat of the Lincoln, their arms and legs wrapped around each other like lovers. Stuck on these back roads and avoiding large cities also bypassed most of the hotels and restaurants accommodating to Black customers listed in the *Green Book*.

That morning, all memory how they both ended up without a stitch of clothing faded into oblivion. With only a blanket to keep away the cold, she wished for a warm body to cuddle against, warm arms around her. His body tepid, barely room temperature, but his skin and muscles felt comforting, so she nestled in, pressing herself against him, ignoring that she woke up in the arms of a corpse.

He stirred. "Oh, you're awake. How do you feel today?"

"Terrible. Did you get the tag number of the truck that ran over me?"

Her quip brought a chuckle. That her silly jokes unfailingly produced such amusement further endeared him to her. "The wine did that to you."

"What wine?"

"Remember, you made me stop and buy that big bottle of Chianti at that roadside stand? The one with the wicker covering woven around it?"

"Oh. Oh, sort of. How much did we drink?"

He rummaged blindly around the floor behind his back until he found the bottle, held it up and tilted it toward her. The sight of a single, blood red drop falling toward her face made her flinch, but only that one came out. He licked the dregs of the bottle off her cheek.

"Tell me we didn't…"

"Didn't what?"

"Eddie, we're naked as two jaybirds."

"Of course not! Do you think I would take that treasure from you while out-of-your-gourd blotto?"

"You're a murderer. You cut a girl in half and set a minister on fire."

"Well, he was going to Hell anyway, so it seemed appropriate."

"Far be it for someone capable of mass murder to take advantage of a drunk girl."

"True." His hand caressed her body, stopping when her eyes closed and she let out a gasp. For an instant, his inappropriate lover's touch made the pain in her head and chest and the aches in every joint of her body melt away with unspeakable pleasure. He pushed her face to his chest, where she tongued the bullet hole until the coppery taste of blood coated it, comforting her. A more powerful wave of pleasure pushed her illness and the wine's revenge further from her mind. "Drink, my dear. Blood is the world's best hangover cure."

†

Somewhere on the high plains of eastern Colorado, he killed a pretty, young blonde over a bathroom.

They stopped at a Gloe Brother's Service Station in the middle of nowhere. After filling up, Eddie pulled the car around back so no one could see her slip inside the ladies' room. As she emerged, a girl maybe a year or two older than her came around the corner at a trot, heading for the ladies' bathroom. The shocking sight of a Black girl stepping out brought her skidding to a halt on the dirt and gravel.

"That's for whites only!"

"Sorry, they don't have a colored bathroom."

The girl gawked like she'd never seen a person with her color skin. "That's because we don't have colored people 'round here."

"Is there a problem?"

Relief spread over the girl's face when a white man arrived to help out. *Now we were getting somewhere—he'll know how to handle an uppity girl like her!* "This Negress was using the ladies' room!"

"Well, we can't have that!"

With a look dripping with superiority and disgust, she turned to Camilla. "Thank you."

"Tell you what," the man said, pinching her cheeks in one hand to crank her head toward him. His fingers wedged her jaw open from the sides; her chocolate-hazel eyes widened and she let out a little squeal. "Why don't I take you far away from this tainted bathroom? Would you like that?"

The girl nodded, although her eyes were still filled with terror.

Camilla assumed she'd run the second Eddie released his grip on her face, but he had gotten inside her brain with that ability he has, and she instead willingly climbed into the back of the Lincoln. As always, he made it a practice to wait outside for her. He tossed over the keys. "Honey, why don't you drive for a spell? I'll keep her company back here."

He did not kill her—not immediately. She was beautiful when she didn't have that hateful expression of superiority on her gorgeous little face. He told Camilla to find a secluded spot. "Where? Do I look like I'm from this neighborhood? She already told you people like me don't live around these parts."

Gentle fingers lifted straw-colored hair behind one ear. "What's your name?"

"Gretchen."

"That's a beautiful name for a beautiful girl." Camilla made a gagging sound but kept driving. "Suppose a visitor from out of town—me, for instance—wanted to date a beautiful girl. In private. Where would they go?"

"Kimble's Lake. Everyone parks out there."

"I suppose everyone will be parked out there tonight, won't they?"

"Nah, it's a school night. Everyone's supposed to be home by now."

"Why are you out this late on a school night?"

"You ain't gonna tell my Paw, are you?"

"Gretchen, the last thing I want is for your Paw to find out I ever met you."

"Whew! Cause he'd wear out my ass with a switch if he finds out I was out after curfew with the Fuller brothers and Kitty Wingo."

"Don't worry, darlin', the only person who's going to touch your little ass tonight is me."

She laughed harshly. "That is some world-class flirting, and I don't even remember your name."

"Be a doll and give our chauffeur directions to Kimble's Lake."

In the quiet broken only by crickets and croaking frogs, Camilla paced to the far edge of the pond. Watching him kill the trucker, the preacher and the others was bad enough, but seeing him with another girl lit a fire in her cheeks and made her whole body go numb. Maybe he wasn't intending to kill her—at least that possibility calmed her a little.

So, she sat and tossed pebbles into the water and waited. And waited.

Something had to have gone wrong. Her jealousy gave way to worry. *What is taking so long?* Worried that this farmer's daughter had somehow turned the tables on him, she rushed back to the car to check. For the rest of her life, she wished she had not.

From inside Peggy Lee crooned *Bali Ha'i* on the radio. There Gretchen sat on Eddie's lap, shirt off and facing away from him while he squeezed her as if trying to fill a milk bucket. Eddie's face was behind her ear, and his body rocked with the same passion when he fed from her. Most of the blonde hair dangling on that side was wet, stained red. The part that shocked her, though, was the girl's face. She was dead, or nearly so, eyes glazed and staring straight ahead as Eddie squeezed her boob while sucking her life from a hole in her neck.

Her lips, so full and luscious back at the gas station, now limp and expressionless. All that bright red lipstick kissed off. They had turned a bluish gray. Dead.

Sickened by the sight as she was, something compelled her to watch. This was her future—both as victim and when he brought her back to be his vampire sidekick.

When the girl's head flopped back and to the side, he rolled her wilted body off him onto the seat. As he moved down to consume more of Gretchen, he spied a shadow peering through the window and smiled at her, his lips and cheek smeared with blood. When he lay down beside her and continued his feeding, he held this dead girl in his arms like a lover.

The rocks scattered around in this excellent Midwest farming soil were too small to weigh her body down, so Eddie floated her into some cattails along one side of the lake. Moonlight reflected brightly off her bare skin as she floated, face down and arms out to the sides. So pale was that skin, she took on the image of a ghost, motionless save for shadowy hair floating around her like a halo or Medusa.

She didn't ask why he took so long to drink the tiny amount of blood in her body. She didn't need to. That girl could not have weighed 95 pounds soaking wet, so he should have finished draining her in a fraction of the time it took to empty his male victims. He may be a vampire, but he was also a man. At least he retained a man's worst parts.

"You'd better drive; you know how sleepy feeding can make me." She snatched the key from his hand. "What's the matter?"

"You killed her."

"You know I need more blood now that I'm feeding for two."

"That's not what I mean, and you know it."

"What do you mean?"

"Is it because she's white, or do you enjoy all the girls that much?"

"Oh, I see. You haven't seen me feed from another woman before."

"What I saw was a hell of a lot more than feeding."

"Pull over."

"Are you nuts? We need to be in the next county by sunrise."

"Pull the damn car over!" When she instead sped up, coaxing the Lincoln's powerful engine down this deserted dirt road, his voice grew more insistent. "There isn't a tree for miles around, if that's your plan. Now, stop the car!"

Nothing but flat corn fields surrounded them; the last tree they saw a willow weeping over the lake, so she mashed the brake pedal hard. Tires locked up and slid a hundred yards over gravel until the car jerked to a halt. Tears streamed down her face. "How could I be stupid enough to think you found me special?"

"You are special!" She jerked away her hand when he tried

to hold it. "If I wanted her instead of you, your body would be floating in that lake. Do you think I give my blood to just any girl?"

"Did you let her drink your blood?"

"Hell no! If I had to spend five more minutes listening to her, I'd be begging for someone to kill me and telling them exactly how to do it."

"How do you do it? How can someone like you be killed?"

"Really?"

"How can I kill you?"

"Just drive, will ya?"

"You told me to stop; I stopped. Stakes don't work, you told me that."

At first, he stared up at the ceiling before turning to her. Somehow, the dashboard lights allowed the two discs staring at her to reflect their color at her. "Fire."

"Fire will kill you?"

"I believe so. You may need to cut my heart out and burn it. Maybe the liver, too. I know that works. There is no manual for this. Now that you know, you can kill me today while I sleep. Do you believe I trust anyone else on this planet enough to tell them exactly how to destroy me?"

For the second time that night, numbness enveloped her entire body. A glow up ahead, a car heading their way, spurred her to get the dead man's Lincoln underway again, across a landscape blurred by tears.

ROCKY MOUNTAIN HIGH

Visitors from the east catch their first view of Denver long before they come near the city limits. The jagged fangs of the Rocky Mountains rise as a menacing backdrop while the lights of the city still lie below the horizon.

The last stop on the western edge of the Great Plains, majestic granite peaks jut skyward to form the city's western city limits. Keep driving, suddenly you find yourself in the mountains and have officially crossed into the Wild West.

She had been sleeping more in the last several days; the illness progressing rapidly. Less blood in her veins each day, and what remained changing. At least, that is how he imagined it works. He massaged her thigh.

"Wake up, Sleeping Beauty."

"Where are we?"

"See light glowing in the distance, at the foot of the mountains? That, my dear, is Denver."

"It's a long way to drive for an omelet."

"They say they're worth it."

Back arched, fingers stretched against the headliner, then she rubbed her eyes. "I never imagined mountains could be so huge!"

"Wait to see them in the daytime—they are magnificent."

"Have you been here before?"

"Only passing through. Spent a few months in Colorado

Springs."

"When was that?"

"A long time ago."

"Look, about that girl a couple of days ago. I get cranky when I'm sick. I'm sorry."

Still holding her thigh, he gave two quick squeezes. "And I am sorry about… I never meant to hurt you."

A couple of miles passed in dark silence. His hand remained on her leg, and she did nothing to discourage him from continuing to massage it. "Can you feel love?"

"Love is a human emotion—I am no longer human." It was a lie, of course, one he almost had convinced himself to accept.

"If you believe only humans can love, the first thing I am going to do when we get to Denver is buy you a puppy. A cute, fuzzy one—a Cocker Spaniel or a poodle tiny enough to fit into the palm of your hand. Let's see how long you stick with that story." A satisfied laugh turned into another coughing fit. The cruelest phase of the illness. One he remembered well.

"It changes your way of thinking, about everything. You'll see."

"Want to know what I think? You're afraid to admit that you are capable of love. Don't ask me to explain why: fear, most likely. Fear of being vulnerable, fear of being alone. Afraid no one will ever love someone who travels around the country killing people." Even in the dim car interior, the way her eyes moved in that side-glance of hers was unmistakably sexy.

"Well, since you know all about how this works, then you must be about ready to complete your transformation."

"Did you mean it when you promised to stay with me through eternity?"

"Sure did." Another squeeze. "Of course, you know how to get rid of me, so we can dispense with divorce if you grow tired of me in four, five hundred years."

A moment in quiet contemplation, jazz playing on the radio. "When I was sleeping a while ago, I had this strange dream, or maybe my brain just wandering."

"About what?"

"How I'd like to die. Well, afterward. How Black Dahlia became a legend because of how she died. I suppose Red Dahlia will, too. Already is, I guess. Did you notice she is in the headlines everywhere we've stopped along the way?"

What he also noticed is Camilla did not mention he appeared in the headlines, too; complete with his mug shot on the front page of papers from coast to coast. Which explained endless back roads through the tiniest of towns, sleeping in the back seat and the looping route traced out all over the fold-up map.

"We might make a proper vampire out of you yet! Not that you need to worry about dying, but how did you decide you'd want to go if you didn't become immortal?"

"Not sure, exactly. Something witchy, I think. Spooky. Not cut in half, though. Black Dahlia is already taken, so they'll have no idea what name to give me, anyway. Hopefully, something more specific will come in the next dream. Anyway, just thought you should know. You made them immortal in their own way."

†

Every passing day deepened snow on jagged peaks to the west, and every passing night those mountaintops glowed brighter in the moonlight. Camilla slept most of the time now, her body failing and frail. Often, she awakened to the sight of him sitting on the bed waiting for her. Once, he waited to share with her the news.

"Are you ready for a party?"

"Surely you jest! I must look like hell."

"To tell the truth, you look beautiful. It is a funny illness in that way."

"What kind of party?"

"Halloween."

"Will they allow a mixed couple at this party?"

"A group of free-thinking Pagans and such hold this

shindig every year. By invite only, and while you were sleeping, guess who scored us both invitations? Sounds like fun. Strange group. Coven, actually. A lot of them call themselves witches."

"Do you really enjoy hanging out with a bunch of weirdos, like witches?"

"You'd expect a person whose boo is a vampire might be a little more open-minded."

"Well, I feel like hell. A party is not at the top of my priorities list."

"Yeah, about that. Will be a shame to return the dress I bought for you. Red and black and sexy; I had to guess your current size." Since buying those dresses for her on their journey, she had shed so much weight, he guessed, two full sizes smaller. "I will feed there—that's the whole point—but I went out and fed earlier so you can feed from me."

"Will it make me feel better?"

Without bothering to unbutton, he peeled his shirt over his head. "Drink as much of my blood as you need to keep you going all night."

†

High atop one foothill on the outskirts of town stands a Victorian mansion overlooking the city rapidly metastasizing in all the other directions across the plains below. Nearly one hundred years old, grim and imposing, its impressive size is all people in the city below knew of the house. Up close, its ornate gingerbread or the round tower at one corner, topped with a conical roof, might have overcome perception of its mass. However, Denver's population kept a safe distance for as long as anyone remembered. It looked too haunted.

The land had been in the mysterious de Gifford family since the city's initial incarnation as Auraria, when a minor gold rush briefly drew prospectors who soon fled to richer strikes elsewhere. A great-granddaughter of the house's original builder now owned it. Hostess of this soiree, she carried out this role by greeting arriving guests in the grand foyer.

"Welcome to Goblin Hall," she swept her arm to usher them in. "I am Eleanor de Gifford."

"Eddie and Camilla," he introduced themselves.

"No last names? How deliciously mysterious! *Entrez vous*! And these costumes—who are your alter-egos for tonight?"

Eddie had also found time to buy himself a formal white dinner jacket and black slacks. "The Count and Countess de Sanguine."

Goblin Hall, their hostess explained in response to Camilla's query, was named after a Norman estate in England where her family originated. "Sadly, nothing but Medieval ruins remain of the namesake. My family practiced necromancy there, so it seemed fitting to name this modern version after the original."

The hostess led Camilla deeper into the mansion by the arm. "My, my, my, you are a vision of loveliness! Is the Count your man?"

The two women turned mirror-image smiles at him. "I guess so."

"That is too bad. Not for you, sugar, but for the rest of us. The men will be as disappointed to learn you are taken as I am you have your claws in Count Sanguine."

To be fair, Eddie's taste in women's clothing was exquisite. If anything, he undersold it. Being a shame to return a dress so beautiful did not capture such a tragic waste—it would have been criminal. His estimate of the size she wore had been perfect, with a few minor alterations.

"If Mama got wind of me wearing a dress this sexy, she'd lock me in my room until I turn twenty-one," She explained when he gave it to her, temporarily filling her with enough energy to do a twirl for his full inspection. "Well? How do I look?"

His hand caressed the shape of her side from ribs to hip. "Dangerous."

Judged by the attention she received entering the parlor

full of witches, most everyone agreed with his assessment. A remarkable few of those looks contained any shred of disapproval as the hostess made her announcement to the coven. "The Count and Countess de Sanguine!"

Among the party-goers were witches of the east and west in black dresses with tall, pointed hats, as well as a smattering of Wiccan priestesses. Witches from Salem in Pilgrim attire and traditional Scottish witches. Three elderly women, undoubtedly sisters, wore gray rags that looked straight out of Mac Beth. Several men wore black robes with pentagrams hanging from their necks. At least half the guests were witches of every imaginable sort, while others were adorned as everything from medieval royalty to a Jack the Ripper laughing with a bearded Carmen Miranda. Well over half the guests were women.

Two women rushed up: one of the Salem witches and a Native American wearing an outfit that looked quite authentic and ancient. "Greetings! I am Goody Prescott and this is Lilith White Bear."

Choosing not to inquire if those were real names or of characters they portrayed—after all, the hostess introduced them as Count and Countess—the stunning Indian woman attracted their full attention. Camilla's eyes went to the intricate and beautiful bead work adorning deerskin covering her from neck to wrist and an ankle-length skirt, while Eddie admired everything else about her. About thirty, and despite her age and physical beauty, Lilith gave off the unmistakable scent of virginity.

Goody Prescott was probably ten years older than the Indian witch, clearly intoxicated and just as clearly enamored with Eddie. "Let's get you some refreshments," she said, hooking the arms of both the Count and Countess in her elbows to lead them to the dining table covered with sumptuous delicacies and a side-table laden with wine bottles and two punch bowls. "I presume vampires prefer red wine?"

Camilla's cheeks reddened. "I'm not old enough, but thank you."

"Don't be silly—we're all old enough here."

Whether any of them had actually harnessed the white or black powers of magic, one fact was indisputable: these witches could throw a party. It would truly be a shame to kill such lovely people.

Eddie observed Lilith held no glass in her hands. "I notice you aren't drinking."

"Alcohol is forbidden; it dulls my medicine," the Native priestess answered. Her natural braids were long enough for the wrapped ends to rest on beaded breasts.

"And her medicine is the best," Goody said, handing Camilla a glass, then Eddie, her other hand rubbing his shoulder. "If you're lucky enough for her to offer you some, try it!"

†

Goody Prescott was far from the only witch intent on seducing Eddie, and when Camilla disappeared with Lilith, a flirtatious crowd encircled him. Whether Eddie or the coquettish coven were more entertained was likely a matter of perspective. Perhaps most intrigued was the elderly witch who invited Eddie the evening he sneaked into her curio shop just before closing. Her acute senses detected a strange kindred spirit, and she knew how a handsome young man such as him would please the younger witches, eager to test out their love spells and perhaps a potion or two.

Eventually, he dragged himself away to track down the Shoshone medicine woman who was deep in conversation with Camilla.

"An *Unk Tehi.*"

"A what?"

"In Lakota tradition, there are spirit creatures who make people disappear. Males are *Unk Tehi* and females are *Unk Cecula.*"

Camilla bumped her shoulder against his arm several times playfully as he came to stand close. "Sounds like our *Unk Tehi* here. He's been known to make a few people disappear."

"Should I let you discuss me in private?" Returning the smile and the bicep bump, Eddie said to Lilith, "As you were saying…"

"Well, since I am Shoshone, not Lakota, don't consider me an expert. What I know is *Unk Cecula* is the horned serpent whose eyes are fire, her voice is thunder, and she has the fangs of a rattlesnake. Clouds of smoke ring her mouth and she cannot be harmed by arrows or war clubs. Anyone who dares to gaze at her will go mad. *Unk Tehi* is her mate."

Camilla repeatedly poked him in the chest. "It's you—*Unk Tehi!*" To Lilith, she said, "Have you noticed his eyes? They glow like those blue flames in the Bunsen burners at school. *Unk Tehi* is better than anything we've got. The closest we have is Uncle Tom."

"*Unk Tehi* is about a million times better," he agreed.

Eventually, he left them to continue their conversation, happy Camilla had found a friend and eager to track down some blood. Goody had been the first to ask if they were actual vampires, which struck him as quite curious, but he dodged coyly each time someone posed the question. A delightful, sinister idea occurred to him, and this seemed the perfect opportunity to try something he never had. When he found himself momentarily alone with the attractive and willing Salem witch, he posed a question of his own.

"Seems to me you are curious about vampires."

One finger, starting at his elbow, ran up his arm to the side of his neck. "Who isn't? When I was about the same age as the countess, *Dracula* played in movie theaters. The Bijoux in my hometown. He has haunted many a dream since. Very naughty dreams. Are you and the countess an item?"

"Very much so."

"She's adorable, for a colored girl. Funny how they seek out others like them."

"What do you mean?"

"Lilith and her. You know, they seem to find one of their own."

"They have more in common than meets the eye." Her abrasive comment gave him pause, but he decided to go ahead with it. "Do you still have those dreams?"

"Sure do, Sugar—or should I call you, Count?"

"This is one instance where Hollywood does not do justice. Reality far surpasses what they are permitted to show on the silver screen."

"Oh, really? Do tell!" Her light brown eyes sparkled, and she rubbed one bosom against his arm.

"Would you prefer I tell you, or show you?" His nose pushed aside her hair, and he placed his lips against her ear for maximum effect. "Bring Lilith with you, and I will make sure your dreams come true."

✝

First, the colors changed.

Lilith's pale tan dress shimmered from blue to green and back again, and her beads flowed down her chest like a stream over a waterfall. Then some witches starting changing shape, similar to how those mirrors in carnival funhouses distort people.

"Wow! It's beautiful!"

Lilith asked, "Are you having visions?"

A look of wonder plastered on her face, Camilla leaned close and stared. "Your eyes are spinning! Are mine as beautiful as yours?"

"Yours are beautiful," she assured the countess, who was moving her hands above her head like clouds, a sight fascinating enough to divert her from spinning eyes.

"What was in that terrible tea?"

"Peyote. Has your vision quest begun?"

Camilla again looked at her, nodding seriously before her face broke into an uncontrollable giggle. Lilith was the most beautiful woman she had ever seen—even if her face formed the exact image of a mountain lion. A forked tongue of a snake flicked through her full lips, making her wonder if it would feel as good on her body as Eddie's did? In answer to her question, the tongue extended the distance to her body, and like two fingers, the forks caressed her bare upper arm. Her shoulder. Her breasts.

Wonderful as they felt, it paled compared to Eddie.

Soon as she thought of him, there he was behind Lilith, feeling her breasts as Lilith's tongue felt hers, and that made her giggle again. "Where is he?"

"Who?" asked the medicine woman.

"Eddie, my Count."

"What do you see?"

"He is making love to you."

"Is he doing anything else?"

"Making love to me, too."

"Is he your lover?"

"No! And we need to do something about that."

"You love him?"

Her head nodded, a shy grin on her lips. "He loves me and I love him, even though he treats me like a child. Honestly, I'm too old to be a virgin!"

"Once a man takes you as a woman, you no longer possess the same magic. It becomes a unique form of magic, but if you wish to retain the power you have now, then you must remain intact long as you can."

"I want new magic!"

Goody Prescott floated up on a cloud behind Lilith, where Eddie had been, and whispered something in her ear. Not that it mattered to her, because the world was perfect, exactly as it existed in that perfect moment. The only time she ever felt such euphoria was when Eddie held her so tenderly in his arms, his skin against hers, tasting her blood as she drank his from his chest. Now, she yearned for Eddie to share in this new form of passion.

"Come." Lilith held out a velveteen hand to help her to her feet. Standing, the world tilted crazily under her like riding waves on the ocean. The two witches surfed gracefully over the earthly waves and kept her afloat. The waves swept her through the mansion and upstairs to the third floor.

✝

"What did you do to her?"

Lilith regarded him differently now. "We drank peyote tea."

Although he did not know exactly what peyote was, he had heard of its mystical, mind-bending qualities. Ordinarily, giving a vulnerable girl like her such powerful drugs might have upset him, but after all she had been through, let her have her fun. And what fun she was having! Soon as Goody brought him to this bedroom on the top floor overlooking Denver spreading out below, Camilla kissed his neck and her hand kneaded his chest over the unhealing wound.

Her lips voracious on his skin, and he pulled her tight to his side. Indian medicine turned this adorable kitten into a black panther, and he saw nothing wrong with that.

"The Count has a proposition for us," Goody informed Lilith, who stood weaving back and forth like a palm tree in a hurricane. Peyote must affect her differently. "He wishes to sample our blood."

"Hold out your tongue," Lilith approached and, taking some bitter powder from a small leather pouch, rubbed it sensuously over his tongue. She did the same to Goody, then with Camilla, although she only gave her a fraction of the powder the others received. Her finger, run the length of Camilla's bright pink tongue leaving a trail of grayish-green powder, sent a chill down his spine. Then she held the pouch open for him and stuck out her own tongue, so he traced a small amount on the pink tongue as she had done on his, from back to the tip.

Her pale tongue curled around his finger and, when he reached the tip, licked a few circles around it before taking his finger up to the second knuckle in her full lips and sucked every remaining trace of peyote from it. Such an erotic display made him marvel at the restraint required for a woman her age to protect her virginity. So much so, he leaned in to smell her blood through the thin skin over her pulsing arteries. The delicious scent left no doubt.

"Goody, shall we start with you?"

To avoid even the remote possibility of influencing her, he had avoided looking into Goody's eyes since they arrived in the room. She gave a nervous little smile and offered her neck, pulling back dark hair out of his way.

"Don't worry, I won't bite. It isn't like the movies." From behind her, his tiny blade sliced through her fragrant vein and his lips wrapped around the gash. Camilla sat, keeping watch from the floor while Lilith swayed in a breeze only she felt, absorbing the sight. His hands caressed her stomach, her breasts. First her eyes rolled back, then her head and she melted into him, which may have been due to the mescaline in his blood —or hers.

A substantial woman with generous breasts and a thin waist, when fully melted, he poured her onto the bed and lay atop her gyrating hips beneath him as if having sex—which, with the peyote's help, may have been how her mind explained the soul-crushing pleasure flooding through her body. The effects of the drug heightened Eddie's pleasure, too, and he had to take special care not to drain her completely.

He left a pallid and panting Goody limp on the bed and also sought to avoid Lilith's eyes, but they were too exotic and lovely. He managed to keep his mind clear, focusing instead on the perfect braid in his hand, fingers following the interlocking pattern all the way to her breast. For a virgin, it surprised him she did not flinch, but the backs of his fingers only brushed her flesh lightly as he fingered her braid and the loose three-inch tail at the end.

"Your blood smells oh so sweet. You are a virgin, are you not?" With his cheek pressed against hers, he felt her head nod, rather than seeing it. "May I taste you, as well?"

"Are you a skin-walker?"

"No."

"You must promise to leave me as you found me, as you have honored this girl."

"I plan to worship you, not defile you."

Camilla was on the bed with Goody, her dark lips against the Salem witch's skin creating a vision of such extraordinary beauty, he had to stop to watch. She, too, watched him as he stepped behind Lilith, hand on her shoulder, the other drawing blood with his small knife, bright red against olive skin. The medicine woman flinched, then tilted her head, and he quickly took her pain into him through his lips and tongue.

Blood sweet as cherries filled his mouth as her supple, firm breast filled his hand. She felt much younger than her apparent age, firm and powerful, and the only blood he recalled for years tasting as sweet came from the tiny girl sucking the life out of the witch on the bed next to them.

Somehow, Lilith remained on her feet. No longer swaying like a wind-swept palm, but like a lover against his aroused body. She moaned and panted along with him, one hand reaching behind her to scratch fingernails lightly over his throat and the soft underside of his chin, and he wanted to make this goddess his lover, as well as his victim.

When her legs finally gave way under the unbearable burden of pleasure enhanced with a healthy dose of mescaline, he took her to the floor and continued fondling and suckling her until he, too, could no longer withstand the ecstasy. Then he dragged the countess in her stunning dress with him, sending tuxedo studs clattering across the floor as he peeled open his shirt for her to feast upon his breast. Both women with him shared in his rapture, although he doubted either reached the dizzying heights he attained.

Inside her buckskin blouse, he found she wore nothing underneath, so even as his pleasure faded, for he had stopped feeding from her, he continued to massage to prolong her pleasure. While continuing to draw blood from his chest,

Camilla pulled on his clothing the way a blind person wearing boxing gloves might untie an intricate knot. Above, an owl watched from a perch at the ceiling. Goody lay motionless on the bed.

The room atop the turret was round, as turrets are, ten feet in diameter. It jutted above the top floor, and although the peaked roof of the mansion partially blocked the view to the west, its four windows otherwise gave a grand panorama of the city and mountains. Any memory of arriving there vanished in a haze, but Camilla had been kissing him for hours. With any luck, she will never stop.

Three chairs arranged in a triangle, and together they occupied one. Because the skirt of her dress fit so tightly, she had it hiked up high so her lovely ebony legs could straddle him. His arm had ensnared a foot, which forced one knee bent up near his face which, based on how wet it was, he may have been kissing it for quite some time, as well. Had she been molded from the chocolate her skin resembled, she would have tasted no more delicious.

Lips open wide and breath warm on the cheek those lips rubbed against, she moaned as her body rubbed against his with increasing desperation. Maybe he tried to stand with her attached to him, but the round room spun and they laughed on the floor. Only their clothes prevented them from fully merging into one. Even the blood coursing through their veins belonged to the other, from the other's body.

He chased her counterclockwise from window to window, her staying just beyond his reach and squealing, swatting his hand away when he touched her. They kissed some more, her legs around his waist and back pressed against the wall, dangerously close to one of the windows. She was beautiful, and that part he knew was not an effect of the magical cactus mingling with her blood in his veins.

Then she was on her feet, braced hands held her up against the wall and he caressed her body sensuously from behind while sucking blood from the slit hidden behind her ear. Her moans bordered on screams. Or were those cries his? Probably both together, their bodies—like their blood—in complete harmony. That was the first time he realized he was naked, vaguely remembering her hands removing his clothes.

She wore only two garments, the dress and panties, and as he drank, with one hand, she removed the panties and pushed back against him.

"Take me," she said as he sucked her life from her neck.

She pulled the dress up, so it hung over her hips as she bent forward, leaning on the wall again. He held those hips in both hands, and how pale they looked against her skin shocked him. She was begging for him now, and he was ready.

"Make me a woman before you kill me."

He may have desired her even more, but no mortal human can comprehend the concept of eternity. At her age, he had found waiting for anything impossible, let alone the fire their feeding had ignited inside her. She reached back, located the zipper and unzipped it halfway down, exposing a dark V of skin, ribs and the ripples of her spine.

"Rid me of my virginity," she pleaded. Her hips in his hands and nothing between their naked bodies made this the easiest wish for him to fulfill he was ever likely to be asked, and he pulled her even tighter against him, if that was possible.

"Is this how you want it?" He thrust his hips forward, as he would have if inside her as she yearned for him to be. "Is this what you want?"

Somehow, he threw her into a chair and knelt before her, kissing above the same knee—or was it the other? She pulled two fists of blonde hair toward her.

"Not this way, my love."

"But you love me, don't you? You told me you do."

"If I didn't love you," he licked her lower lip, "I would do as you ask. This is not how you want this."

"But I love you, Eddie. Don't let me die this way!"

Under the window facing south, she lay curled in a fragile ball, vomiting and crying. A pool of red in front of her—blood mixed with wine—and he pulled her hair back to not fall into it, wondering how she got into this position. A shocking volume of vomit. He covered her down to mid-thigh with her dress for modesty.

Spidery arms clung around his neck as he carried her down a narrow staircase, her head tucked under his chin. He took care to pin her dress in place between his arm and her legs, because her panties were gone, a vision returning of them floating in the mountain breeze from the window.

He had no business driving, but he did. White and red bars of light like neon tubes shared the road with him, light trails left by cars driven by sober citizens. Somehow, he missed all of them.

Camilla's face was limp, her eyes partially open white slits as he tucked her into bed. Aware of how furious she would be if she awoke to find her dress stained with blood, he draped it over the back of a chair. Better to vomit on him, which he could shower off, so he held her on her side in his arms to protect her.

How much peyote had she consumed? What amount is fatal? Hopefully, he drank enough of it with her blood, like sucking the venom from a snakebite. He held her tight in his arms, hoping for her skin to warm him, but she felt cool to the touch.

THE CIRCLE OF DEATH

Precious weight fell away rapidly, before his eyes, thinner each day. More still from one night of abandon. Clothes which fit perfectly only days before now hung from her body like sacks and her face lost its plumpness, leaving it the disturbing image of a skull. Still strikingly beautiful, just no longer her.

When she awoke, she lay shivering, so he held her against him as if his body possessed warmth to give. Then he drew a hot bath and carefully lowered her to it. That steaming water brought a rare smile to taut lips.

"At least you made it a bubble bath, so you can't sit there staring at me."

"I can still stare at you," he grinned, eyes locked onto hers. "Can you remember last night?"

"Not much—why?"

"There were no bubbles last night."

Foamy hands covered her face. "Oh, no. What did we do?"

"Not what you begged me to do, trust me."

She peeked between two hands of spread fingers. "What did I ask you to do?"

"*Rid me of my virginity.* That's an exact quote, best as I can remember it. A lot is fuzzy for me, too."

"I did not! I do not talk like that." She splashed him with bubbles, but that took so much of her energy, it left her drained. Then a series of coughs racked her, and the enormous toll each excruciating spasm took on her body manifested on her exquisite face. He stroked her cheek, her hair, her swan-like neck, her shoulder. Steam still rose when the last remnants of bubbles popped, but by then she had long ceased caring—not after he recounted in painful detail the tower scene. Their licentiousness and agonizing restraint.

Too weak to stand, he dried her body for her and, after swaddling her in a robe, carried her back to the bed and let her suckle blood from his veins.

†

"Seems to me you killed the wrong person." Had she bitten a maggoty chunk from a rotten apple, Camilla would have worn the same expression.

Open hands looping in aimless circles, palms-up, staring at the floor as if some rational explanation might write upon it by a mystical hand, an excuse a reasonable person might accept, Eddie was at a loss for words. "He just… disappeared. Dead? Run somewhere—New York? Chicago? Canada? G-men can't track down mobsters who go on the lam; how am I supposed to find one?"

"Well, unless he ran to Colorado to learn how to ski, you probably won't find him here."

"What can I do about it?"

Camilla had finally asked him the one question she had avoided since the night he kidnapped her. Whether she at last trusted him enough to ask or her dire condition had emboldened her, even she could not say. In response, he told her everything. How he killed Leslie Haas and turned her into the Red Dahlia. And why? Shocking as it was, his crime had a certain logic to it. A logic perhaps only one who had become accustomed to feeding upon blood was likely to understand.

Logical as his explanation had been, it contained one glaring flaw.

"Go back there and find him. Soon as he is sure you are gone, he'll be back. Trust me—we've got crooks on our side of the Troost wall, so I've seen it many times. Once the coast is clear, they are back on the same corners selling girls or heroin, breaking into houses or whatever they did before becoming lamisters. Don't assume he's any different just because he's with the Italian mob."

"That's what I figured. Somebody will muscle him out of his operation if he stays away too long."

"Those guys don't even bother to hide from the cops in New York—do you think he's gone forever just because some guy wants him dead? Heck, he's probably got a contract on your head right now." She threw her head back, laughing. "And we know how that will turn out. He'll be more disappointed than me when I shot you right here." One finger bullet poked him several times. Lively vigorous pokes, at that.

†

"I bought you something."

Her eyes lit like Christmas lights, eager to see what he carried hidden in the bag imprinted *Harold & Co., Stationers*. From inside, she pulled a box of stationery. Thick bond paper in a lovely lavender. "My favorite color!"

"There's something else."

She dug her hand inside to retrieve a long, slender box which, when opened, revealed a silver fountain pen lying on a black velvet bed. "This must have been expensive!"

"I bought a lap tray, too, but it's too bit to fit in the bag."

"What is all this for?"

"I thought you may want to write a letter."

A melancholy smile spread over her lovely, gaunt face. "Thank you."

†

The illness treated Camilla with particular malevolence from early on.

It robbed from her the lovely songbird voice that sang so beautifully. It must have been the way singing vibrates the vocal cords that ignited bouts of painful coughing, because it silenced her after a bar or two, enough to convince her to no longer try.

But her sudden turn for the worse was most puzzling and defied explanation. Her body must all have flushed the last traces of peyote from her system days ago. Her mind functioned fine, still better than most, yet her body failed inexorably since that night. Only one thing made sense. What if her body was not yet ready for human blood? Perhaps she was only able to ingest his own tainted blood.

Before he died, he only consumed the blood his sister offered him. Her own. He had no way of understanding at the time, nor had the first seed of suspicion begun its germination that she had become a vampire, but only Lena's blood passed his lips until after he was dead and buried. There must be some difference between blood of the living and the dead to deliver such starkly dissimilar deaths.

If so, what harm was Goody's blood causing inside her precious body? How long does the poison of living, human blood last? From the look of it, it must speed up this mortal sentence. And it corrupted her, and not just her skeletal face. Her entire body had deteriorated into little more than a skeleton. Every rib showed through desiccated skin stretched over protruding shoulder bones and pelvis. Her knees massive bulges compared to the shriveled calves or even her thighs.

Although spared of the agony of experiencing this sentence imposed upon Lena, he had witnessed it since. Too many times. Sooner or later, they all perished this way. His body had wasted away, too. Almost to nothing. Not at such a rapid pace and, of course, his perspective different for his demise, not the insidious suffering played out before him. It is entirely possible he looked this awful, this pitiful. He must have—he was dying then, too.

†

Dearest Mother and Father,

First, let me apologize for not writing to you sooner. I love you and miss you both, and my brother and sisters so much! I am sorry but, as you know by now, the police were hunting us and we knew they will use any mail I sent to help track us down.

Don't believe what the papers say. It is not true. Most of it, at least. The truth is, I am with the man you know as John Doe, the Red Dahlia killer. He takes excellent care of me and is not the monster portrayed in the newspapers. Quite the contrary. I am safe, and he has treated me with respect. Do not worry that he has molested me, because he has not. Nor are we lovers, as some of the more tawdry stories claim. In fact, we are so much more than lovers, but he has never dishonored me.

Just so you know, he is not telling me what to write. This is me, and I write this freely to tell you the truth.

There is so much to explain, and I suspect you are as ~~furious~~ upset that I am with a white man as you are that I am accused of murder. It still shocks me sometimes, too, but the details are so much harder to explain, so I won't even try. Just trust my judgment, and know that the truth is not the stories they write about me. It pains my heart if I have shamed you and the rest of the family, for what I have done should not bring shame to you.

The surprise is, life is more complicated than you expect, and only skin is black or white. Everything is somewhere in between, some shade of gray, sometimes different shades on different days or when viewed from slightly different angles. I promise I did not kill that man they claim I killed. The wreck hurt me badly, and I almost died. By the time I woke up afterward, I was miles away. "John Doe" saved my life that night, and a few times since. He does not want anyone to know his real name, so I'll call him that. But I know who he is and his life story.

I know what you are thinking: I can turn him in and the police won't prosecute me, but it is not so simple.

The reason I have written little about myself is I can't lie to you. It's been rough, and I have been ill, but I am improving and soon will be good as new. I almost did not tell you this, but you deserve the whole, unvarnished truth. It's not serious, and it is NOT a baby! That is impossible because I have not done that—with John Doe or anyone else.

I have seen so much of this country and met interesting people. When I see you again, what stories will I tell!

Here I must end, for now. Do not expect me to write again soon, but I will write when I can. I know it is wasting my time to add this, but do not worry about me, and please believe me that every word I have told you is true and my own. And know my thoughts are of you when you think of me!

Your loving daughter,
Camilla

†

Fifty years. A lifetime on his own. Half a century. Closer to sixty now, a difference without meaning. In that time, rarely had he known anyone longer than five or six years. When the first ripples of rumor about his unchanging appearance, the name Dorian Gray pops up in conversation—time to move on. Meant well, usually falling somewhere in the territory between compliment and jealousy, but to him, these jokes pack every bit the danger of a fire alarm or policeman's whistle.

The only other time he trusted a person with his life story, she once had also lain emaciated and dying before him. In a moment of unforgivable panic, he delivered her to a hospital. There she died. Two days later, from behind the hollowed trunk of a distant dying oak, he watched them lower her coffin into the ground. Later—two or three in the morning—he scaled the wrought-iron fence surrounding the graveyard to dig her up. Only when her body began reeking of death did he abandon everything he owned except the car which carried him far away from that cursed place. He drove cross-country to L.A., stopping only to kill someone for food and to rebury the woman he loved in the beautiful Arizona desert.

A few weeks later, he met George Hodel.

Alcohol no longer possessed the power it once did. Peyote

held promising allure, but might take a very long time to purge the sour aftertaste from his mouth should she perish. No doctor to turn to, no preacher or priest or rabbi. He had no one but the lovely girl wasting away under a blanket in his bedroom.

And she had no one to blame but him.

THE DEMISE

Shortly before dawn, a lavender envelope disappeared into the slot in the side of an anonymous blue box on an anonymous corner. No one saw who dropped it there, any more than they noticed the postman empty the box at 2 p.m. sharp. No one ever notices the ordinary things taking place daily around them.

The only thing anyone noticed that day was Ethel Parker.

Between the time the envelope slipped through the slot and the postman went about his normal rounds, a driver delivered six cases of Ballentine Beer to the rear door of a bar two blocks down. The same amount, give or take, he delivered day in, day out to the dive some creative genius named The Corner Bar shortly after Prohibition's glorious repeal sixteen years before. Like the name, nothing much had changed in this serious watering hole for serious drinkers during those years, save for the deterioration that eventually tarnishes every Corner Bar in every city.

Ethel was a regular, where she drank beer or vodka and met men. On good nights, she left early enough with her first to reel in her third before last call. The night before began as one of those nights, a well-dressed gentleman chatting her up and springing for drinks soon as she returned from her first date. They left together shortly after ten, plenty of time for her to return for one more.

Turns out, the gentleman was Ethel Parker's last date.

The next person to see her was the deliveryman pushing a dolly loaded high with Ballentine. Something caught his eye over behind a stack of crates in the alley, near a jumble of rusty garbage cans. Something white and cold.

There, atop an old tarpaulin, lay Ethel.

The police arrived and interviewed the delivery driver, who had pissed his pants when he saw her body up close, shirt open and one pale tit staring out of her black bra. Her gray eyes were open and stared unseeing up at the clouds. Her mouth also wide open, like someone cut off her last scream in the middle.

It didn't take the police long to determine she bled to death —that was obvious the minute they saw the washed-out color of her skin. A strange thing, though—a thorough search of the alley, then expanding to the block surrounding the Corner Bar, failed to locate so much as a single drop of spilled blood.

The tiny laceration behind her ear took longer to find.

†

Soon after they arrived in Denver, he realized all the tracks left behind led here. A little trail of breadcrumbs leading across the Great Plains. Police may envision themselves stealthy, but he had been on the run longer than most criminals' lifetimes, and at almost six decades, longer than any cop was ever on the job. By then he could smell them—figuratively, if not literally. His carelessness unintentional yet hardly forgivable. Sloppy. Each time he fled, when the heat was on, he absconded with a plan. Each time but this one.

This time, everything was different.

A few short months ago, he surrendered all hope. The struggle after L.A. and his slide into utter degeneracy interrupted for the briefest of moments. The respite lasted only long enough to watch his adored beauties—his source of the unblemished nectar that filled him again with life—burn before his eyes. That two-bit gangster should have paid with his life, but ran like the coward he was. Eddie knew even killing that thug would have failed to satisfy him. He wanted more. He needed it to end. Until his moment of clarity in that fetid jail cell.

Camilla coughed. Weakly now, because her strength was

ebbing. He dabbed her forehead with cool water, refreshing enough that her eyes flickered. He gripped her hand tight enough to hold her in this world. "You're back, I see."

"Can't get rid of me, can you?"

"Who would want to get rid of you?"

He didn't ask how she felt. He knew. All too well. Once, he too had died. "Can I get you anything?"

"I'd kill for some blood."

"Drink as much as you want." After unbuttoning his shirt, he leaned over her, because she no longer had the strength to lift her head. Soft, flaccid lips suckled him. Like a baby now, he imagined, although babies likely had more strength. His head fell and his eyes closed as the pleasure built inside him. Her hips moved enough to show she felt it, too.

Then she let go and gasped. "Thank you."

Her face pale, a shocking departure from what had been such an elegant ebony. Every fiber of his being desired her blood. Hers was the sweetest he ever tasted, yet he knew every drop he drained hastened her demise, and in recent days, his worry had grown to the point of abject terror.

What if she failed to return to him?

†

Police must have picked up their trail, likely from gas stations and fool-hearty stops at roadside diners. Too many witnesses to identify an escaped prisoner wanted for the most sensational of crimes. Too easy. A gangly blond kid and a long-legged Black girl of striking beauty sure to attract attention no matter what, but with his mug shot plastered all over the cover of every newspaper in the country?

So he retreated to the darkness now, more the traditional creature of the night from movies and popular books, simply because creatures own the night. Dark shadows are so useful for what they conceal.

He need only keep his head down until she died. Then

they'd slip away together for somewhere new. This escape harder, perhaps, but such places still existed. Canada, maybe, or Mexico. On many Caribbean islands, he'd heard, Camilla might find a more accepting home. How to travel there was another story, but one problem at a time. And the one luxury they had in unlimited quantities is time.

Sometimes, he visited the witches, particularly the Native medicine woman, Lilith, whose untainted blood also carried a heavenly sweet essence. She was no fool, and knew exactly who he was, but he gave her forbidden pleasures while leaving her intact for her magic, so she held his secrets while taking from him worldly ecstasy. She called him Count, with a wink and a grin, to prolong the charade. Each visit, he took only a taste, only what he needed to survive. And he gave her all the pleasure she desired.

But he saw police everywhere, and since she lived so far across town, eventually gave up his Lilith.

He hunted by night, but was careful to leave no bodies behind.

†

Human nature is curious. How quickly people forget and move on with their lives is simply amazing. Some unscrupulous politician should take note, for, if handled properly, might manufacture an unending source of moving on until no one remembered anything by the time election day rolled around.

The trail grew cold. For two weeks, no sightings came in of the Red Dahlia killer or the pretty Black girl, Camilla Singleton, either his prisoner or accomplice—and the opinion was pretty evenly split on which. However, the authorities had far less disagreement over the reason the pair dropped off the face of the earth.

The killer was gone.

Where he went was much less clear. Most assumed he was holed up somewhere in the mountains, while his absence convinced others he made the dash down to Mexico, crossing the border somewhere in the desert south. Or southwest. Some even assumed him dead, although the lack of a body cast significant doubt on that theory.

The last sighting was by a woman who claimed he accosted her in her sleep, waking to find him kissing her, but her story was too strange and frankly non-believable. The Denver Police concluded she must have literally dreamed it up. Nothing like a search for an escaped killer to shake crazies from the trees!

So, with plenty of local crimes to worry about, the cops lost interest in the search. It shifted west, with park rangers and sheriffs of mountain counties on higher alert than the Denver P.D. Warnings went out to New Mexico and Arizona to keep a watch on their borders, although if he chose to visit Chihuahua or Baja California, few would be sorry to see him go.

The last thing any sheriff in America wanted was for this slippery murderer to escape from their jail next.

†

It never occurred to him how difficult procuring raven feathers might prove to be. Turns out, it is much harder than feeding.

Sure, you can always pick up one or two in parks where ravens scavenge for scraps dropped by picnickers, but being out and about in a public place like a park was extremely low on his list of bright ideas right then. Magic and occult shops sold them, too, but in very limited quantities.

Far less than the quantity required.

†

One person might have what he needed.

For the most-wanted man west of the Mississippi to sneak unnoticed to the opposite side of town, though, that raised the difficulty several notches. The wisdom of investing in some clever form of disguise flashed through his head for a moment, but he was too tall and too blond to pull it off.

His best bet was to borrow a car. With any luck, the night would pass before its hapless owner reported it stolen. Two blocks away, a beat-up Model A parked on a slight rise provided the perfect opportunity. He let it roll half a block, building up enough speed for the engine to kick over when he popped the clutch. Half an hour driving slowly and carefully on residential streets, eyes sharp for police and drunks swerving home from a night at the pub, but he made it without incident.

Locating it was no trouble, even in the dark. He remembered the route well. His heart sank when he found the windows dark. Had this trip—this tremendous risk—been for naught?

Given the slim hope she may return home, he waited. Despite the growing plague of cars since the war, now that everyone could afford one, a spot along the curb right out front offered a perfect view of the door, to see if she arrived. There he sat, shivering, less from the chilly night air than from a lack of blood to warm him. Patiently waiting and watching. The oddest sensation came over him—one of being watched himself.

Had he been spotted?

On the drive over, his attention focused fully on where he went and on the lookout for police along the route, he easily could have been tailed. Any other car parked on this street could be an unmarked police car. His acute vision picked up the slightest of movement, so he waited. To his right, he detected motion in the shadows. Head still, he allowed his eyes to turn toward the duplex.

A curtain fluttered, and although no lights were burning inside, he had the eyes of a nocturnal animal, enough to make the silhouette out clearly. Long hair flowed, unbraided, the way Lilith normally wore hers. And she was looking directly at him. How did she know he was here?

She met him at the door, opened only a crack. "May I come in?"

"If I say no, will it prevent you from entering?"

"No more than mirrors not reflecting my image. That's Hollywood."

"And if I slam the door in your face like any rational person?"

"You never struck me as a rude person."

"Every cop in the state is searching for you. You're a wanted man."

"Then why do I feel so unwanted?" Her best efforts could not keep a twitch from the corners of her mouth. "I will not harm you."

"Get in here before someone sees you." The door shut after she quickly checked both directions. "Do you need blood?"

"No. Well, yes, but blood is not why I'm here. I need a favor."

"Let me guess: you need someone to drive you halfway across the country while you hide in the trunk, and an Indian girl is the last person anyone will suspect."

He shook his finger at her. "I like how you think. Kinda wish I thought of that myself, and it may be exactly what I need, but I'm not ready to leave yet."

"You're not here for my body—well, my blood, at least—or my skill as a getaway driver, so you must need Indian medicine."

"Again, not my plan, but now that you mention it…"

"Well, don't get your hopes up about some invisibility spell or turning you into a skinwalker. My medicine is not that powerful."

"Do any Indian rituals involve feathers? Crow or raven feathers, to be exact?"

"In fact, some do. They are important to the Pueblo and other nations. Many tribes revere crows for their intelligence and mischief and are symbolic of transformation. The keeper of the law. Some nations view crows differently, more darkly, creatures who steal souls. My people revere them, though, as a symbol of rebirth. The Cherokee even practice *Koga Nvwati*, or crow medicine. To them, the crow is a shapeshifter, a spirit guide who leads them through darkness, opens them to transformation."

"So you can get some for me?"

"I have a few in back. How many do you need?"

"How many can you get?" Sapphires alight with a beautiful glow bore into her ebony eyes, and he added, "It's for Camilla."

"How is she?"

"In desperate need of *Koga Nvwati*, I'm afraid."

"Give me a few days to track some down. Are we talking a few dozen or…?"

"Is a few hundred too many?"

Her eyes widened as her head tilted to one side. "Make that a week. Maybe more."

One hand reached out and touched her shoulder. "Thank you."

"Now, what about you?"

"Don't worry about me; I am fine."

"The message written on your face disagrees. Drawn, even paler than usual—when my ancestors spoke of White Man, I doubt any were white as you. Weariness. Defeat."

"If only you have medicine for me."

"That medicine is pumping through my veins."

He knew, for the delectable aroma overwhelmed him the moment she cracked open her door. "I'm afraid my mood prevents me from thinking of such things."

"But you see, my sacred duty is to provide medicine and healing, both of which you direly need. Besides, it is not purely for your benefit. Taking my blood has given me something—a power or insight which is helpful in my medicine."

So that is how she knew I was lurking outside, he thought. "Is it power you wish me to give you, or something of a baser nature?"

"I must admit, the pleasure you possess is powerful. Of a kind otherwise denied of me. Any other man giving me such ecstasy would also take portions of my power, not giving me some of his in return."

"Is this your price for two hundred crow feathers?"

"Two hundred? Seems a small price for so many sacred crow feathers. A price, if memory serves, should be a rather pleasant one for you to pay, as well."

Through silken hair that glistened in the reflection of an overhead bulb, the still-unhealed gash behind her ear waited for his lips. In pulling those sable locks out of the way, behind her shoulder, his fingers stroked those waist-length strands. "So beautiful. I am glad you did not braid it like you did for your costume."

Her body leaned back, anticipating what was to come, almost collapsing against his chest. "You aren't planning to kill me, are you?"

"Never."

"Camilla is dead, isn't she?"

"How do you know?"

"Do you so easily forget who I am? The feathers are to transform her?"

"One way or another." Her aromas filled his nostrils, and the subtle pulsations in her neck sped to twice per second.

"Then give me your power and your pleasure, and I will do everything possible to help you transform her."

The fulfilling taste of virgin blood lit his senses, flowing over his tongue, exploding in an instant head rush. Insufferably long days had passed since his last feeding, which may have made her essence even more compelling. Her knees failed, forcing him to hold her, braced high on her waist to press her weight against him. Mere inches below her breasts. When he took those in his hungry hands, his legs again turned to spaghetti.

He got her gently onto the floor, then rolled her onto him to avoid crushing her delicate frame. Through only the flimsy cotton of her nightgown, her breasts stoked deep within him a fire. Her blood, her body, her scent, the hair flowing down his neck, its weight on the arm around her drove him to a quick frenzy. Not his alone, for her body writhing against him communicated with an efficiency words lack.

Her body bucked like a wild animal in a rare moment of unbridled freedom. More powerful than any woman's response while he fed. They shared a unique symbiosis, receiving from him something in exchange for the life he took from her. Something mystical and unfathomable, as far beyond his comprehension as what she gave to him was to her.

Her body shook in short, staccato quakes seemingly as powerful as the waves wracking his. What powers might she take from him if she consumed his blood?

He forced himself to stop feeding of her, perhaps having already taken more than he should, but his hands continued giving her pleasure. The response of her body, again shuddering as a result, her round bottom against him in such a lurid manner, gave him a different, more human form of bliss, and he held her in his arms long after her throes of passion came to an end.

THE ANGEL

Since they moved in, not one person knocked at their door. His door, now. Even vacuum salesmen avoided this apartment. So, the knocking surprised him. Forceful without being loud. Insistent. A salesman. Either that or a cop. He never missed having a peephole more in his life.

Salesman, no doubt, because no cop worth his salt gave up easily as his visitor. He relaxed when the rapping ceased. Only they did not give up. After a fleeting minute of peace and quiet, the knocking resumed, only this time softer. Three taps, then a voice.

"Count? I know you are in there."

"Lilith? Is that you?"

"Does the count receive many visitors?" Halfway through the sentence, the door opened to unmuffle her soft voice. A box large as a steamer trunk nearly eclipsed her behind it, and soon as he confirmed no one else was around, pulled it in and her along with it.

"What's in the box?"

"You wanted crow feathers? You got crow feathers."

"I didn't expect them for a few more days."

"What can I say? I aim to please." A box full of feathers weighed more than he expected; it thumped on the worn table that came with the flat. "Where is she?"

"The bedroom. Want to see her?"

A nod, so he took her there. Laid out on the bed, hands folded like a corpse, she looked beautiful. "This makeup is wonderful—did you do this yourself?"

"It isn't makeup."

Over her shoulder, Lilith narrowed her eyes at him, then bent low, holding her hair to keep it from spilling over Camilla's face. She sniffed. "How long has she been dead?"

"Five days."

"Five days?"

"I know. Still looks alive, doesn't she?"

"Why is her body not decaying?"

"That is why I hope your medicine or magic or whatever powers you have might be all we need. Because I don't believe she is fully dead."

"Somewhere in between? Trapped?"

"Neither dead nor undead."

"The power to raise the dead is not unheard of, although not the form of medicine I have."

"Do you know how?"

"The calls, the songs, what words to seek favor from the gods—yes. But the power?"

"But you will try?"

"Let me get some things from the car I brought with me, just in case."

Scents of sage and some other sweet herb Eddie could not identify burned in clay censors and filled the air with their fragrant smoke. For two hours straight, after changing into a long robe of animal hide, Lilith prayed and chanted, exhorting the earth spirits to complete Camilla's resurrection. Prayers and exhortations she had heard but never imagined herself participating in. This was forbidden magic.

Then again, who imagines being summoned to raise the dead? Or the undead?

Mournful calls to the ancient spirits were, to Eddie, recognizable only by the emotion lifting them. Gone was the flat, measured tone of Lilith's usual speech. Tears streamed down her face. Her voice carried the sorrow of generations. Back to his childhood and beyond.

Perhaps some kindred spirit bonds Native Americans with

descendants of slaves, like Camilla. Or even with someone like him, a mythical beast of nature like the others in Native mythology. The Firebird, Sasquatch, the wood elves they call Canoti, the winged serpent. Not to mention the *Unk Tehi*.

It may go both ways. Sure, Camilla's charms spoke for themselves. Beauty, intelligence, the sweet flavor of her virgin blood. But the power of his bond to her defied straightforward explanation. Bound to him by blood, but every woman he fed upon paled in comparison. Was it a kinship born of his being an outsider, too? Hers of race, his a somewhat more esoteric line separating him from society that, by appearance, he should belong to.

But while he may have learned the secrets of walking undetected among them, he no longer was of them. To think: the Klansmen and Dixiecrats who hate Camilla because of her gorgeous chocolate skin would welcome him, quite oblivious to the reality that he was the monster. An irony surely doomed to be lost upon them were they ever to discover the truth. An irony perhaps but one person could understand, if only she could awaken. To arise again, to laugh with him about such foolishness.

This holy woman chanting incantations, whose ancestors were slaughtered or shipped off to reservations because they stood in the way of progress—might she also understand?

None of the words she sang and chanted made sense, yet he understood. Ceremony or spell or whatever it was—it resonated deep within, in a place where words do not matter. She called upon the spirits of the butterfly for transformation, the buffalo as life-builder. The hawk for its ability to stop time. The hummingbird, for it represents beauty and miracles. On the snake for its power of transformation.

Days went by, chanting and drenched with sweat. Cursed hours of promise and disappointment, broken only by precious few hours' sleep. Periodically, tears streamed down her cheeks. Camilla did not stir, but that only seemed to further motivate Lilith. Some of her chants began to sound familiar, so he did his best to echo them, because in a primal way, he understood.

In the end, neither her medicine nor his curse bestowed immortality upon the fallen young beauty. The corruption his deadly kiss gave failed to stave off the final corruption of death. Lilith stayed with him in the run-down tenement he took because they asked no questions and accepted cash. No one knew Lilith was there with him, which may be why she remained, unconcerned about the impropriety of a virginal priestess staying under a man's roof for days.

She stayed until the signs became unmistakable.

Death claimed Camilla.

"I knew her only a short time," Lilith lamented, "but she was the sweetest girl."

Eddie sat silently. Despite her complete inexperience with his kind and wary that losing his lover may unleash some demon akin to the Navajo legend of *'ánti'įhnii,* the most malevolent form of skinwalker, Lilith stayed with them. After all, her magic had failed along with his.

She stayed to prepare the funeral which the girl wanted.

†

"I am not afraid of you."

After abandoning hope, Camilla's beau had kept mostly silent, speaking only as much as necessary for their preparations. A fairly typical reaction to the death of a loved one, in her experience. Comfortable with quiet herself, she allowed him time with his thoughts. Why she blurted this out confounded her. When his eyebrows lowered to form an unspoken question, she felt compelled to explain.

"Most people are, I suppose. Not me. Funny, in a way. The night we met, you spoke honestly to me about what you were, so that may be why. The honesty."

"I told you Camilla was also a vampire, which, as is abundantly clear, was a lie."

"A lie is known to be untrue, meant to deceive. In your

heart, you believed her to be like you. If you believe something is true, intend to speak the truth but it turns out otherwise, that is nothing worse than a mistake."

"So this," his hand waved over the beautiful body of his dark, virgin lover laid on the bed with care, "this was a mistake?"

"It is never a mistake to try to save one who you love."

"Are you afraid this is your future, too?"

"Were you not listening when I told you I am not afraid?" Their eyes met across Camilla's corpse. "Will this happen to me?"

"No," he assured her, "there is no danger if I take only a small amount. And if you do not take blood from me."

"Is that how it is done? You gave Camilla your blood in the hope she would become like you?"

"I believed so, but it is not the reason. That is what was done to me, but when I try to give someone this gift, it brings only death. A terrible death filled with agony." While he spoke, he gazed with sorrow at Camilla, then his eyes lifted to her. "What I have taken from you does not cause harm, so you have nothing to fear."

"I shouldn't believe you, but I do. This is why I should be afraid. I know what you are capable of, what you need to survive, that my life is in your hands, yet I trust you. With my life. Without fear. Stranger still, since Indians have nothing like vampires in our traditions."

"No?"

"It seems this is another curse Europeans brought with them. Yet, when you asked to take my blood and touched me in ways no man has touched me, I knew you were not going to harm me. That is my gift. I rarely tell people the nature of my gift, but I have insight into people's minds and hearts, their spirit. This is how I knew how dangerous you are, but that you mean me no harm."

"And now that you know I kill even those closest to me?"

"Yet I am not dying."

"Camilla was dying. I barely knew her then. When she learned who I was—some of it—and a little of what I have done, she tried to kill me by crashing her car. She ended up being hurt, not me, so I gave her my blood to heal her, so she might live. I truly believed…"

"I owe you an apology for not telling you the act of taking my blood has opened my mind. Each time you do, it nourishes you and also my spirit. Much like you, I cannot explain, only that my abilities have strengthened. Not only does it weave us more tightly together, it allows me to sense your spirit more clearly. Others, too."

"How is this possible?"

"If not for the wolf, will a deer be as fast? Will she hear so clearly in the forest, far better than we human beings can hear? The wolf gives the deer her speed and hearing because he takes her life. In turn, the deer teaches the wolf humility."

"Is that why you allow me to feed upon you?"

"Does that surprise you? That I give to you and take from you? Camilla also took from you, in her way. The raven does not seek the speed or strength or beauty of other creatures, but accepts the gifts it receives. They are the most honest animal."

He looked down at the raven feathers on the table. "But I took everything from her."

"She also gave herself to you, as I do. And from you she took happiness, as well as a chance to become like you."

"Is that what you want, to become like me?"

"My spirit is different from yours. A hunter asks an animal's spirit before he will take it as food, for each is a thread in the web of life. Where those threads meet, as yours and hers did, they each become stronger. Her spirit allowed you to take from her, as does mine."

Neither spoke for a while, instead focusing on their work. It was again Lilith who broke the reverential silence. "I will no longer take power from you without your permission, as I am guilty of doing."

†

The church was neither large nor modern. For the hundreds of Denver residents who passed by each day, nothing about it attracted their attention. Its whitewashed clapboard sides and the style, with its short, stocky steeple, reminded him of Chestnut Hill Baptist Church in Exeter. His first two sisters buried there alongside his mother and, presumably by now, his father. Perhaps even his youngest sister, Hope, almost seventy if she still lived.

When built, this sanctuary stood on the outskirts of town, and this church bore witness to the tide of a city growing closer over the decades until eventually sweeping by. Now it stood only blocks from the tenement built in the heyday of the Roaring Twenties, where two strangers lived since arriving in Denver.

Where Camilla died.

Deacon Oliver Simmons habitually arrived early on Sunday mornings, tasked with making sure everything was in tip-top shape for the 8:30 service. Normally this meant little more than turning on the lights and now that cold weather was here, feeding the furnace.

Nothing was normal about this morning.

After switching on all the lights, a floral scent captured his attention. Like a funeral, although funerals are never held on Sundays. So accustomed to finding everything in order, he had not bothered to look around, but the pleasant scent, out of place as it was, sent a chill down his spine. So did the sight of flowers surrounding the altar.

Roses, mostly, although sprinkled with other varieties, most not displayed in vases but laid in bundles like someone pulled them straight from those buckets the flower vendors have out at the market. Armfuls of roses and baby's breath. And there was something else, some dark shape hidden among those loose bouquets.

"What in the hell..." Oliver swore under his breath, then caught himself. "Heck?"

An intuition loud as a voice warned him to stay away from the altar, but this was his job. His duty. The early arrivals only a few minutes away and with the reverend due at any second, he had his work cut out for him. All those flowers needed to be cleared away before the congregation arrived. He doubted he had enough time to pull vases from the storeroom, fill them with water and arrange these flowers into the kind of displays normally reserved for weddings and Easter, but he'd let Rev. Pirkle make that call.

A few feet away from the altar, he stopped short. The dark shape was a dress, mostly black with a crimson pattern. And were those feathers?

By this point, every instinct in his body screamed at him to stop, but his sense of responsibility drove him forward. Up the altar steps until able to see past the mountains of flowers.

It was a woman. A girl, really, a pretty one, if thin to the point of emaciation, as if she starved to death. More disturbing—if that was possible—to each side, adorned with wings fashioned of pure black feathers. Like an angel.

A spider web of a handwoven Indian dreamcatcher amulet lay on her chest, just above her crossed hands.

Oliver ran breathless from the sanctuary toward the rectory next door, where Rev. Pirkle had a telephone. In his haste, the idea of closing and locking all the doors he unlocked soon as he arrived did not occur to him. Before he had even had a chance to explain the horror laid out on the altar to the preacher, already dressed in his cassock, a shriek arose from inside the church.

The first of the parishioners had arrived.

THE PAY BACK

Newspaper headlines across the country were predictable.

When Eddie created the Red Dahlia, he knew this was how Leslie Haas would be forever remembered. As obvious to editors as if the killer had dictated his own moniker for her. Which, in a sense, he had.

This time had been no different. Camilla wanted something witchy, and she got it. The Angel of Death.

Less prominently spelled out in the papers was the letter found on the altar exonerating her of any crime. His confession. Written in the real murderer's own hand, Eddie proclaimed Camilla's innocence. He admitted to killing Cletus McFarlane, as he subsequently found out had been the name of the farmer who came upon their accident scene with ill intent that night.

Camilla Singleton heroically risked her life trying to stop me, his letter explained, and when Cletus found her bleeding and unconscious, *he decided raping an injured young girl was how he intended to spend his night. I stopped him.*

Taking her for medical attention was not possible, he explained, not while he was the Missouri's most wanted man, so he tried to nurse her back to health. An effort which ended in miserable failure. Camilla was no criminal, but even at risk of her life tried to shoot him with a gun he foolishly left unattended. She was a heroine, and he—the Red Dahlia killer—was responsible for her death, as well.

This stymied the coroner, who was at a loss to explain anything his examination of the Angel of Death's body revealed. Nothing in his post-mortem exam disproved any of it, yet raised more questions than answers.

Camilla Singleton had indeed suffered a severe head injury, just as the confession explained, which her parents confirmed had not been there the night she vanished. Yet, the huge gash above her hairline had healed—years ago, from the looks at it. Far more extensive healing than explainable by the scant weeks between the kidnapping and her discovery in the little church six hundred miles away. Six of her ribs also had fractures, although her parents adamantly denied she had ever broken a single rib in her life.

Over the years, the coroner had become familiar with chest injuries similar to hers, commonly suffered in auto accidents. Typically, those suffering crushing to their chest cavities died from those injuries, usually within days, if not minutes. The heart and lungs cannot survive such severe damage.

Like her lacerated scalp, Camilla's ribs, too, had fully healed and resembled fractures from years ago.

More troubling was her cause of death. Quickly able to rule out those injuries from the accident, he and several Denver doctors called in for consultations could not determine what, in fact, killed her. Her fragile body weighed a mere 94 pounds, an astonishing ten pounds lighter than her normal weight, yet showing none of the usual signs of malnutrition which could explain such rapid weight loss.

Then came the problem of when she died.

According to the coroner, she had been dead for weeks. Perhaps months. Even though decay had barely set in, other signs pointed to death long before. Her heart and some other organs desiccated far beyond what could be explained naturally.

"It almost looks like she has undergone some natural form of mummification, like those they found in the Andes fifty years ago," the coroner explained, shaking his head. "But there are no signs this body has been frozen."

Denver police were desperate to charge the Red Dahlia killer with another heinous murder, but in the end, the best the coroner could do was categorize the cause of Camilla's demise as death by misadventure.

Not that it mattered, for Missouri had dibs on him. If he ever turns up somewhere.

†

With a grunt, he tossed his heavy bags into the trunk of his sky-blue and white Buick before noticing that the tires were flat.

"Need help changing those?"

There stood The Kid, tire iron in hand. He must have been waiting, but Joey's mind struggled to explain how he could sneak up on him so easily.

"Kid, uh, I didn't expect to see you here."

"Like the Phoenix, risen from the ashes?"

"The papers said you were out west somewhere."

"Sorry, I meant to mail you a post card."

A frantic Joey Four Fingers looked around, even though he knew they were miles away from the nearest human being. Until that very moment, the seclusion is what Joey loved about this cabin hidden deep in the Ozarks. Up here, he could take target practice with his war surplus Grease Gun, broads could sunbathe naked in the yard or the occasional ungrateful whore could scream bloody murder and nobody was the wiser.

"Look, Kid, I, uh…"

"Do you know who was in that car? Two girls. The older girl was twenty-three years old. All that was left of them was a few bones, small enough to fit into biscuit tins."

"I didn't expect them to be driving your car, Kid, you know that."

"Of course, you expected me to drive, knowing full well they might be riding in there with me. But that didn't bother you, did it? What was it you said to me? I'm getting too big for my britches?"

"What, you going to work me over with that?" Joey's dark,

beady eyes went to the tire iron at his side.

"Thought about it, and I just might. Not that I need anything. In fact," he tossed the tire iron into the weeds, "where's the fun in that, when I have my own two hands?"

Joey reached behind his back for the snub-nosed .38 tucked into his belt at the small of his back. The Kid charged him, but Joey had the gun out first and fired three times. He had no time to aim, but when he squeezed off the first shot, The Kid was two steps away and right on top of him by the third, much too close for even the stubby, inaccurate two-inch barrel on this piece to miss. Despite three chunks of hot lead in his chest, The Kid hit him like a train, sending Joey flying straight back while the Smith & Wesson flew off in some other direction.

They landed past the front end of the car twenty feet away, which probably would not have made any sense to Joey's brain if he'd been able to think it through. But the impact knocked the breath from him, so his only thoughts focused on how badly he needed to inhale after it was all knocked out of him and how this Kid was still moving with three slugs in his chest.

He was not handsome, not snarling over him like a rabid dog the way he was. Fists rained down in such a flurry and with such precision, he lost count. Did The Kid land five punches or fifty? His head swam and one eye socket filled with blood, turning The Kid red in his view.

"They were good girls, you asshole. Sweet, innocent girls."

"Until you got hold of 'em, right, Kid?" Joey spat out bloody saliva. "Tell me, what do you do with 'em? The secret is ours; I won't tell anyone."

"You got that right, you rat bastard. It's killing you, isn't it? Wondering what I do with the girls I save from you and the other pimps? Eating you up inside. I protect them, keep them safe from the likes of you. That's what I did. In return, they give me their lives, but I take only what I need, so they suffer no harm."

"Protect them? That's rich," Joey said, his remaining teeth bloody, revealed as he chuckled for effect. "How'd that turn out? If you left them to me, those bimbos would be alive today, drinking cocktails downtown and living high on the hog."

"Other than the two you murdered, all my gals are alive. For those two, tonight you will pay a heavy price."

He spat out a thick ball of bloody spit which left a connecting thread hanging off his chin. "How the fuck did I miss you with all three shots?

"What makes you think you missed?"

The pimp's rodent-like eyes scanned his torso, where he'd pointed the barrel, and for the first time, saw small holes in his shirt, each stained with a modest amount of blood. None near any vital organs, one appearing to be little more than a graze to the side of his chest near his left underarm. Still, while not fatal, two slugs should have put him out of action. Punches as vicious as had pounded his face to a pulp should have been impossible with the wound near his right collarbone.

"What the hell? I didn't miss? Who are you—*what* are you?"

"For a minute there, I thought you knew what I was. I assumed you tried to fire-bomb me because you figured out how to get rid of me."

The pimp snorted. "I've been making fire bombs since I was twelve. They're most sophisticated these days."

"Well, if you don't already know, there's no point in telling you who I am, let alone what I am." Eddie stood and jerked Joey up by his collar, ratcheting his arm into a hammerlock. "If you move, I'll break it, so please, give me an excuse."

The pimp offered no resistance when led away, turning with each guiding pressure on his twisted arm much more readily than a donkey responds to reigns. Eddie marched him through the front door of the pimp's cabin. On paper, the cabin belonged to Joey Four Fingers' elderly housekeeper, and he supposed Joey's lawyer thoughtfully drew her up a will—free of charge, of course—leaving it to him on her death.

The door closed behind them, and Joey's vision instantly went black.

✝

As badly as he wanted to wipe his eyes, Joey's arms refused to cooperate. The back of his skull ached where Eddie had blackjacked him. It took him several seconds to realize his arms and legs were tied to the legs of a chair. His living room smelled like a bar at closing time on Saturday night.

"Hey! Where the fuck are you, Kid?"

A heavy smack to his right ear came from behind. "Find me yet?"

"What's that smell?"

Something crunched under the leather sole of Eddie's shoe as he stepped around to where the bound criminal could see him. "You have excellent taste in alcohol, Joey. Nice collection you had here. Sorry." Eddie said, head tilting to urge the pimp to look around at shards of shattered glass littering the floor. "Some of them broke."

He continued circling until he stood in front of the hog-tied pimp. "Personally, I'm more of a wine drinker. Alcohol doesn't have the same effect on me as it did when I was younger, but I love the taste. Now I prefer blood, but you can't order it at a bar, can you?"

Beady eyes narrowed under a furrowed brow as he tried to make sense of these comments, following along as The Kid picked up an unopened bottle of Wild Turkey and smashed it on the wooden floor at Joey's feet. Glass and bourbon sprayed his ankles.

"What the hell? Okay, I get your point. It's over; I'll tell everyone you and your girls are off limits. A permanent truce."

"Tell you what, Joey: you decided when to start it, but I'll decide when it's over. And how it ends."

"What do you want?"

He bent low, face twisted almost unrecognizable by fury inches from the pimp's. "What I want is two beautiful, intelligent, lovely young women back. But you destroyed any chance of having them by torching them in a fire. Give me a second choice, Joey."

"Kid, I didn't mean to hurt them. Honest. I feel terrible it happened to them."

"It didn't *happen to them*, Joey. You did it to them! You lit those two innocent girls on fire. I am the sucker who watched them burn, who heard their screams, watched their hands on the glass feeling for an open window to escape the flames. Tell me, when you were twelve, were you close enough to smell what a burning body smells like?"

"I'm sorry, Kid."

Eddie smacked him with the heel of his palm across the face, hard enough that something inside made a loud crack as it broke. "I asked you a fucking question."

"No."

"Burning human flesh is the worst smell you can imagine. Once you inhale it, you can never get it out of your nostrils—not completely. It's been here inside mine for a lifetime, and it never goes away." From the coffee table beside him, Eddie picked up a bottle of twenty-one-year-old Glenfiddich, twisted off the cork, and held it near Joey's smashed and bleeding lips. "This looks like good stuff. Have a swig."

He drank deeply from the offered bottle, which Eddie teasingly tipped up several times to encourage him to drink up. He poured until the pimp began choking and amber liquid spewed from his nose. Then he pulled it away.

For the first time since Joey saw the bullet holes in his shirt, Eddie cracked a smile. Without a word, he held the bottle high over his head and doused Joey with it, the crook's face tightening into a grimace as the alcohol stung every wound on his shattered face. The empty bottle bounced at his feet.

"Kat and Grace."

"What?"

"Those were their names. The beautiful young women you burned alive. Kat and Grace."

At the door, Eddie turned and pulled a matchbook from his pocket. One match flared and settled into a steady orange flame, which he held up. In the other hand, he folded the cover back and held it to the lit match. The entire pack flared.

"Say their names."

"What?"

Lowered to a menacing growl, Eddie repeated, "Say their names."

"Kat and Grace. Now stop this shit and cut me loose!"

Joey's screams and pleas had no effect on Eddie. "This may be slower than whatever you used on them. Sorry, had to work with what's in your liquor cabinet."

So much alcohol covered the floor only a few dry spots remained. The matchbook flew in a graceful arc, landing at his bound feet in a puddle of expensive liquor. Blue flames sprouted, spreading around his feet, under the chair, up his Scotch-soaked leg. His feet kicked out against nautical-firm knots in the rope holding him tightly in place. The screams rose in pitch and desperation.

Eddie did not stick around for the grand finale, although screams wailed as he made his way through the woods to where he left his car. This time, he did not stick around to smell burning human flesh. Famished as he was, it pleased him to have not sullied his body with such foul blood carrying an essence that likely would have infected his mind in some unforeseeable way.

Visible from miles away, smoke drifted from a fire somewhere deep in the forest, far from any homes or places of business. If anyone saw the smoke, they did not call in a report of fire.

By morning, the flames had burned themselves out.

†

Say what you will about these modern cars with their sensuous, rounded shapes influenced by the new jet airplanes which were rapidly making obsolete the beautiful Mustangs and Lightnings and Thunderbolts which only four years before ruled the skies over Germany and Japan, but Eddie still loved the old cars. The Packards and Cadillacs like the old gangsters used to drive.

Those old, golden age gangsters were mostly gone now, too. When Al Capone died two years before, it brought an era to an end, one Eddie had drifted through like a ghost. For most Americans, the future looked bright, although Stalin coming up with his own A-bomb that summer had ignited a growing sense of unease across the country.

Change came so rapidly now, halfway through the twentieth century, but Eddie still found useful what others had moved past. One luxury the gangsters loved was the privacy those old cars afforded with their curtained rear seats to hide the identities of the passengers. Those curtains also did a great job holding back the sun.

Eddie climbed into the rear seat of a gargantuan 1937 Cadillac Series 70, complete with blackout curtains along all the windows behind the front seat. "Ready?"

"Where to?"

"It's up to you."

The driver adjusted the rear-view mirror until Eddie came into view in the shadows. From there, only Lilith's exotic obsidian eyes and a bit of her nose reflected back to him. "Are you sure this will work?"

He was not sure about anything. Not anymore, but there was no need to let her know that. "Sure as I'll ever be."

Curtains blocked the morning sun on the passenger side of the car. North, he realized, nodding his head.

THE END

Other works by T.A. Bound
Available at: https://books2read.com/ap/xbkzdL/TA-Bound

SHARKANO

A sci-fi/horror adventure now on sale on Amazon
in paperback, e-book and KindleUnlimited!
https://books2read.com/b/Sharkano

Red Dahlia is not the end!
Watch for the upcoming sequel:

Deceased

Coming in late 2022—Sample below

Read the origin story, based on actual events:
The Last Vampire

On Sale Now at your favorite bookseller!
The Last Vampire

Deceased
Part I
Bloodlust

*"One of the artifices of Satan is, to induce men
to believe that he does not exist."*
John Wilkinson, Quakerism Examined, 1836

Chapter 1
Welcome Home (Sanitarium)

1987

The squeak was neither loud nor overly distracting. To most seated in the quaint sanctuary, it went unnoticed, and those who heard paid it no heed. Of the hundred-odd mourners filling the pews to near capacity inside the diminutive church, those reciting the Scripture with closed eyes saw nothing, while others reading along in the prayer book intent on following the words of the Psalm. Only one head turned.

In the second pew, Aunt Barbara wiped her eyes with a starched linen handkerchief behind two identical cascades of extravagant orange curls in the front pew, the one reserved for the closest family members. The billowing, colorful mop in her direct line of sight spun, revealing the pale, freckled face of her niece lured to glance over her shoulder. Brilliant violet eyes focused beyond her, toward the door at the rear of the sanctuary. A color so rare and striking, the twins' eyes inspired admiration and awe since they were infants.

More annoying to Aunt Barbara than her inattentiveness was the shamelessness of the teen's pristine makeup. Not a streak in her eyeliner. Way too much eyeliner, at that. Woeful impropriety for the funeral of her grandfather. Attempts to communicate her disapproval of the teenager's disrespect by clearing her throat three or four times went unacknowledged, so the elderly woman tried signaling her by waving a soggy, wadded handkerchief toward the casket and the minister up on the pulpit behind it. If the teen noticed the surrender flag, she ignored it.

Curious what diversion had captured her niece's attention, the woman also turned toward the main entrance in time to see a tall, wiry young man with tousled blond hair taking his seat in the last pew. Dressed all in black, handsome—although Aunt Barbara did not recognize him, he bore a striking resemblance to several members of the Brown family, enough for her to conclude he must somehow be kin. Strange, for she knew everyone in the family. Few were still alive.

"Everyone turn in your hymnals to William Brown' favorite hymn, *It is Well With My Soul*, and stand as we sing."

In the front pew, Angelique turned to her twin. "Did you see him?"

"Who?"

"The eye-candy who wandered in late."

Celeste, seated on the twin's other side appearing tired and emotional, turned to her daughters, piercing eyes of absinthe green flashing with anger. "Do you need a hymnal?"

Angelique confirmed her hymnal's existence by lifting it a few inches, cradling it while her sister flipped to the proper page to the sound of the organist launching into the opening bars. "He must be our relative. Looks like one of us," she said in her softest voice, enticing her sister to turn so she could take in her sister's eye candy for herself. From way in the back, the stranger flashed a brief smile, acknowledging their curiosity before returning his attention to the pages and joining in the singing.

"My sin—oh, the bliss of this glorious thought. My sin not in part, but the whole..." the sisters sang together in one voice, waiting for the brief musical interlude leading into the second verse to steal another glance over their shoulders. Turning as mirror images, the blue eyes of the stranger met them across twelve rows of pews. The girls' heads jerked back to the page. Having lost her place, the smitten one gave the other a side-glance, a helpful neon pink nail pointing her to the proper line. Their shoulders bumped together, exchanging a grin, although Angelique's came easily and more enthusiastic. Her sister had taken their grandfather's death much harder.

At the conclusion of the service, family, friends and neighbors surrounded the Brown family, offering their deepest condolences. Lost in a crowd too lofty to peer above despite her two-inch heels, she craned up on tip-toes, lifting her narrow heel off the ground, struggling to locate the stranger who had disappeared. The assemblage of bereaved dwindled, all heading outside to the adjacent graveyard.

"Let's go, girls." George placed an arm across Angelique's shoulder, steering her toward the double doors on the side, the direct route reserved for family to avoid delay. The same doors through which the deceased leave feet-first on their one-way journey to the grave waiting especially for them. Their mother ventured nowhere near him, so this gruff firmness gave away that he had not missed their distraction during the funeral, either. Outside, she again reconnoitered for the mystery man. Only when the coffin hung suspended above the fresh rectangular hole in the ground, the preacher reciting more rote words over their grandfather's corpse, did Angelique spot him.

There, standing alone in the old section near headstones worn smooth by generations of rain, snow and hail in the now-full plot containing the graves of her ancient Brown family ancestors. Must be a hundred feet distant, though observing with keen interest from afar. An elbow jabbed into her twin's side, followed by a swivel of her eyes, directing her attention to the man. Watching. Even at this distance, the sisters realized his stared back at them. Hard to believe, but the way the late spring light lit them, blue irises reflected the sun back toward them.

"Earth to earth, ashes to ashes, dust to dust," the preacher said. The solemnity of the moment drew the twins' attention, despite themselves. "I*n sure and certain hope of the Resurrection* *to eternal life, through our Lord Jesus Christ; who shall change our vile body, that it may be like unto his glorious body, according to the mighty working, whereby he is able to subdue all things to himself."*

"Amen," the assembled mourners spoke in unison. The instant they finished, Angelique hurried past the circle of huddled bereaved surrounding the grave toward the old cemetery and its historic Brown graves.

No one was there. A frantic scan of the flat, open ground of the graveyard confirmed her fears.

The stranger had vanished.

In the few seconds her attention had been distracted by the preacher and his concluding words at the graveside, where could he have gone? Her family and neighbors regarded her with curiosity, wondering what had so captured her attention, but that did not faze her. In fact, she hardly noticed.

"Ashes to ashes, funk to funky, we know Major Tom's a junkie," sang the more tempestuous twin under her breath as she scanned the surroundings. "Why does that song get stuck in my brain at every funeral?"

"Daddy hears you singing that at Grandpa's funeral and there will be something else sticking from your brain." Images of David Bowie costumed as a spacy Pagliacci had infected her mind as her sister launched into the tune.

Wind tossed curls across their faces as they lowered their grandfather into the ground. The twins slipped away unnoticed through a slight haze of dust the sudden breeze kicked up. Upon reentering the church, a lone deacon gathered up discarded funeral programs in an otherwise empty building. Dejected at the handsome specter's disappearance, they made their way back outside. "Missed your chance," her sister taunted her.

"Who do you suppose he was?"

"Some stranger? The kid who mowed Grampa's lawn ten years ago? Who knows?"

"But we knew everyone who worked for Grampa."

"Whoever he was, he's gone now. Come on, they'll be heading to the house soon." Together, the twins rejoined the dispersing crowd to find their family. From a distance, dressed in identical short black dresses and walking with elbows locked together, even those who knew them best could not tell them apart.

†

Seemingly insignificant events can irrevocably alter destiny.

Simple decisions often steer the ultimate course of history. Every crashed plane contains at least one empty seat meant for a passenger who missed their flight or decided on the spur of the moment to grab an earlier one. What's one more beer before driving home? Lincoln chose to attend a play. Even a decision whether to answer a firm knock on the door carries enough potential to change the world.

Celeste fought against her instinct. Not that she was too busy mincing onions in the kitchen. Instead, it was the anger. At that moment, she did not wish to speak to anyone, let alone someone who felt the need to knock. The only face she wished to see was one who could help get this mess ready. Bernie was at baseball practice, and Lord knows where the twins were. George called to say he was running late. Timed to reach the answering machine when he knew she was out. After everything else that had gone on, that cold, tinny voice on a micro-cassette that made it sound even more phony is what set her off. Too cowardly to speak to her, because he knew how upset every late return home makes her.

But the insistent knocking drew her as a magnet to iron.

"Hi. By any chance, are you Mrs. Brown?"

For a moment, she wondered if a Mormon missionary had dropped by. The young man standing there looked about college age, devilishly handsome, blonde hair pleasantly unkempt and bordering on need of a haircut, and he might have had the most piercing azure eyes she ever saw. One side of his mouth lifted in an arresting crooked smile. Had he been wearing a short-sleeved white shirt with a black tie, she might have slammed the door in his face. Judging by the preppy white oxford shirt, olive green chinos and penny loafers sans socks, he must be a frat boy calling for one of the twins.

"Now is not a good time. The girls aren't home yet. Leave your name and I'll let them know you dropped by."

"Oh, no, ma'am. I'm here to see you—and your husband, if he's here."

"Honey, whatever you are selling, we ain't buying. If I don't get back to stirring, my sauce will catch on."

"I'm sorry. It's just that—I'm Eddie Brown. Edwin, actually. I believe we're distant cousins. Well, your husband is, anyway, and I'm passing through and took a chance to stop by to meet you. Someone in town told me this place is still in the family."

Horrible as his timing might be, she could not turn away a relative—even one she never heard of. Her mother raised her better than that. He looked harmless enough and, now upon closer inspection, a family resemblance was undeniable. In fact, the similarity to George's father was rather remarkable. "Okay, come in. But I'm afraid I can't offer much company right now. Seems I bit off more than I can chew with this new recipe."

"Perhaps I can help? I know my way around a kitchen. In fact, sauces are a bit of a specialty. Don't let the summer I spent studying culinary arts in France go to waste."

"Let me find you an apron." Celeste, smiling for the first time, closed the door behind the handsome visitor.

✝

Bernie returned first. Celeste introduced him to his new, long-lost cousin, but after a brief conversation, her son rushed off to shower before dinner. Eddie sure knew how to cook, but even had he been a novice, a second pair of hands to slice and stir unburdened hers. Charming, too. And funny. When her husband arrived, she did not hear him at first, because Eddie was right in the middle of a hilarious story about getting lost on the New

York City subway earlier this summer on his way up to Rhode Island.

George missed the joke and found nothing at all humorous about his wife yucking it up with a handsome stranger in the kitchen. "Am I interrupting something?"

"Oh, there you are! Eddie, this is your cousin, George."

George's eyes narrowed. "Cousin? I have no cousin named Eddie."

After a quick hand-wipe on a towel, Eddie extended his with a wide grin. "Distant cousins. Celeste and I tried to figure it out. What did we decide? Second cousins three times removed?"

"Third cousins, twice removed," she corrected him. The last traces of her anger had melted like a tablespoon of butter in a pan while they cooked together, her tone cheerful.

George hesitated, but took the offered hand, gripping like a vice when he did. "We don't have many cousins. We're a small family. How do you figure we are related?"

"Our great grandfather, Edwin Brown, Jr. Our grandfathers were brothers. My grandfather was Ernest Brown."

"Ernest? He disappeared. No one knows what happened to him."

"Eddie does," she said with a wink. "It's a fascinating story, although I only got part of it. Doesn't he look like your father?"

Now that she mentioned it, he did. The shape of his face, the nose, his eyes. "Maybe a little. I'd be interested in hearing that story."

"The whole thing is too long," Celeste said. "But since your cousin is staying for dinner, there will be plenty of time for him to explain the entire family tree. Dinner will be ready in five minutes or so."

With a puzzled expression, George asked, "He will?"

"If you don't mind. I came to Exeter on a quest to meet you."

"Of course he doesn't mind, do you, dear?" The iciness of the tone indicated the only acceptable response was to give his consent.

"No. No, I am interested to hear all about this."

"Oh, it is interesting, alright," she said.

"This family has plenty of interesting stories, if nothing else!" Eddie added, then turned toward the rest of the house. "Your wife says the front of this house is the original dating from the early 1800s, but you added this whole rear section?"

"Well, my father added some, but we built it out. My mother was still alive and staying with us, and we had three young children, so we needed to add a few rooms. Renovated the entire interior, too." George beamed with pride.

"From inside, you could never tell it is that old. The front, though, it looks… original."

"The town is big on retaining its historical charm. They would have blocked us if we tried to change the appearance. Every few years there is talk about designating it an historical landmark. Like our little family home is historically significant enough for that!"

"You should be proud," Eddie said, still intently inspecting the ceilings and floors.

"Oh, we are. Never really considered changing the exterior, but the old part of the house looked like a barn when I grew up here. Could not wait to update everything. Drywall, new hardwood floors, updated wiring and A/C-heat." George showed him around. This kid had a way of making you feel at ease. Few people struck George that way. Must be some family connection.

"Celeste says you have other work in addition to running the farm. What business are you in?"

"I own a Shakey's Pizza franchise up in West Warwick."

Eddie nodded. "Player pianos and picnic tables. Sure. They started up in Sacramento, not far from where I'm from."

Pleased with himself, George said, "That's right. Best pizza around, too."

"How is business?"

"Good, good. Future looks unlimited, although we're currently going through a rough patch. Requires some travel, particularly these days. They're always having meetings at the regional office, if not the home office. Lots of competition. The economy's tough all over."

"Too bad."

"Yeah, the farm is not much of a money-maker these days. We decided to turn much of it into a Christmas tree farm a few years back. Low overhead, but it cranks out a small yet steady profit, if only for about six weeks."

"Still have some fruit trees, I see."

"A few. The apples and one of the pears date back to before the turn of the century. Might need to get rid of them. The girls used to sell their fruit by the roadside when they were kids, but outgrew that long ago. My son never had an interest."

"Be a shame to lose such ancient trees," Eddie said.

"Nostalgia is a poor business strategy. How much apple pie can a man eat? Know what I mean?" George patted a plump stomach straining his belt. "Money's tight, and we cannot pick them. I'm not hiring Mexicans to pick only a few trees. Besides, they're Greenings. Too tart to eat, and cooking apples just don't sell. So, most of it goes to waste."

"Don't Greenings apples make excellent cider?"

"Who knows? Back in the day, they say the Browns made cider, so it does make sense. Can't stand the stuff, myself. Give me an Old Milwaukee and I'm happy. I suppose you decided to stay for dinner since you helped Celeste with it? The twins better be home soon or they'll miss it."

"She invited me, if you do not object."

"Object? No, I already told you, seeing how we're family."

Minutes later, the sound of Madonna blasting from an approaching car ended abruptly near the kitchen door. "That will be the twins," Celeste announced as she dished the last of the meal onto serving platters. Eddie had finished setting the table while George watched Vanna turn letters on *Wheel of Fortune* on TV, beer in hand.

The four had just taken their seats when the front door opened. Deep in conversation with one sister trailing a few steps behind, in they breezed, oblivious to Eddie standing there. Their mother said, "Girls, come meet your cousin Eddie."

The twins stopped dead in their tracks, one's eyes comically wide with her jaw hanging open. Neither one spoke.

"You look like you've seen a ghost," her father said.

"I know you. At Grampa's funeral a few days ago."

"Yup, that was me. Had I known who you were, I would have introduced myself. As it was, I had pressing business that required my attention before the service ended, or else we would have properly met. That and my Irish propensity to burn after only a few minutes in full sun. Please accept my apologies for such unforgivable rudeness."

"I did not see you there," Celeste said.

"He sneaked in late," her daughter explained.

"I only planned a quick visit to town that day, and when I got here heard tell that a distant relative's funeral was being held that morning. I underestimated how long a determined preacher can eulogize."

"Everyone, sit down before the food gets cold. Your cousin Eddie helped me cook."

Up close, the girls' fine features created the impression of matching china dolls, impossible to tell apart. Only slight differences in facial expressions gave any hint they were not, in fact, some clever trick with mirrors. Transparent alabaster complexions complimented brilliant hair cascading several inches past slender shoulders, with full rosy lips, faint wisps of eyebrows and narrow, turned-up noses that—if partial to freckles—might well be perfect. But it was those eyes of delicate lilac that were capable of ensnaring the unwary.

"Hello, Cousin Eddie, I'm Angelique," the talkative one said, her warm hand taking his in what passed for shaking, which she held longer than necessary. His eyes followed her as she walked past, a gaze she returned by swiveling her head. "Sit next to me so we can get to know each other. Josette, sit over there." She pointed to the spot across from their cousin.

The other twin offered a much more formal handshake. One of Eddie's eyebrows raised high. "Josette?"

"Mother didn't tell you? She named her twin babies after her two favorite characters on *Dark Shadows*."

Crimson spilled down Celeste's heart-shaped face towards her neck. "When I was their age, I was a huge fan. And with our family history… They are pretty names, though."

"Beautiful," Eddie agreed.

Face settling in a pink deep as blush wine, Celeste continued, compelled to explain. "I loved the names!"

"We put our foot down when she tried to name our baby brother Barnabas," Angelique said. "That's how he got stuck with Bernie—it's as close as we allowed."

"Hey," her mother laughed, "I'll have you know, the mansion they show in the opening is right over in Newport. Blame you grandparents—they took me to see it because of my addiction to the show."

"No need to explain," Eddie smiled with a jocular wave. "They truly are lovely names."

Josette gave him fair warning. "Don't make the mistake of shortening hers to Angel. She hates that, and will hate you for it if you do."

"Got it," he said with a wink, although curious why. Maybe for the obvious reason, but with the sense of humor her mother claimed she possessed, shouldn't any juxtaposition strike her as a fun play on her melodic name?

"Strange names run in the family," George blurted out, flailing for relevance in the conversation. "Honey, tell our cousin your full name."

Her pupils flared into green flames, the color of burning copper. "First, there is nothing strange about my name, George. Second, if I recall correctly, you didn't state any qualms about our daughters' names when we put them on their birth certificates." Tense brows relaxed when she turned to their guest. "My full name is Mary Celeste, as in…"

Her husband completed it for her, twisting the knife. "The ghost ship."

More than a century before, back in 1872, a passing vessel

found the infamous Mary Celeste drifting derelict in the Atlantic hundreds of miles from the nearest land. Other than minor damage to her sails, the ship otherwise appeared in perfect, normal order when another ship came upon her. Only when the other vessel drew close did it become clear that this ship was anything but normal. The crew and passengers were gone, vanished without a trace, and for no apparent reason. In the hundred years since, investigators have found no satisfactory solution matching the documented evidence, creating one of the most baffling and enduring seafaring mysteries.

"Okay, what you need to understand is the Brown family—well, my branch of it, at least—has a long history of naming their daughters Mary, then calling them by their middle name. So, my parents intended for me to be called Celeste, not Mary Celeste."

Eddie grinned. "It's a lovely name. If I'm not mistaken, isn't it Latin for heavenly?"

A satisfied smirk on her face, Celeste aimed the green torches back at her husband.

"That story about Brown women's names? I've heard that before," Eddie continued. "Mary Olive, Mercy Brown's sister, is a classic example. Did you know no one ever called Mercy by her first name, either? To those who knew her, she was Lena, so even the most famous woman in our family followed that tradition."

Angelique placed her napkin in her lap, a formality unseen in their home, and prodded the table in a new direction. "Tell me all about yourself, Eddie. Where are you from? What brings you here? Why haven't we heard of you before this surprise visit?"

"I'm from Coloma, California. Home of the Gold Rush. I decided to come East for the summer, to see where my family originated. As for why you haven't heard of me, most likely for the same reason I never heard of you and Josette. Old family secrets involving a grandfather everyone here believed was dead, but instead went West to seek his fortune. Cut off from his family."

"Sounds mysterious," Josette said.

"He's already told your father and I the story, but it is a

good one. Maybe you can tell the kids after dinner?"

"Ooh, I cannot wait," Angelique said. "Family secrets sound so… naughty!"

"And I suppose they are. Darker than naughty, perhaps. Why don't you tell me about yourselves? I traveled all the way across the country to see the Brown farm, never dreaming to find long-lost relatives still lived on it."

Bernie took it all in, not saying much as he devoured a pile of food on his plate. His expression almost concealed a hatred of being around his sisters while they flirted. Especially Angelique. The sickening way she acted around the popular guys in school inspired him to express how eagerly he awaited their graduation so he needn't be subjected to it daily. Then they ended up attending University of Rhode Island at Kingston which, the way she told it, was better than Yale. The fact that the twins were top students despite hardly trying filled Bernie with the urge to puke. "May I be excused?" Without waiting for an answer, he picked up his plate, took it to the kitchen, and hurried upstairs.

"Nice talking to you," Josette called up after him.

"Oh yeah, nice to meet you," Bernie called down from the stairs.

"He's such a twerp," Angelique said.

"That's enough!" George's voice came out as a shout. Controlling himself, he continued, "Your cousin did not come all this way to hear your constant sniping at each other."

"He's the one who ran off without saying a word to our handsome guest," Angelique said, defending herself. Upon hearing the flirty compliment, George glared a warning at his daughter, but thought twice about yelling again. After clearing the table, the five of them sat in the living room, chatting. Celeste brewed coffee.

"I hope this won't keep you up all night," she said, placing a cup of their lovely heirloom china in front of Eddie. Staring at it, Eddie's entire countenance changed, his pleasant expression draining away.

"No, it's… I'm a night owl."

"Where are you staying, Eddie?"

"I have reservations at a bed & breakfast over in Pawcatuck, the Morgan Inn."

Celeste's eyes lit up. "Impressive—spoken like a true Rhode Islander. Most visitors have no idea how to pronounce it."

Angelique snickered. "Tourists normally make it sound like a dirty word."

"That must be twenty miles from here," her sister said.

"Thereabout," he confirmed.

Angelique asked innocently, "Hey, why don't you stay here?"

"Oh no, I cannot possibly impose upon you like that."

"It's no imposition," Celeste said. "Is it, George?"

"I'm sure he would prefer some peace and quiet. Some privacy."

"Nonsense." It was Angelique again, her interest transparent. "He is family! And he came all this way to see the farm, why not let him stay at it for a few days? He can sleep down in the guest room."

Celeste beamed. "What a wonderful idea! Yes, why don't you? It will give us all a chance to get better acquainted, won't it, George?"

His face refused to belie the fact that having this stranger staying under his roof would not only be an imposition, but a burden. "Well…"

"Listen, I will not dream of it," Eddie said. "Unless you will allow me to pay. The same as the bed & breakfast is charging. It's only fair, and I will not take no for an answer."

This offer sweetened the deal and brightened George's receptiveness. "Well, if you insist…"

Celeste objected, but Eddie held firm, so the deal was struck. "Let me retrieve my things from the room, and I will be honored to stay here in the Brown ancestral home."

An hour later, Eddie returned with his luggage. One small decision to answer the door led to a new family member. A paying guest even George welcomed.

†

Someone must have left the light burning for their guest in case he got up in the dead of night. This realization slowed Josette's descent, bare feet slapping quietly against the old wood of the stairs. When she awakened, their visitor slipped her mind. For an instant, tempted to return for a robe, but thirst compelled her onward. A tall glass of chilled water from the filter pitcher her mother stored in the fridge did the trick, sending chills through her body in the process. Two steps from the stairs, a rustle from the living room made her jump and spin toward it.

"Sorry, didn't mean to startle you." Her cousin sat in her father's comfortable chair in the corner. A beam aimed at him from halogen track lights cast his face in harsh light and shadow, distorting his features into an unrecognizable sight.

Heart pounding crazily, she let out a deep breath upon catching sight of an open book on the crook of his crossed leg. "Shit! Don't do that!" Then, lowering her voice, she pointed toward the ceiling. "My parents' room is right there."

"That's why I didn't say anything. Figured you might scream. At least you aren't armed." The shadows contorted his grin into a Jack-o'-lantern grimace. "Care to keep me company? I was just reading." A vague wave toward the bookshelf in the corner, where a gap stood out like a snaggletooth from the removed book.

"No, I was just…," then stopped, realizing his spot in the corner offered an unobstructed view through to the kitchen. That's the moment she wished she was not half-naked, wearing only a thin tee-shirt emblazoned EWG Knights Cheerleading, one size too big, so it hung just long enough to cover her panties. Not appropriate for a conversation with a male stranger she met hours ago who claimed to be a mystery cousin, even before chilling her body with ice water. But curiosity took over. "What did you find to read here?"

"Somebody keeps a fascinating collection of Reader's

Digest Condensed Books here in your parlor," he explained, closing the book and holding it up to read from its spine. *"Captain of the Queens, Beloved, In My Father's House* and *The Last Hurrah*, all in one volume!"

"My father's. Claims he's read the classics when all he reads are Cliff's Notes for lazy adults. Which one were you reading?"

"In My Father's House. It's not what I hoped for."

"What were you hoping for?"

With mock seriousness, he answered, "The kind of thing Reader's Digest doesn't publish."

"Stop it! They'll hear us laughing and come downstairs to see what we're up to."

"Then come sit down over here where we won't have to shout to each other." His head shifted, the shadows under his brows and nose now less sinister.

"I'm not exactly dressed for hanging out with a guy I just met."

Shadows lengthened as his head angled down toward her feet, then back up. "Ever been to the beach?"

Since the shirt did cover more than a bikini, Josette chose a chair facing the same direction to avoid offering him too good a view, stifling a humorous realization to avoid answering what struck her so funny. Something about her cousin could charm the pants off her—if she was wearing any. "We've got better books upstairs. My father's taste is, shall we say, lacking. My sister and I read. Real books, not condensed."

"What about your mother?"

"She is literate, but not much of a reader. Never had time for it with three kids, I guess."

"Your brother must have plenty of time to read, being a mute and all."

"Oh my god, wait till I tell Angelique that one! She'll think that's the funniest thing ever. No, his best conversation is when he is cursing out Nintendo. There is nothing worse than teenage boys."

"I can think of a few worse things. A broken leg, acne…"

"Wrong. So, what's your first impression of our little branch of dysfunction in your family tree?"

"Honestly? The women seem friendly, intelligent. Sure are pretty."

Warmth on her face only suggested the color at his compliment. "And the guys?"

"Well, they don't seem to take to me all that well. Your sister can be a bit overpowering…"

"That's one word for it."

"At least she is funny."

"All the guys say so—the reason she's so popular—well, one of them. Stay on her good side, though. Her sense of humor can turn biting like that." A snap of her fingers made the point clear.

"Noted. Not that a little bite ever scared me off."

Was he flirting with Angelique while she wasn't even here? "No, I don't suppose it does."

"You, though," he pointed, lowering his head like sighting a gun at her chest still chilled from her drink, "the quiet ones are who you need to watch out for. Taking everything in, analyzing, intelligent enough to know sometimes stillness can be ruined by words. Deep. And they say, the deeper the water, the more dangerous it is. Don't know if it's true."

It came out as a question unasked, his intense eyes bearing a physical presence, real as a hand reaching out, touching her. Reaching inside her. A shudder ran through her, further tightening her skin, so she crossed her arms over her chest. "It's late, and someone will hear us if we keep this up. Let me go back upstairs," she said, standing, pointing unnecessarily toward the second floor while tugging the tail of her shirt to belatedly cover where it got hung up on one side of her bum when she stood.

"Well, I'll stick around for a while. I'm curious to find out what happens *In My Father's House*," he said, even the shadows unable to disguise his smile as wry. "Goodnight!"

"'Night," she said, scurrying up the safety of the staircase.

ABOUT THE AUTHOR

T.A. Bound's debut Young Adult adventure, SHARKANO, was published in 2020 by Solstice Publishing. In 2022, he published THE LAST VAMPIRE: The Strange Legend of Mercy Brown. An attorney by trade, he has also published a non-fiction book on insurance claims. Raised on the Gulf Coast of Florida, after attending college and Law School in South Carolina, he moved to Marietta, Georgia, his current home. There he lives with his wife and their adopted dog Maksim Gorky, named after the Soviet author, where he enjoys cooking, writing and reading: history, biography, horror and thrillers—particularly historical fiction.

He is currently working on additional sequels to *The Last Vampire*, as well as other stories.